INTO THIS WORLD

ALSO BY SYBIL BAKER

Talismans

The Life Plan

INTO THIS WORLD

WORLD

a novel

SYBIL BAKER

9 Dec 2012

Nicole,

Thanks for coming out
I hope you enjoy!

all best

Sybil.

Engine Books
Indianapolis

Engine Books
PO Box 44167
Indianapolis, IN 46244
enginebooks.org

The author gratefully acknowledges the support of University of Chattanooga Summer Fellowship, which allowed her to research and write much of the novel. She also wishes to thank George Conley for sharing his experience as a GI in Korea in the late 1970s, and The Hunter Museum of American Art for exhibiting Hughie Lee-Smith's *Confrontation*, which provided the inspiration for the novel.

For romanization of Korean words, the author chose to use the Revised Romanization of Korean, the official Korean language romanization system in South Korea. To maintain consistency, this system is used in the text even when historically other romanization systems were used.

Also available in eBook formats from Engine Books.

Printed in the United States of America
10   9   8   7   6   5   4   3   2   1

ISBN: 978-1-938126-01-7
Library of Congress Control Number: 2012930506

For Rowan

CHAPTER 1

You're giving up stability for the unknown." Allison's father, Wayne, guided a piece of bloody steak into his mouth. He sat at one end of the cherry wood table, the only kitchen table Allison could remember. Bonnie, Allison's mother, sat across from him. The chair opposite Allison was empty.

She had told them she'd quit her job of thirteen years. She'd come home late, holding up dinner by an hour. It had been her turn to cook.

The phone rang.

"Don't answer," Allison said. She was afraid her boss—ex-boss—Ray was calling. She had quit at the spur of the moment, neglecting the exit paperwork required to vacate a job with a security clearance. She'd turned off her cell phone, but it would be easy for Ray to dig up her home number from her personnel file.

"What did Ray say? You were such an asset to him." Bonnie cut a palm-sized piece of steak for her plate; she was expert at portion control. She permitted herself one spoonful of mashed potatoes and filled the rest of her plate with salad. Despite her efforts, at fifty-six, she was fighting a losing battle against middle-age spread.

"I just couldn't take it anymore," Allison said.

"Honey, you've been working there since you graduated," Bonnie said. "What couldn't you take? Stable job, good benefits. Now you'll have to start over."

The phone rang again.

Allison toyed with her mashed potatoes. "How about a little support here? You know, belief and optimism in your talented daughter?"

"Now, honey," Bonnie said. She worked as a file clerk with the county. "In this economy, beggars can't be choosers."

"Sometimes it's better to be happy with what you have," Wayne said. She'd heard him say so before, but for the first time she wondered if he was right.

The answering machine, a relic her parents had never replaced, picked up after the fourth ring.

"Are you my father?"

The voice was slurred, barely audible above traffic crackling in the background. Wayne shot out of his chair. He spat steak into the sink and picked up the phone.

"Mina? Of course I'm your father."

Bonnie was in the kitchen now, her hand on Wayne's back. The clock read ten before nine. Almost eleven in the morning in Seoul.

"Just come home okay?" Wayne said. "It's not safe there."

Bonnie left the kitchen and picked up the family room extension. "Honey, it's Mom. Dad's right. If you're having problems, just come home." They talked in this manner for a few more minutes before Mina hung up.

"Goddammit," Wayne said. "Where's her phone number?"

Bonnie rejoined him in the kitchen and rooted around in the drawer by the phone. Allison watched from the table as Wayne frantically punched the digits on the cordless handset. She went into the family room and picked up the phone Bonnie had been using. The phone rang, but Mina did not answer. They hung up and returned to the table, but no one ate. Wayne carried his plate to the kitchen.

"I don't like her in that country." He scraped bits of mashed potato down the disposal and turned it on.

"That country?" Bonnie said, her voice rising. "That country is where you spent two years of our marriage. Two hardship tours there, the second time you begged to go back. That country is where Mina was born."

"I was in the army," Wayne said, as if that explained everything. "Korea's not stable. I don't trust those people." He rinsed his plate and placed it in the dishwasher. He sat back down at the table, pressing his fingertips together as if in prayer.

"Your daughter is one of those people." All that remained on

Bonnie's plate were tiny bites of steak like rabbit turds.

Allison stacked the rest of the dishes. "You can't trust her."

Wayne followed her to the kitchen. "Don't say that about your sister." His voice was soft, pleading.

Bonnie wrapped the leftover steak in aluminum foil. "It was delicious, honey." She scooped the rest of the leftovers into Tupperware containers and turned on the dishwasher. "So why did you quit?"

"It was time to move on." Allison no longer felt like talking about it. What would she tell them now anyway? Once again, Mina, as if by some chilling clairvoyance, had managed to not only incite Allison to quit her job but then to prevent her from even explaining it to their parents.

When Allison turned she saw Wayne back at the kitchen table, resuming his position of prayer. She paused before breaking his contemplation.

"Dad, *Hee Haw's* on."

"I don't feel like it tonight," Wayne said, standing. He walked down the hall to Mina's old room. He used her computer to play war games, hearts, and solitaire. Bonnie disappeared into their bedroom.

In an empty family room, Allison turned the TV on to a station broadcasting decades-old episodes of *Hee Haw*, the show she used to watch with her dad, before Mina. She'd sit on his lap after dinner and when the two men with pitchforks came on the set, she'd join in singing. *Where oh where are you tonight, why did you leave me here all alone. I'd searched the world over and thought I'd found true love, you met another and pfft you was gone.* When she said *pfft* she blew the tiniest drop of spit in the air, like the guys on TV. Her dad laughed when she did it with the song, but once she made the noise at dinner, and he thumped her hand and her mom said it was unladylike. She remembered nights when, after dinner, they'd go to the family room, push the furniture aside, and her dad would lie on the floor. Allison would run and jump onto his feet and he'd sail her over to the other side of the floor where she always landed safely.

Now Allison took the couch even though Wayne's recliner was empty, inviting. She flipped stations during the commercials to reruns of happy, joking families; of drama-filled hospitals, police stations, law offices run by beautiful people; of murder and mayhem solved in the final minutes. But after the commercials were over, she'd switch back to *Hee Haw*, waiting for her song, singing it under her breath. *"Pfft you was gone."*

When she knew that her parents were asleep, Allison shifted to Wayne's recliner and carefully unfolded the sheet of paper tucked beneath her watch band. The words were still there: nothing could be undone. That afternoon she'd stopped by Ray's office to tell him she was finished with a manual she'd been working on. He was out but would be back soon; the administrative assistant told her it was okay for her to wait. She was about to sit when she saw the piece of paper near the trashcan, picked it up to throw away, but for some reason, perhaps because it was folded into a tiny square, not crumpled, she unfolded it instead. She recognized Ray's scratchy handwriting immediately.

Five things I don't want to admit to myself (this is hard)—
I'm a mediocre middle manager who will never meet Merry's ambitions.
My penis is small. Women see a tall guy like me and expect something larger.
I use my looks and charm to manipulate people.
I like to be spanked.
I have cheated on my wife. With Mina, Justine, Amber, Courtney, and a woman from the bank whose name begins with J.

Mina. The summer of Allison's second miscarriage Mina had interned at Allison's office. Had they had an affair then, without Allison even suspecting? She'd been keeping her pregnancy a secret, but she was preoccupied with fatigue and nausea and fantasies of her child growing up friends with Ray's and Merry's girl, who was not yet a year old.

Ray walked in just as she palmed the list. He sat at his desk, clasping his hands behind his neck, waiting for her to speak. His light blue oxford was clean, pressed, his sleeves rolled just once, revealing the gold watch Merry had given him for his fortieth birthday last year. A hint of downy golden hair framed the edge of the cuffs. Allison remembered being surprised at how hairy his chest was compared to the wispy hair on his head. Now he was balding at the back. In a few years he'd probably have nothing on top. Behind him was a photo of Merry, a woman who possessed many things Allison coveted. Such an old-fashioned word, covet. A Sunday school word. *Thou Shall Not*

Covet. But covet Allison did. She coveted Merry's lithe body, her blonde bobbed hair that grazed the tips of her shoulders, the clean, simple lines of her clothes cut from expensive fabrics imported from foreign lands. She coveted the two daughters Merry and Ray were raising, their spacious house, its expansive deck perfect for summer barbeques she was rarely invited to. Most of all, she coveted the shake of Ray's head when he'd pick up the photo on top of his file cabinet and say, "How'd I'd get so lucky?"

"What's up?" he finally said. What he meant was, *why are you here?*

There was no reason for her to be there, none at all. "I'm such an idiot," she said. "I quit." She walked out his office, past her own cubicle, out the glass doors to the stairs which she walked three flights down instead of taking the elevator, and only when she was on the street did she remember she'd left her favorite sweater behind, a gray sweater Ray had given her twelve long years ago after he'd broken up with her, an Angora consolation prize, which she kept draped over her chair and wore most of the year because this was an office where, despite the time or the season, the air was always stale, chilly. She reminded herself that the sweater was an ugly sweater, always shedding its hairs, and it was better, so obviously symbolic, that she'd left it behind.

Their affair twelve years before had been brief and lopsided, with Allison's devotion weighing in on the side of obsession, his on the side of disinterest. She was still ashamed at her dishonesty, when she'd gone off the pill and hadn't told him. The night she was going to tell him she was pregnant he told her he was in love with someone else, a woman named Merry, who, Allison would soon learn, was as perfect as he claimed. So she never told him about their baby or the abortion she got the next day.

Allison pushed the recliner back, closed her eyes. Grandpa was announcing the supper menu on *Hee Haw:* turtle stew with onions and crackers, wild greens, stewed okra, and bread pudding. "Yum, yum," Allison murmured with the cast. After Ray and Merry married, Allison met Ted. Their marriage had lasted not quite nine years, sliced out like a tumor soon forgotten, the reason she'd moved back home six months ago. The doctors had told them there was no reason for her miscarriages, to keep trying. Secretly, Allison believed Ray's baby would have made it, if only she'd chosen the baby over Ray. But she hadn't, and then Ray married Merry and she married Ted, and she'd loved him for a while and he'd loved her, but by the fifth time, when the baby had been further along, when they were out of danger, when they had optimistically taped the blurred ultrasound to the refrigerator—a boy, a boy—she'd awakened one night convinced she was drowning, and she didn't even have to touch her legs to know it had happened again. They agreed not to name the baby, stillborn, and then Allison woke up one day and asked for a divorce.

She pushed herself off Wayne's recliner, walking through the darkness into the kitchen, where she smoothed Ray's list on the counter. She carefully punched in the numbers for Mina's cell phone.

"What?" Mina croaked. Her voice sounded scraped, raw, far away.

"It's me."

"Ally," she whispered. "He lies."

"That's why I quit."

"Your job? I mean Dad."

"Listen," Allison said. "I was thinking about coming to Korea. What do you think?"

"You never visit me. Even when I lived in LA."

"We have a lot to talk about."

Mina paused. "You really want to know?"

"I do."

They hung up and Allison went to bed. She didn't fall asleep until the sky started to turn pink, but she had nowhere to be that morning. Whether she were awake when the sun rose or set didn't really matter.

CHAPTER 2

The flight from Dulles to Seoul was fourteen and a half hours, double the time of the two longest flights Allison had taken before. One was to London, the other to Vancouver, with Ted for a convention. She'd been ovulating, and by that stage she and Ted were relying more on superstition than science. Perhaps a conception in a different time zone would bring a magic pregnancy that did not shrivel on the vine. So they'd had sex in the convention hotel, courtesy of the FCC, under a dark sky that never permitted the sun to shine, where the streets were covered in a thin mist that never quite became rain. And she'd gotten pregnant—that had never been the problem. That one lasted four weeks.

The plane was half full of Koreans, some families, women with children, and businessmen who transitioned between English and Korean with an ease and fluency she admired. She slept fitfully, her head nodding to the right, then the left. After a few minutes, her head would bob to one side and she'd snap awake from dreams that the passengers sitting next to her were sent to spy on her.

Allison had told her parents she was booking a ticket to Korea to check up on Mina. Bonnie had set her coffee cup down and wrapped her arms around Allison in a full hug. "Thank you, honey," she said. "Please, try to bring her back with you."

Wayne cleared his throat, grabbed Allison's free hand. "I appreciate it," he said. "I really do. I'm getting older. I want to know my girls aren't a world away from me if something happens."

Wayne looked at Bonnie and she nodded encouragement. "Ally,

there's something we've been wanting to tell you," Wayne said, "and now seems as good a time as any. Our latest contract didn't get renewed, and my position is being eliminated. I've been offered early retirement, and I'm taking it."

"You're retiring?"

"Back home to Hillsdale," Bonnie said. "Found a house for almost nothing when we were visiting last summer."

"It's time for us to enjoy our lives, be near family, live in a house in the hills with trees and sunshine and not much else. Heck, we'd planned to do that years ago, then got sucked into life here." He paused. "The only problem is Mina."

"We can't settle in someplace new until we know Mina's back here, safe," Bonnie said.

"If you can bring Mina back, Bonnie and I can get on with our own lives. I know you've suffered, Ally, and we know we don't worry about you as much as we should, with your divorce and all, but you've always been the stable one. We wanted to show you we appreciate all you've done. We'll give you this house, free and clear. You won't have to save a down payment to buy some dumpy condo. You can have this."

Allison told them she couldn't make Mina do anything, they knew that. She told them she wasn't even sure if she wanted the house, though deep down she did. She could never afford something like this on her own. She told them she'd try, but she didn't know how. Even now, on the plane, she had a vague plan at best. Find Mina, reassure her parents all was well, confront Mina about Ray, extract an explanation as to why she had sex with the one man Allison had loved, and then… Then what? Convince her to come back to the States so that Allison could have the house? Or tell their parents about Mina's affair with Ray—a married man, Allison's boss—so that they'd finally see what kind of girl Mina was?

Allison thought about the house. The first thing she'd do would be to pull up the carpet that hid polished oak floors in the living room. She'd strip the wallpaper and paint the rooms in pale earth tones. She wondered if even with new furniture, paint, floors, if she could change enough to make it hers instead of theirs. Did she want the house enough to bring Mina back, to never mention Mina and Ray to her parents? Because that's what it meant. If she didn't bring Mina back, if she told them what Mina had done, would they stay in that house, the family home, until things were right? Allison would have to stay with them at least another year while she found a new job and saved money for her own place, a dumpy condo, as Wayne had said, while her parents waited for Mina to come back, which might never happen.

By the time they landed in Incheon, her head felt thick and slow from the plane air and lack of sleep. She filed through immigration, her three-month tourist visa stamped in her pristine passport, and followed the others to the baggage claim, past customs, through sliding glass doors into the open expanse of Arrivals. She would have been happy to follow these people the rest of her life, not having to make any decisions, but the passengers dissipated and she had no one to follow. Incheon Airport, she'd read in the in-flight magazine, was less than a decade old, but it seemed even newer, all clean and spare, with storefronts yet to be filled, smelling vaguely antiseptic. She was faced with dozens of Koreans, some waving signs in English or Korean. She searched for Mina, who had promised to meet her, and when she couldn't find her, she scanned the signs, but she couldn't find her name.

A Korean man in khakis and a blazer approached her. He was of delicate build and indeterminate age, in his thirties, she guessed. He held out his hand to her.

"Allison?" He waved a photo from last Christmas in front of her. "I'm Mina's friend, Jason."

She slung her handbag on her shoulder and took his hand, which was faintly damp and cool. He was slight, a few inches taller than she was, with pale skin that emitted the vaguest scent of cigarettes, cologne, and garlic. His hair had a few strands of gray, a deep side part, and bangs that almost flopped over his eyes, which were obscured by the slightly misted lenses of boxy black glasses.

"Where's Mina?"

"Teaching. She didn't tell you I was coming instead?"

Typical, Allison thought, but she just shook her head. Jason gently prodded the large suitcase from her and eased the oversized duffel bag off her shoulder. His manner was so graceful she didn't notice she'd been unburdened from her belongings until she resumed walking. She stayed close to him, this stranger carrying her bags, already moving quickly through the airport. Relieved of her luggage, Allison suddenly realized how tired she was.

"Are we going to your car?" she asked.

"We're taking the bus."

Except for the bus she'd ridden in elementary school, Allison had never even been on one. She'd been afraid of them since she'd watched *Urban Cowboy* and Ratso had died on the bus to Florida with Buck. Wayne had told her some stories of the *kimchi* buses he had taken while he was at Camp Humphreys—the Hump he called it—buses packed with the squalor of humanity, and pigs, and chickens, that careened through dirt roads, almost toppling over. She decided if the bus looked that bad she would refuse to get on. She'd spend her last dime to take a taxi to Seoul if it meant she didn't have to worry about dying on a bus with farm animals.

They waited at one of the many stops just outside the airport. Jason joined the other men smoking cigarettes near an oversized ashtray. Other men, airport workers, she guessed, ran past her with urgency. There were women, too, dressed up, and students in skinny jeans and Converses. The late March air was colder than in Virginia, and she wondered if she should have brought a heavier coat. Taxi drivers lined up and loitered next to their cars, which were parked in long rows.

Until she'd boarded the plane, she'd not really heard Korean spoken before. Mina had spoken a little when she first arrived, but she stopped when no one responded. Allison remembered how frustrated Mina had been, jabbering in Korean, sometimes yelling, and all of them, including Wayne, looking at her blankly. Bonnie had suggested bringing one of the Korean families over for translation, but Wayne had been adamant. "She's an American now, so the faster she learns English, the better." They asked Allison, who had started first grade, to read to her, but Allison had refused. What was the point if the girl couldn't understand? And so for the first weeks Allison had listened to Mina cry and jabber until she decided not to speak at all. This lasted a few months until almost as abruptly she began speaking English as if she'd known it her whole life.

The morning Mina started speaking English, Bonnie had made pancakes, a special request of Wayne's. She'd placed a hot stack on the table with a plate of sausage links and Aunt Jemima syrup. Mina, still tiny for her age (she'd just turned three), was strapped in her high chair, with Allison's old bib that read "Daddy's Girl" secure around her neck. They bowed heads and Wayne said grace, thanking God for the food on their table, for family, for safety, for being American. When he said Amen, Allison was sure she heard Mina echo the two syllables, a guttural whisper, like she was using her voice for the first time. Allison looked at the girl, her new sister, with her thick dark hair blunt cut at her jaw. Mina's eyes looked so large, when Allison had been expecting small slits instead of those round moons.

"Pancake please," Mina said. "Juice please."

Silence. Wayne held a stabbed pancake on his fork, hovering over his plate.

"Mimi hungry. Pancake please." Mina's smile was something new, a smile given to please others rather than a smile to please herself, but Allison thought later, most people never noticed the difference. Their father shook his head and reached over, fork in air, and plopped the pancake on her plate.

"How's that, Mimi?" Wayne asked.

Mina nodded, her mouth already sugary from the syrup, cheeks full of pancake pieces. And that was how Mina became Mimi, and Mimi she was until last year when she told them she was going to Korea to find her identity and that she would like to be called her Korean name from now on.

After that morning, Mina couldn't stop talking. English spilled out of her mouth fully assembled, as if the words and sounds had been nurturing themselves in some part of her brain, waiting until they were ready for the world. Six months later, when the family was at the mall, a Korean woman walked up to Mina and began speaking Korean. Mina stared, then ran to hide behind Wayne's legs. The Korean woman laughed nervously, hurrying away.

As a large bus pulled up, Jason mashed his cigarette out. He hoisted one bag over his shoulder, and pulled the suitcase toward the back of the bus. Jason looped tags on her luggage and hefted them into the luggage compartment. Allison, not moving from the bench, felt heavy, dizzy, stiff limbed, weighted by the dense, unfamiliar air. Sounds swirled around her, none that she could recognize, and she prayed that Jason would not leave her. She wondered if this was how Mina had felt when she'd first come to the United States from Korea, not yet three years old, suddenly surrounded by people speaking a language she didn't know, her native language no longer worthy of meaning.

Jason gestured to her. The line to board the bus was thinning, and Allison willed herself to move. Breathe. Stand. Jason walked over, touched her elbow, and then released her as soon as she was steady.

"You can rest on the bus," he said. Allison nodded, biting her lip. So dependent was she on this stranger's kindness. She was crazy to come here, a place she did not belong, where Mina was the one who blended in. Two other young women as thin and almost as pretty as Mina had boarded the bus ahead of Allison. Their hair was the same, middle parted, straight, and she wondered if that was how all the girls here looked.

The bus was large, clean, spacious, with padded chairs that reclined with the push of a lever. A flat screen TV above the driver's seat played scenes of Korean mountains and people in traditional dress playing instruments and spinning colored ribbons from hats on their heads. No pigs or chickens. No smell but a vague woodsy scent she guessed came from a can. She rested her head against the rain-splattered window. Although she'd planned to take in as much of this world as she could, she next felt Jason's arm on her shoulder waking her for their stop.

Allison wiped the drool from her mouth. "How long did I sleep?"

"A little over an hour."

"Felt like ten minutes." She rubbed her neck.

"Jet lag," Jason said. "You are tired."

She grabbed his elbow this time, following him to the front of the bus. Jason said a few words to the driver as he pulled to a stop on a busy street where they disembarked, luggage in tow. "Let me carry this." Allison tugged at the duffel bag on his shoulder.

"No, no, it's okay." His pace quickened.

"I feel like an old lady. At least let me carry my duffel bag."

Jason stopped. He smiled for the first time and let the straps fall from his shoulder. "Just a few more blocks."

He led her down the busiest street she'd ever seen, much busier than any in DC, a street packed with young Korean women in dresses or tight jeans and heels, and men in skinny jeans and Converses, couples and groups with arms linked, sharing umbrellas, talking on cell phones, chattering to friends. It seemed that every other store was a coffee shop—some like Starbucks and Coffee Bean & Tea Leaf, others with names she didn't recognize, Angel-In-Us and A Twosome Place. The coffee shops were more than one level, with big windows through which she could see tables crowded with girls in pleated miniskirts and pastel trench coats. She gazed down at her own sturdy shoes, the loose, drab pants, the oversized navy cardigan she'd worn because of the draft on planes, her shapeless coat, a waterproof, insulated jacket ordered from the LL Bean catalog years ago. Mina called it her grandmother wardrobe, and now she understood why. She tried not to dawdle or stare too much, for she was afraid she'd lose Jason, and if she lost him, she wasn't sure what she'd do. Mina's phone number was in the suitcase Jason was pulling, and her cell phone didn't work here. If she lost him, she'd have to call home and get Mina's number. She hadn't seen a phone booth yet. Then a few Westerners walked past, and she heard slips and snippets of English waft by. She wanted to reach out, grab the words, and shove them into her mouth so she'd have them. Just in case.

He turned off the main street onto weaving, narrow roads, crowded with compact half-sized trucks and people everywhere. And then Jason stopped in front of a four story brick building.

"Second floor." He climbed the stairs, carrying the suitcase. "It's heavy," Allison warned. She'd stopped at the bottom of the steps to catch her breath.

Jason continued to the second floor, waiting for Allison to reach him. He pushed in some numbers on the keypad and the door opened. Jason took off his shoes, which joined what Allison recognized as Mina's trademark Keds and a pair of shiny black boots. Allison carefully unlaced her brown leather shoes. Jason pushed open a door on their left.

"Bathroom." He wheeled the suitcase past a closed door through a small kitchen area to a living room. "This is where you'll sleep. Couch folds out." Besides the blue fold-out, the room had a desk with a computer, a TV, and a coffee table topped with a newspaper and a half-full ashtray. She collapsed on the couch.

"Great," she said. "Thanks." Her body ached, the dull fog of fatigue returning. She was afraid to close her eyes, afraid she might not wake up for days, wondering what world she'd been transported to, forever lost. "When can I see Mina?"

"When she gets off work. In an hour or so." Jason slid a window open. "Mind if I smoke?" She shook her head. This was not her country. Not her apartment. "Can I go see her?"

Jason lit his cigarette, exhaled close to the window. He was older than she'd first thought; though his face was pale and unlined, the slivers of gray, the slight puff under his eyes showed he was closer to her age—thirty-five. He shrugged, seemed to be watching some kind of drama on the street that she could not see. "You don't want to rest? If we go see her we're out for the night."

"I promised Dad I'd check on her right away."

Jason nodded. Allison didn't know what he was to Mina. There were so many men carelessly strewn about Mina's life, men who were protectors pretending to be lovers, lovers pretending to be friends, manipulators pretending to be friends, men hovering on the sidelines, angling for something.

She yawned, standing. "Besides, if I fall asleep now, I might never wake up." She excused herself to the bathroom. There was no bath or shower proper, just a hose and shower head suspended between the sink and the toilet, with a drain on the wet, tiled floor. Plastic slippers in large and small sizes lined the door. Allison eased her feet into the larger size and clopped two steps to the toilet, its lid spotted with shower spray. At the sink, she splashed her face with cold water. Her bangs were separated, greasy from the long flight, and a burgeoning pimple claimed an angry red spot on her chin. "I don't usually look this bad," she said to the mirror, trying to convince herself.

Jason led her back into the labyrinth of now darkened streets. The night sky was almost obliterated by buildings and lights that seemed to defy time. Neon lights flashed, syncopated music blared out of restaurants and bars with their speakers turned outside to the streets, men outside restaurants hawked their wares like carnival barkers. Koreans spilled from wide, cracked sidewalks onto car-clogged streets. Allison wanted to ask if there was some kind of celebration or holiday. She wondered how long they'd been walking—she couldn't remember not being on this street, not following him.

Finally they stopped at a building with an ice cream shop and Dunkin' Donuts on the first floor. They took the elevator to the sixth floor, where the doors opened to a hall with bright colors and animal posters in the windows. Above the entrance a sign read "Leaping Frog English School." Behind the glass entrance, a young woman in what looked like a flight attendant uniform chatted on the phone. She nodded to Jason as he bowed slightly to her and pointed toward a back room. She waved a tiny half wave to Allison, as if they were shy new friends. As they approached the classroom Allison could hear singing. English, but not. Rhyming words that formed shapes she almost understood, animals or numbers or vegetables. Through the glass walls of the classroom, Allison saw Mina waving her arms like a frantic choir director, miming the animal or vegetable or number they were singing.

Mina had never liked children, and even at thirty-two, had never expressed a desire to marry or have her own. She had always been a waitress or a salesperson or held a basic office job secured by her friends until she got bored and quit. She had always lived off of men and the general kindness of others who wanted her to be in their world. But here she was singing a song about sun and rain and snow with a bunch of kids.

She looked even thinner and more frail than the last time Allison had seen her, two Christmases ago, when their parents bought Mina a ticket home for the holidays. Allison and Ted had been a month away from separating. January brought them to that point. But at Christmas they were still pretending they might go on, that a miracle or magic would save them.

Mina was still searching for her magic. After years of taking classes sporadically, she'd finally finished her undergraduate degree in LA, and that Christmas she told them she was moving to Korea next year to find her identity, her "lost self," she called it. Their father had been strangely angry, defensive. Her identity was easy, he said, she was a Morehouse. She was their daughter. They'd adopted her from an orphanage where children were left to wither and survive on the fringes of Korean society. There was nothing for her there. She was an American. Had they not given her everything? Korea was dangerous, he added, especially for girls who looked like her.

"What do you mean, look like me?" Mina had cried. The presents were still unwrapped under the tree. Allison was sipping hot chocolate at the kitchen table, trying to listen to Christmas carols on the radio. Ted sat across from her reading the *Post*'s sports section. Bonnie hovered between the kitchen and the living room, where the battle was starting.

"I mean attractive. Men will take advantage of you. No doesn't mean no there."

"I'm tired of this racist shit. You can't stop me from going."

"Come on, Mimi," he said.

"Mina. My name is Mina." She walked out of the house, slamming the door. Allison sipped her hot chocolate. Bonnie was in the living room now, trying to calm him. "Go after her, someone," Bonnie called into the kitchen. Ted never looked up from the paper. Slowly, Allison rose, fished for her car keys, slipped on her coat. Her hot chocolate would be cold when she got back, whether she found Mina or not.

And here she was in Seoul, tracking down her runaway sister again. When they were young, Allison could easily spot Mina on the playground, the only Asian girl in their white neighborhood. Now, it was Allison who would be easy to find. After the kids finished the song, Jason opened the door to the classroom. Mina greeted them in an exaggerated, dramatic voice.

"We have a surprise today. My sister flew all the way from Washington, DC." The children whispered and giggled as they turned to Allison, who stood at the entrance of the classroom.

She'd not been prepared for the little Minas chiming hello at her.

"She's not your sister," one of the children said. "You're Korean. She's American."

"She is my sister. I'm adopted." Mina then said a word Allison assumed was Korean and the students murmured again. "English!" Mina said. "Show my sister your English!"

"What your name?" a boy asked. The class giggled.

"My name is Allison. What's yours?"

"My name is Tommy. Nice to meet you," the boy said.

"Nice to meet you."

"Where you from?" another child asked.

"I'm from Washington, DC. Virginia actually but, DC is close enough." She saw Mina shake her head slightly. The kids stared at her.

"DC. The president. My home."

"How long you visit Korea?"

"One month."

"Do you marry?"

"Not anymore."

The children looked at Mina again.

"Remember, no personal questions," Mina said.

"Do you have baby?"

Allison opened her mouth. She shook her head. "No baby."

"I said no more personal questions. Very rude," Mina said, and then used another Korean word. "Let's sing another song for my sister Allison." Allison turned to Jason, who was outside the classroom watching them, his head pressed against the glass. She waved at him, her new friend, her only friend here, and listened to the children sing a song about the colors of a rainbow.

CHAPTER 3

After the class, Allison, Mina, and Jason walked to one of the nearby Korean barbeque places for a late dinner. Mina had taken Allison to Korean restaurants in Virginia a few times, but this was not like any she'd seen. A man dropped a large glowing coal in the middle of their table and placed a grill on top. A plate of sliced pork called *samgyeopsal* was brought out with plates of lettuce, *kimchi*, onions, garlic. Jason lifted the tongs and laid the slabs of meat on the grill. Mina was on her cell phone giving directions to a group of friends who were meeting them. *Soju* and beer were ordered and the first shots and cheers already delivered when the others arrived.

"To my sister. I never thought you'd come here." Mina pushed the drink to her.

"Me neither." They clinked glasses. Mina, as always, looked stunning. Even here among all the Koreans, she still inhabited a different orbit. Even here there was a certain edge to her beauty. But Allison could see a cloud of dullness around Mina's eyes, her sunken cheeks, and Allison knew Mina was not eating or sleeping enough. It was not a great time to talk to their parents, but Wayne had made her promise she'd call as soon as she could.

Allison borrowed Mina's phone to call them. Wayne had purchased a phone plan where Mina's calls would be charged to him, in the hope that she'd call more. It was morning there; Wayne should have been at work, but he answered the home phone on the first ring.

"I was beginning to worry," he said.

"Mina's here." Allison paused. "She's fine."

"Can I talk to her?"

Allison held the phone to Mina, but she shook her head. "Not now. We're out having dinner. Seoul's nothing like you said. It's rich. And there's no pigs on the buses." Jason smiled slightly. He plucked a piece of meat from the grill, dipped it in sesame oil and salt, dropped it in the middle of a leaf, then added garlic before folding the leaf like a burrito and popping the entire thing into his mouth. She thought she heard him oink. "Mina's fine. She teaches children just like she said— they sang me a song."

"That I'd have to see," he said. "Tell her I just want to hear her voice."

"Another time Dad, okay?"

"Hey, that boss of yours called. Ray Shifflet."

"Ex-boss."

"Sounded important. You might want to call him."

She'd deal with the paperwork and debriefing when she was back in Virginia. "Okay Dad. Got to go. Love you, too."

Mina was chatting with two friends, nodding and arranging places for them at the table. Allison knew Mina had probably been half listening to the call but wouldn't ask about it. Mina introduced her friends. Tom, from London, a teacher at her school. Gary, a Canadian who played soccer with Sam, and Kayla, an Australian from Perth who taught at the same university as Jason.

"I'm just an English lecturer. A *gang sa*," Kayla said. "But Jason's a real professor, with a PhD from UCLA. He's developing robots who teach English—out to make us obsolete." Allison turned to Jason, whose face remained expressionless. She'd not even thought to ask him what he did or who he was, and while she could blame her rudeness or lack of concern on jet lag, she knew it was because she'd only seen him as one of Mina's guys, whose purpose in life was to cater to Mina's whims and desires. She was about to ask him about these robots he'd studied, but the conversation had already shifted to a discussion of where they would go next. They decided on a bar a few buildings away.

"You sure you want to come?" Mina said to Allison. "You must be really tired."

She didn't feel tired exactly. More like clotted, like her body was heavy and weighted, like a thin veil separated her from the world.

She'd known Seoul would be different, but she was not prepared for the absence of anything that referred to her life back home. What was so alien to her about it was how easily everyone else moved through it, even Mina and her foreign friends, as if this was the way the world was supposed to be, with its careless crowds and cacophony of techno music and knots of people spanning the road. That this was the way life was really lived, on the streets, outside of the domestic domain. That it was normal to share bits of food cooked over hot coals at ten at night, drink rice alcohol from tiny shot glasses, make plans for a night that would last until the sun rose. And that Allison's world of moving singularly and smoothly from kitchen to living room to bedroom, from house to car to office and home again was the life that was strange, foreign, perplexing.

Mina raised her *soju* glass and stood. "A toast, to my sister who came all the way to Korea just to bring me back to good ol' America." Everyone laughed except Jason. Allison wondered what their father had told Mina, if he had perhaps bribed her, too, with something to bend her will.

She went with them because even though she was exhausted, she knew she would not be able to sleep, that her frayed nerves had been sparked, that her senses, overloaded, wanted more. And she was determined to watch Mina in this world she now inhabited.

She could not remember the last time she'd stayed up past midnight, and when she next checked her watch she was in a bar called Noli. It was three in the morning Korean time, which meant it was two the next afternoon in Virginia. She'd been up for thirty-five hours. She'd gotten drunk and sobered up several times in the course of the evening. She'd never been a big drinker, so a few shots of the vile *soju* and a couple of beers were all it took, while the others drank endless pitchers of Korean draft beer and drained bottles of *soju* with alacrity. At Woodstock, a bar lined with albums that played songs from their father's era, Mina had clinked Allison's *soju* glass with hers and leaned into her ear so that she could be heard above the din.

"Why didn't you do this with me in the States?"

"I don't know, job, marriage, pregnancies, miscarriages. I had other things on my plate." Besides, Mina was the wild one in the family, the one their parents fawned and fretted over, and Allison had always figured there was only room in the family for one Mina. But here in Korea, what did it matter if she became a different person for a little while, became part of Mina's crowd, so that she could gain Mina's confidence, some intimacy, before she laid bare all she'd learned of Mina's affair with Ray?

It was at Noli that another person arrived, a tall, thin man with chocolate skin and a face with such perfect symmetry it could have easily graced a magazine cover. Mina was dancing with no one and everyone. Her shirt rose and fell with each sway, revealing a flat stomach and a glittering belly ring. She was as entrancing and hypnotic as a snake charmer, so that the dance floor seemed to orbit around her and her hips and her hair, which she pulled up with her hands to cool her neck before letting it fall again, like a dark and heavy curtain on a hidden stage. Though she seemed to be in her own world, when the man came in, leaning languidly near the entrance, she ran to him, jumping into his arms. He was the one, Allison knew then, who for the moment at least, was the source of Mina's pleasure and pain in the world, the reason for her sunken eyes and gaunt cheeks. Once he arrived, Mina was ready to go home, so the three of them walked back to the apartment. His name was Robert. He and Mina went straight to her bedroom while Allison fell onto the sofa, not even bothering to pull it out.

The next day, Allison awoke to Mina holding a cup of coffee in front of her face. She'd smelled the coffee first, and she thought she was back home waking to the pot Bonnie made every morning. Allison sat up and sipped from the cup.

"It's instant but it's not bad," Mina said. She stood over Allison, watching her. Robert brought two more mugs. Mina motioned for Allison to move so she could sit down. He handed a mug to Mina then moved to the window. He slid the panel, stuck his fingers through the bars, nudged the window open, allowing cool air into the room.

"Robert's from Trinidad, originally," Mina said. "American citizen. US Army, enlisted." Mina never cared if the guy she was with was rich or poor, what his education or background was. He just had to have a certain dangerous sexiness, a charisma and charm that matched hers.

Robert nodded. He was even more beautiful in the daylight—darker, taller, all angles and planes. He had not said much on the walk home, just hellos and whispers into Mina's ear.

Allison tried to think of something to say that would make him talk. *Wh-* questions—she'd read that in more than one women's magazine. "How long have you been in Korea?"

"Six months."

Not technically a *Wh-* question. She tried again. "What do you think of it?"

"It's okay," he said. His voice was deep and accented, like an old coworker who had immigrated from the Bahamas. Robert showed little desire to make an impression on her, displaying none of the solicitousness of Jason or the camaraderie of Kayla and the others.

Mina went to Robert and put her hand around his waist. Even though Mina was 5'7", her head only touched his shoulder. "First time I've seen him in a few weeks. They're always sending him away."

Robert said nothing, just looked out the window. "I've got to get going." He pecked the top of her head, above her messy ponytail. "I'll call you when I get back." Mina walked with him out of the apartment. Allison took a shower and dressed. By the time Mina had come back it was already early afternoon. Allison had never slept in that late her whole life.

"Let's get something to eat and I'll show you around a bit," Mina said. "I'm starving."

Allison was, too. Out on the street, busy with Saturday shoppers in high heels and dresses and skinny pants and tight T-shirts, they walked a few blocks to a restaurant full of customers huddled over black stone bowls of steaming soup. Soon they were seated, and Mina, not even asking for a menu or what Allison wanted, ordered for them. A few minutes later, hot barley tea was poured into their plastic cups while side dishes of marinated seaweed, *kimchi*, bean sprouts, and two small fried fish, whole, arrived. Mina showed Allison how to peel the fish bones away with her chopsticks to reveal white, delicate meat. Allison couldn't face the fish head, crispy, eyes closed, mouth a downward slit. She closed her eyes when she ate the fish. Two earthenware bowls of boiling red soup were set in front of them. Mina cracked an egg in hers then stirred it up, instructing Allison to do the same. *Soon du bu*, tofu soup, thick with red pepper and soft tofu, with pieces of seafood mixed in. Mina scooped rice into an empty bowl. She poured hot water into the pot. The rice stuck to the sides and bits of it loosened and floated, brewing a weak broth. Allison thought it tasted like toasted hot water, but Mina insisted it was a delicacy that Koreans loved.

"He's going on a mission, that's why he had to leave," Mina said, as if she were answering a question Allison had just asked.

"Where?"

Mina shrugged. "Can't say exactly. I think he goes into North Korea. He lives in the woods for days at a time."

"Sounds dangerous."

"He's going to help me find my mother."

"If she's alive," Allison said.

"She is," Mina said.

"You know something?"

Mina stared at her across the dishes. "I'll tell you later, when I'm sure."

Sure about what, Allison wondered. Sure she could be trusted? Sure she had the answers? Either way, Allison didn't ask. She wasn't sure herself that she was ready to hear what Mina would tell her. After lunch they walked to the subway station, which was more labyrinthine and chaotic than the aging Metro Allison was used to. Mina bought a rechargeable subway card for Allison to use during her stay and led her through clotted passageways to their train. They rode for three stops, squeezed in the middle of a crowded car that smelled of garlic and alcohol. They transferred trains, emerging into cold bright sun and a small stream below them that ran through the city. They stood on one of the small, sloping bridges that overlooked the stream, called the Cheongyecheon, with young families and couples holding hands, admiring the trimmed trees, still bare, and modern sculptures, the environs cultivated to accommodate those thousands who had descended on the stream for an afternoon stroll.

"After the Korean war, this stream was filled with trash and dead things. Only the poorest would live here. In the seventies, they paved the stream over and built a highway. What you see is only five years old. Dad doesn't know how much has changed."

Even in the chilly weather, people lounged in the grassy park along the stream while children hopped from one stone to the other. Everyone looked so calm and peaceful, it was hard for Allison to imagine the world Mina described being here before. "He worries about you."

"For all the wrong reasons."

"You don't mind the crowds?" Above the bank of the stream rose the skyscrapers of downtown Seoul.

"I kind of like them. Lots of energy. And easier to disappear. I couldn't do that in the States."

"Why would you want to disappear?" Allison turned to Mina, who suddenly seemed to be peering a little too far over the bridge.

"I didn't say that."

Allison gently gripped Mina's arm, as if she could somehow rein her sister in. "I quit my job."

"Good."

"What?" Her hold on Mina tightened.

Mina didn't answer at first. Her eyes were closed and she seemed to be listening, perhaps to the stream's gurgle underneath the sounds of the city. "I'm glad you came," she finally said, covering her hand over Allison's.

"Me, too."

They joined the crowds and walked along the stream, the late March wind still fierce on Allison's ears and nose. On the way back, the subway station seemed even more crowded. Allison struggled to keep up with Mina, who negotiated the crowds with assuredness and certainty. Sometimes she gripped Mina's skinny forearm, so she wouldn't lose her. When they approached the transfer car, the bell was ringing, and Mina lurched into the crowded car, making a space for them, but Allison lost her hold. The doors closed before she could get on and the train swept Mina away, only the tip of her head visible above the masses. A hand shot up, waving, Mina's perhaps, a greeting or a goodbye or a signal of distress.

Allison panicked. She didn't have a cell phone yet, and even if she did, she didn't know Mina's number or anyone else's. If she had a phone she could have called Wayne, but what could he do, except yell at her for being stupid, for not watching herself in this dangerous country? Should she wait for Mina to return? Would she? Could anyone here speak English, and if they could, how could they help her? Was there a lost children booth, where Allison would wait for her baby sister to pick her up, give her a lollipop, take her home? She leaned against the wall, listened to the rush of air in the subway tunnel, the bell clanging on the other side of the tracks. Her throat constricted. She wanted to cry. She remembered the day Mina had arrived, three years old. She must have felt like the lost child then.

Allison was turning six that year, and had to stay home with a sitter while Bonnie picked up Wayne and Mina from the airport. She ran to her dad as soon as the front door opened, but he didn't pick her up and swing her around as he used to. A girl with short black hair wearing a pink frilly dress and black patent leather shoes was sleeping on his shoulder. Allison hugged his knees, and he handed the girl over to her mom. He wrapped his arms around Allison, but didn't pick her up.

"She doesn't look like me," Allison said.

"Doesn't matter. She's your sister now." Her mom stroked the sleeping girl's jet black hair.

She had awakened the next morning to find the girl standing over her. They'd removed Allison's toy chest and replaced it with a small bed for Mina. "Sisters share, that's the fun of it," her mom had said as Allison helped her make Mina's bed the day of her arrival. Mina had a butterfly bedspread, gauzy with yellows and blues while Allison's was splattered with large flowers the colors of earth and sand.

Mina stood above her in a white sleeveless nightgown. She gripped one of Allison's Barbies and had the head in her mouth. "*Omma*," the girl said. "*Bego pa*."

"Speak English," Allison said.

The girl sucked on the Barbie head.

"Mina mouse," Allison said. "Minnie Mouse."

The girl jabbered again, the words sounds Allison had never heard before. She grabbed the Barbie. "That's mine. No play."

The girl started crying. "*Omma*," she wailed. "*Omma*."

Allison's mom arrived then. She scooped the girl in her arms and soothed her. "It's alright Mina. Poor thing." She cupped the girl's head to her shoulder, looked at Allison. "What did you do to her?"

"Nothing," Allison said. "She doesn't even speak English."

She waited that morning to see her dad, but he slept until lunch time. Only after he'd eaten did he call her to where he sat in his recliner.

He looked the same as she remembered, except that he needed a shave and he seemed a little shorter, and the small belly she used to rest her head on was gone. Mina was sleeping in the bedroom, after crying off and on all morning, and the house was for once quiet.

"What do you think of your new sister?" he asked her.

What did she think? She was already tired of her, wanted her to go back to Korea, wanted her room and her parents to herself. "She can't speak English," Allison said.

"She has to learn it. You can help her."

Allison rubbed his cheeks. "You need to shave."

He sighed. "I'm taking the day off."

"Is *Hee Haw* on tonight?" Allison asked.

Her dad smiled slightly, kept his eyes closed. "Well I don't know. But we can find out Ally-gator."

"I'm not a gator. I'm your little girl," she said. She climbed up in his lap even though he groaned dramatically about how big she was, going into first grade. She didn't care. She would stay there forever if she could.

Then Mina was crying again, yelling, in Korean Allison guessed, and she wondered why the girl couldn't just be quiet for a while. Her dad pushed himself off the recliner and disappeared down the hall. Allison waited for him to return, but when he didn't, she went to her bedroom. Mina was sitting in his lap, a small manageable bundle, and he was rocking her. Her mom was in the room as well, rooting around Allison's closet until she came up with an old baby doll with white blonde hair and glassy blue eyes. Mina curled her arm around the doll and whimpered herself back to sleep. Her dad told Allison to play quietly in the family room, that Mina and he were jet lagged. When she asked what that meant, he said that they'd flown for a long time and night was day and day was night and the body didn't know what to do when.

Sure enough, Allison awoke that night with Mina sleeping with her in her bed. Jet lagging, Allison thought. She pushed Mina off the bed, so that she fell with a thump to the floor. She readied herself for Mina's wailing and the subsequent whipping she'd get. She told herself it was worth it. But Mina did not cry. Instead she stood quietly, hovering over Allison in the dark. She felt the girl's presence, her low,

33

shallow breathing tickling her bare arm. And then Mina lay down on the floor next to the bed. Allison closed her eyes, praying that Mina would be gone in the morning, that she was just a ghost or a spirit that needed to be returned to its rightful place.

When Allison awoke, Mina was still on the floor, sleeping, holding the white-haired baby doll she must have retrieved sometime in the night. Allison went to her parents' room and tried to crawl in bed with them. She told them she'd had a nightmare, but Wayne said it was not yet morning, that she was a big girl now. He told her to return to her room and go back to sleep.

But her room was no longer her room, her world no longer her world. Instead, she sat in the hallway in front of her parents' bedroom door, waiting for them to find her.

Of course she was just six then, but now Allison, lost in Seoul, regretted what she'd done to Mina, felt that she was getting some kind of karmic comeuppance. It served her right if Mina didn't come back for her. She took a breath, exhaled. She was not three years old, or six even. She was not in danger. She would sit and wait and come up with a plan. She had some change in her pocket and bought an instant coffee from a machine for fifty cents. She held the small cup in her hands and blew on the steam.

"Be careful, that stuff's addictive."

Allison turned and offered Mina her coffee. "Your reward for coming back for me."

"You think I wouldn't? What kind of sister do you think I am?"

That first week Allison settled into Mina's apartment, using the living room and its fold-out couch as a makeshift bedroom. She spoke to Wayne and Bonnie several times, assuring them that Mina was doing well, and that she'd seen nothing that reflected that night Mina had called wailing and weeping. She told them that Mina had a regular job, good friends, and a boyfriend, and that perhaps they should just accept that she was doing okay. She didn't mention Mina's plan to find her mother, that there was something shady about Robert, or that she was out every night until the sun came up. Those details would not help anyone.

During the day Allison wandered the strange alleyways and streets of the city, each time venturing slightly farther, making sure she'd remember her way back. Jason helped her buy a used cell phone, so if she got lost she could call Mina, or, more reliably, him. Gary had also given her his number that first Saturday night, telling her to call him if she needed anything. He'd been drunk when he'd done it, so she held off, not sure if he'd even remember her name.

She traversed the neighborhoods, stopping every few hours at one of the hundreds of coffee shops, sipping coffee and studying the twenty-seven letters that made up the Korean language, *Hangeul*, from the appendix of a travel guide. Soon she was slowly sounding out the letters on signs, storefronts, and menus, though she had no idea what the sounds meant. She'd been surprised to hear Mina speak Korean so fluently the night she arrived, as if she'd been able to conjure all the Korean she lost and then some. Her mother tongue. She spoke to the restaurant and bar attendants with ease, and occasionally she switched into fast, choppy Korean with Jason. "When did you learn to speak so well?" Allison asked her. Mina shrugged, saying she'd started learning when she moved to LA. "It's not that hard, at least the basic stuff. It feels kind of natural to speak it."

Her ticket was for a month, and after the first week Allison didn't know what she would do with the rest of her time. She had expected Mina to be more difficult, in some sort of trouble that would take time to untangle, on some kind of emotional precipice she'd have to pull her away from. Both had happened before, more than once.

One was on a Saturday night when Mina was still in high school. Allison was a freshman at George Mason University, commuting from home. Mina, as always, was at a party. Allison was already asleep, planning to get up early and study for an exam on Monday when Bonnie's cry, sharp, high-pitched, woke her. Wayne was speaking rapidly as well, although Allison could not make out his words. She heard the bathroom tap turn on, and then, she was pretty sure, Mina's soft sobs. Her mind still foggy, Allison shuffled to the bathroom. Mina sat on the toilet, her head tipped back as Bonnie dabbed with a cotton ball the blood that dotted her face. Only after Bonnie had cottoned off the blood and Mina agreed to go to the doctor did they decide not to call an ambulance or, at Mina's insistence, the police. She'd been attacked by some white girls at her school, girls jealous because they'd heard their boyfriends talking about her one night, about how they thought she was the hottest girl at school. They called her a chink, slant-eye, and other names Mina would not repeat. Two girls held her while one hit her on the head with a bottle, hoping to permanently scar her. But Mina was a fighter, she'd been in fights before, and had just earned her first degree black belt in Tae Kwon Do, the Korean martial art she'd been studying since sixth grade. She escaped, and now she was squeezing back tears as Bonnie dabbed antiseptic into the cuts. Allison stood in the doorway, her pajamas slightly damp from the warmth of deep sleep, and she couldn't help but wonder if Mina had told the whole story, if there weren't something more than the boys' talk or the girls' jealousy, but there was nothing she could say. When she saw that she wasn't needed, she padded back to bed. When she woke up, Bonnie told her Mina had gotten twelve stitches on her scalp, but her face was not permanently scarred.

That was more than fifteen years ago, a world away for both of them. For the first time in Allison's memory, Mina had not only her usual group of male admirers, but a few female friends as well. She seemed settled into her life in a way Allison had not seen her before, rooted in this rootless world of itinerant internationals, many who were only in Korea for a year or two before moving on to travel around China, Thailand, Taiwan, Vietnam. Allison didn't need three weeks to find the right moment to confront her sister about Ray. To bring her home or convince her to never come back. To get the house and a new job and resume her life, be the good sister, or to return without Mina, face Wayne's disappointment, then tell them about Mina and Ray, and be done with Mina once and for all.

CHAPTER 4

Two US Army officers were killed with their own axes on August 25, 1976, five months before Wayne arrived in Korea for his tour of duty. The argument had been over a poplar tree in the Joint Security Area at the Demilitarized Zone that divided North and South Korea. North Korea's esteemed leader, Kim Jong Il, had planted it years before, and the North Korean commander said he had an order from the top for no one to touch the sacred tree. But US Captain Bonifas ignored their request to stop pruning, and commanded that the operation continue. Calmly, the North Korean commander removed his watch and wrapped it in a handkerchief. Then he struck Bonifas with a karate chop to the neck, grabbed his axe, and hacked him and another officer who was also overseeing the pruning. In the chaos, the North Korean soldiers fled back across the Bridge of No Return to North Korean soil. Three days after the killings, Operation Paul Bunyan was carried out with the combined support of more than eight hundred US and Republic of Korea soldiers. The poplar tree was successfully chopped down.

Now it was January 1977, and the country was still on lockdown, with all US military personnel and Korean citizens under a midnight curfew. Wayne was told off the record that if the North Koreans took Seoul, there were men under command to shoot him and everyone else who worked in Intel. He was terrified he would die, forsaking his young wife and baby girl, who he liked to believe could not manage without him.

He'd married Bonnie a year out of high school in the Baptist church in their hometown of Hillsdale, Tennessee. It took a year and a half for her to get pregnant, though it wasn't for lack of trying. Sometimes things just happen that way, she'd told him. He secretly despaired that they might not have a family, that something might be wrong with her, but then one day after he'd come home from work, she told him simply that she'd been to the doctor, that she was pregnant, and then she started crying. He wrapped his arms around her and cried with her. He hadn't realized until then how hard it had been for both of them.

In her eighth month, Bonnie was having problems breathing and her blood pressure was dangerously high, so she quit her job at the Piggly Wiggly for a month of doctor-ordered bed rest. Allison was born two weeks early, a difficult labor that left Bonnie so weak that the doctor told her she should think twice about having any more. There was no discussion of her working—where they came from, a mother stayed home with her baby. Wayne was working as a drywall helper, and was a year away from being on his own as a drywall hanger, so they left their rented apartment and moved back in with Wayne's parents. They lived in a dark room on the second floor, and Bonnie spent most of her time there with Allison, dreaming of the house they'd rent in a year, how she'd paint the kitchen yellow and the furniture white, and leave no room darkened or secret.

But when that year was almost up, Wayne could not reconcile himself with a life of hanging drywall in their hometown. There was nothing wrong with Hillsdale, but both sets of parents were always interfering, telling Bonnie how to take care of Allison, fighting for time with their granddaughter. Bonnie felt she had no say in how her daughter was raised. Wayne thought he should expand his horizons and provide for his family, so he enlisted. By then, it was 1975. Vietnam was winding down and he figured it would be a few more years before the US geared up for something else. He didn't have an appetite for war, and he'd seen the damage Vietnam had done to some of his buddies who came back broken, if at all. But the possibilities and the allure of the uniform in a peacetime role appealed to him. He signed up for the standard five years, and after that he could get out if he wanted to, with a skill that might take him farther than hanging drywall. Bonnie agreed that now was as good a time as any to give them a change of scenery. Besides, she said, there was some kind of romantic allure to being a military wife.

In November 1975, they moved to Fort Polk, Louisiana, where Wayne was stationed for thirteen months. Fort Puke. Little Vietnam. They trained in marshes, the air so heavy with heat and water that his skin felt slicked with oil. The boys returning from Vietnam were stationed there, sad, crazy men who took to the heat and swamps like a place so deep in memory and re-living that they'd never be comfortable again anywhere else. For thirteen months he toiled there. Bonnie and Allison lived with him in housing on base, poor as they'd ever been, but strangely unburdened from place and family, of their oppression and compassion, for the first time in their lives. They didn't talk about the broken souls around them, ghosts of a war already wanting to be forgotten, and when Wayne learned he'd be stationed in Korea for a year and would get hardship duty pay because his family had to stay behind, he thought, well, it's just a year.

And so he bid Bonnie and Allison farewell, already missing them before he'd let go of their hands, already lighter than he'd ever felt, finally untethered from the place and people he'd loved and known, and for him, barely twenty-two, knowing and loving were still the same thing, inseparable in his mind of loyalties and allegiances.

He and the group of GIs on his flight were met at Seoul's Kimpo airport by military officials who read off everyone's name from a list, like a roll call at school. He was already assaulted by the smells of garlic, sewage, and something like old shoes. He was going to Camp Humphreys. The guy who'd sat beside him on the plane, Tyrone from Detroit, nudged Wayne's ribs. "Man, you lucky, word is the Hump is the best place to be. Me, I'm going to a shithole." One of the military men pointed to Tyrone, who was unshaven, his hair shooting up in different directions. "Clean this guy up, he's a mess." And that was the last Wayne saw of him.

The whole country smelled. It stank. Even in the sharp bite of the January wind, blowing straight from Siberia, the smells seeped into his clothing, sat on his skin. Smells of dead things rotting. Sewage seeping from drains in the streets. Shit. Not the mild, slightly sweet tang of cow and horse dung back home. This shit was acrid and sharp, smelling of illness and bad food and vomit. He wondered if the smell would ever go away, but it didn't; it only abated as they pulled onto the base.

He was assigned a bunk and a bunk boy, Mr. Park, a small stooped man as old as Wayne's father, who for twenty dollars a month would shine Wayne's shoes, make his bunk, press his uniform. All of those responsibilities he'd learned in basic were essential to being an Army man had now been relegated to someone else who needed the work and the money even more than he did. Vietnam was over, and Wayne was already sensing that everyone, including the military officers, just wanted to relax, to let the air out. He spent the first few days sleeping off his jet lag and getting used to his job in the photo lab developing airplane reconnaissance photos. The third day he got his pass to leave Camp Humphreys, and his fellow GIs were waiting to show him the village outside the base, the Ville.

"The first thing you got to get is a hooch," one of guys said as soon as they'd left the gates. "Only twenty bucks a month and you've got your own pad, for not much more you get a *yobasayo* and rice."

"A yobo say what?" Wayne said.

The guys laughed. Wayne was already annoyed at how superior they felt, when they'd only arrived in Korea a few months before he had.

"It means hello in Korean," a boy named Sam said. "But that's what we call the girls."

"I don't need no whore," Wayne said. "I got me a wife and a pretty baby girl back home."

The boys laughed again. They were just out of high school, eighteen or nineteen, and Wayne suddenly felt so much older than them with his responsibilities and family, already formed and blossoming.

An old woman approached him. She was wearing a mismatched voluminous cotton shirt and baggy pants, both decorated in clashing flower patterns. Wayne thought the primary colors of the woman's clothes looked garish in the desolate, washed-out landscape before him.

"You want blow job, short time, long time, good price." The woman gave a half-toothed grin. Her black hair was curled into tiny permed cones.

"With you?"

The guys laughed. "You really are green," Sam said. "She's the *mama-san*. The pimp."

"Go away, old woman," a guy named Lenny said.

"New blood. That's you," another guy said. "But don't use them. The girls are cheap but they all got VD. And they're ugly. We'll show you how to get the good ones."

"I told you," Wayne said. "I'm a married man. I don't pay for sex."

"Hell, I'm married too," Lenny said. "I'm telling you man, twelve months is a long time."

"What happens in Korea stays in Korea," said another.

Ahead of them stretched one narrow paved road stiff from the frost that covered the land like an eggshell. The buildings were one or two stories, their tops netted in a mass of crisscrossing wires. *Hangeul*, the Korean alphabet, decorated the doors and signs of the stores, and Wayne, who had not yet bothered to learn the letters, felt like he'd fallen into a strange dream that offered neither compass nor refuge. Soon, signs in English appeared: bars called Seven, Duffy's, Top Hat, Maxim, Soul Brother, the bar for the black GIs, and T-boys for the whites. Young, pretty Korean women crowded in, some with cards around their necks. Outside many of the bars, a sign posted by the US military read: *Makgeolli* Kills.

"Who's Mah Ko Lee?" Wayne said.

Again, the knowing laughter. "It's some old shit Korean alcohol made from rice. The farmers drink it. Tastes like spoiled milk. Stay away from it."

"Does it really kill you?" Wayne said.

"Does the US military lie?" Sam said.

"It stinks to high heaven here," Wayne said.

"It's from the rice paddies. They use shit to fertilize them. You'll get used to it."

"Just watch out for the honey wagon. That's when they suck up all the sewage. A man could die if he got too near that."

Except for Wayne, all of the men were in a good mood. He wanted to go home. Not to Bonnie and Allison, whom he loved but who would not allow him a moment's rest. For the first time since he'd left it, he wanted to go back to Hillsdale, where hills rolled so far that he felt he was riding an ocean wave whenever he looked at them for too long. He missed his horse, Lady, who was probably dead now, the last he'd heard she was near to it, and all those people and places he'd up until that very moment been glad to be away from. He wanted to ride his horse into the hills and lie in the grass and breathe in that green and stare at the open sky for so long that he imagined he was up there looking down on his small, sweet life.

It did not take Wayne long to learn about the Ville. There was Grubbies, run by an ex-GI hippie who sold rolling papers and made his own ripped jeans by shooting holes in them. Soul Brothers was the blacks-only club, where the *tuigi's,* children of the devil, worked. They were women born to Korean mothers, abandoned or never even claimed by their American GI fathers.

That first night they took Wayne to Duffy's and introduced him to the owner, Mr. Lee. He brought them a round of Korean beer called OB in large brown bottles and poured the beer into glasses. The Rolling Stones blared from the speakers. Some Korean women sat at their table. They were pretty enough, with effortless long hair and slim figures, but he'd never even thought about Asian women before or ascertained their special appeal. He couldn't understand what was wrong with the women back home.

"This here's Sue, and this is Kimmy, and this is Jin," Lenny said.

The girls nodded and giggled. "So handsome," one of them said.

"They're full of shit, but we don't care. We all play the game." Sam lit a cigarette and patted for one of the girls to sit on his lap. He ordered a cocktail for her, which she sipped slowly from a straw. "Which one do you like? It's good to make a down payment, otherwise the best ones get taken. Like Kimmy here, see I bought her a drink and I'm slipping her a dollar too, just so she knows who to come to at the end of the night."

The girl called Sue was draped on Lenny, laughing at anything he said, even if it wasn't funny. "Where's your card?" he asked her.

"I forgot it."

"Bullshit. No card, no money." Sue stopped mid-laugh, stood up, and stomped away. "Don't ever let them pull that shit on you," Lenny said. "If they don't have their card, that means they got the clap. I learned the hard way—got it every month the first three I was here. I try not to get too drunk to remember now." The boys laughed again and drained their beers in unison.

Wayne's head was spinning. All the stuff he'd scoffed at in English class came back to him—he was falling down the rabbit hole, he was descending into the circles of hell, he was not in Kansas anymore. He was afraid he'd catch a disease just by being in this bar. He thought of Bonnie at this very moment vacuuming as she liked to do mid-mornings while Allison played with stuffed animals in her crib, the apartment clean and tidy, smelling of lemons. A truck rolled by the bar and he swore he could smell the shit steaming out of it.

"Y'all are going to hell." Wayne stood. He'd seen bars before, but nothing like this. He wondered if it was because they'd abandoned God by coming here.

"Don't be such a pussy."

"I give him two weeks," Lenny said.

Wayne ran out of the bar onto the street, crowded with soldiers he didn't know. He hurried back to base, fell into his bunk, and wrote Bonnie a rambling letter of childhood longing, of how when he was a little boy, he'd watch the show of shadows play across his room, of how he was too terrified to sleep. Then he prayed to God and asked for strength and forgiveness, of which, he already feared, he would need much in the year to come.

CHAPTER 5

After that first week in Seoul, Allison understood more clearly what Mina's world must have been like growing up. On the afternoons when she explored tiny alleyways of crumbling houses, the old women with their short, permed hair staring impassively at her, the men squatting in the streets smoking cigarettes and appraising her without shame, she guessed how it felt. To be the only one. To be noticed whether you wanted to or not. To not be able to disappear. Even on the main streets where Starbucks sold tiny cups of coffee for twice as much as back home and Italian bistros and Turkish kebab joints filled their seats with eager Koreans, even there, in a world she understood more, where she was greeted in English and given extra attention, she was still, quite obviously, a *way-gook*. Outside person. And this was how, despite her parents' efforts, Mina must have felt every day of her life.

But whenever Allison started to feel some peeling away of her resentment, a possible surrendering to her sister, she imagined Mina and Ray having sex in some hotel room or even on his desk, her lean legs spread and inviting. Yet she wasn't ready to confront her, either. So for the rest of the week, when Mina asked her to go out with them, Allison declined, blaming lingering jet lag.

Then, Friday morning, just as Allison was dressed to go out on one of her forays, Mina padded into the living room, wrapped in a towel.

"Are you ready to get naked?"

"Are you still drunk?" It was just after ten, a time when Mina usually still sleeping off the night's fun. She worked from three to eight weekdays, a perfect schedule for nightly bar hopping.

"Nope, came home early last night so I could take you to a Korean sauna. Best thing for jet lag. Give me five minutes to dress."

Allison couldn't remember them being naked before. When Mina had first arrived, Allison said she was too old to take a bath with her little sister. Even when they shared a room in the early years, Allison had always changed in the bathroom, and when she finally got her own room, she double-checked her bedroom door lock before she undressed. Mina was the opposite. Bonnie was forever chasing her around the house with a towel after her bath, Mina's small wet feet leaving damp marks on the tiled floors. She'd run outside in her pale nightgown claiming it was a dress, or she'd insist on removing her top because Daddy wasn't wearing one.

Allison remembered her parents talking about it one night after dinner, not long after Mina had been adopted.

"Maybe she just has a wild streak," Bonnie said. "Like her father." Bonnie laughed then, but Wayne didn't.

"You don't know what those people from those little villages are like," Wayne had said. "Savages. They use human shit to fertilize their rice paddies, the boys piss wherever they want, and they all wash in one big bath house. That's where she gets it from. Give her a few more months, she'll adapt."

Now Mina met Allison at the door, her long hair pulled back and loosely piled on her head. She wore baggy, faded jeans and the same Navy hoodie that Allison had on. Presents from Wayne that last Christmas they were together. In cursive gold script the letters spelled "Daddy's Girl."

"I didn't know you still had yours," Allison said. Mina said nothing, just slipped her feet into her canvas sneakers and led her down the street.

At the front desk they were each charged six thousand won, almost six dollars, and were given two locker keys and four towels not much larger than washcloths, which, Mina explained, they were to use for washing and drying. She followed Mina to the lockers that matched the numbers on their keys. Mina pulled off her hoodie and threw it in the locker. Her rib cage was as narrow and bony as a child's.

"In LA you'd pay sixty bucks for this."

Allison still had her jacket on. "Isn't this just a little bit weird for you?"

"Why?" Mina shimmied out of her jeans. She was wearing no underwear.

"I don't know, the whole naked thing?"

"So?"

Allison shrugged off her jacket and hung it on the one hanger in her locker. She took off her own hoodie and jeans so that she was just down to her beige bra and blue underwear.

"If you'd told me we were coming here, I'd at least have made sure they matched."

"Nobody cares, trust me." Mina, naked, was sitting on the bench now, crossed legs swinging impatiently. Her hand waved in the air, as if it were holding a cigarette. Like a painting: Study of naked woman smoking at a café.

Allison clamped the towel between her neck and chest as she unfastened her bra and then pulled down her underwear. She folded her clothes and stacked them in the locker.

Mina was already walking to the sauna, carrying the little packets of soaps and shampoos she'd bought at the front desk. Mina showed Allison around the sauna like a proud homeowner. "Here's the green tea pool, and the geranium pool, and the really hot pool, and the cold pool. And *Hinoki tang*—a pool with special Japanese wood. Then here's the crystal sauna, the mud sauna, and the salt sauna. We'll do a few of these to prepare the skin for them—the death scrubbers." She turned toward two older women whose sagging breasts were cupped in loose black bras. Their stomachs doubled over the bands of their black lace underwear, but their legs were muscular and toned. One was scooping yogurt out of a container and rubbing it on a woman's body. The other was scrubbing a woman's back with a green mitt. "But before the saunas we have to wash and ready our skin," Mina said.

"We have to wash before we're washed? Isn't that like cleaning before the maid comes?"

"Kind of. You don't want to get the pools dirty, right?"

On the left were rows of plastic stools and spigots with hoses attached. Mina placed the packets on the tile between them and sprayed the stools, which looked like chairs from a pre-school.

Through the soft filter of steam, the women's sauna looked like a straight guy's porn fantasy. Dozens of naked women showered, scrubbed, soaked, laughed, and lounged as if at a Sapphic resort. The problem was, for the porn fantasy part at least, the women were real and not blurred and steamy, and any close ups would reveal stomach scars and deflated breasts, bellies that distended and rolled like a man's. Even the good looking ones, the ones who might have made the final cut for the sauna fantasy movie scene, were not flawless. In Allison's opinion at least, their breasts were too small, the half-cone shape too pointed, the hip and shoulder bones too sharp, the skin too mottled with ghost trails of stretch marks canvassing stomachs and thighs. These women, so perfect when fully clothed, were reassuringly human—real—to Allison, although she still felt self-conscious. She was the only white woman, and her breasts, somewhat average in her opinion, looked swollen and pendulous. And the women's legs, all of them, even the older grandmothers whose stomachs doubled or trebled with hilly folds, boasted shapely calves, toned thighs, and, miraculously, no cellulite.

"Now I know why you have such great legs," Allison said.

"All Korean women do," Mina said. "It helps to keep men from noticing our flat asses."

Mina and some of the other girls looked cadaverously thin to Allison. Jutting hipbones, ribs like keys on a piano. She wanted to bake something for them, a chocolate cake or apple pie, and feed them tiny forkfuls the way you might feed a baby bird through a dropper.

"Wash my back?" Mina turned so that her spine, with its knots and visible ribs, made her look from the back like an old woman. Allison dipped her scrubber into a round tub of soapy water, then gently touched her sister's back.

"Harder," Mina said. "I can't feel anything."

"You have a half moon," Allison said. She touched each of the tiny moles at the base of Mina's back.

"I say it's a dolphin. Didn't you know?"

"I guess not," Allison said.

"Okay, you don't have to scrub me raw," Mina said. "That's what the *ajummas* are for. Rinse me." Mina shifted forward on her stool as Allison sprayed Mina's back with bursts of warm water. "Your turn."

They changed positions. Allison braced for Mina's scraping, but her pressure was firm, not painful.

"I wish I had your skin," Mina said. "Creamy. Like milk."

"And it burns and blushes way too easily. I'll trade my skin for your body."

Mina laughed, quickly. "I guess I could finally figure out what it's like to be in yours. My body is the only one I know."

"What's it like to sleep with so many guys?" Allison said.

"You've got a lot of dead skin." Mina squirted the hose on her back, rinsing off the suds. "I don't know if it's so many. Not that I've counted. What about you? Were you a virgin when you married Ted?"

"Oh, God no."

Mina laughed. "That's good to hear."

"Have you ever slept with a married man?"

"Once or twice." Mina stood. "When I was younger. I don't pull that shit now." She took the tiny towel and wrapped it on her head. "You have a luscious body. You should experiment a little now that you're single."

"No way." Allison draped her towel in front of her.

"Whatever." Mina sounded bored with the conversation. "Let's go rub salt on ourselves then." As Allison followed her to the salt sauna, she wondered if that was true, that if Allison asked her about Ray she'd shrug her shoulders, wonder what the big deal was. That would be even worse, that Ray was so insignificant that the repercussions for Allison had never even crossed her mind. That something that Allison dreamed of having only in the darkest, quietest moments of the night was of no consequence to Mina, that to Mina Ray was just a fly, a shrug, a penny dropped on the ground not worth picking up.

Allison knew, though, that Mina understood her feelings from the day she first set foot in the office. Mina interviewed for the summer job on a rainy April morning. She'd stopped by Allison's cubicle five minutes late, dripping water from her hair onto the printout of a report Allison was editing: Mina didn't believe in umbrellas. She'd worn a sapphire silk blouse that was now clinging like a second skin, revealing the points of Mina's tiny nipples.

"Metro was delayed, as usual," Mina said. She looked around the room, stuffed with cubicles like Allison's. "So this is it, huh. Where's the all-powerful Ray's office?"

"You can't go in like that," Allison said.

"I wore a skirt like you asked me." Mina's bare legs were slick and shiny from the rain. She set her purse down next to Allison's computer. It was one of those large bucket purses with no dividers or pockets so that Mina's cigarettes, brush, makeup wallet, keys, and music player were tangled in one dark mess.

"I can see your nipples."

Mina grabbed the ends of her hair, squeezing them so that a few drops landed on Allison's report, then placed them over her breasts. "Happy?"

"Don't embarrass me."

"I won't ruin your precious little job." Mina patted her hair down. "Let's get this over with."

Afterward, Allison walked Mina to the front of the building. The rain had stopped but the streets were still wet, glistening under the sun. Mina's blouse was drying in patches so that she looked like some exotic black and blue spotted animal. Allison leaned against the brick wall, pulling her sweater tighter around her waist as she waited for Mina to light a cigarette.

"So?" Allison finally said.

"Ray's kind of weaselly. I expected a bit more from the Allison crush."

"I don't have a crush on Ray. He's a friend and my boss. And he's not weaselly."

Mina shrugged. "I've seen his type before. That ridiculous photo of his wife, like she just happened to be sitting in that field with the sun and her makeup perfect. Like that photo makes up for his fucking around on her."

Allison wanted to slap her. If they were alone, she might have, but there were too many people, some coworkers, leaving and entering the building. Instead she hugged her sweater tighter. "Just because you're a slut doesn't mean every good looking person is."

Mina opened her mouth, then closed it, shaking her head. She flicked her cigarette on the ground and rubbed it with her shoe. "I got the job."

"Please don't mess it up. Ray's opinion is important to me."

"He's a rat, Allison. He doesn't deserve your time."

"You don't know a damn thing about Ray. I do. He's a good man, honest, loyal, and hard working. He's not just my boss. He's a friend."

She looked up at Allison and studied her. "You're in love with him."

"Don't be ridiculous. I'm married. And pregnant."

"Oh God, Ally." Mina stepped over to hug her. "Congratulations. Why didn't you say something?"

"It's still early. And the last time, you know, it didn't happen." Allison swallowed.

"Look, Ted seems like a good guy. This time I'm sure it—the baby—will work out. I don't see why you can't be happy with that."

"I am." Allison bit her lip, wiped the sides of her eyes to stem the tears. "Hormones."

A llison admitted that she felt better after the sauna, more than cleansed, almost reborn. She'd thought about confronting Mina. What if she threatened to tell their parents and Mina said, *whatever.* So she kept her mouth shut and agreed to meet Mina and her friends for drinks that night. Robert was away on a mission, as he was a few weekends every month, so Mina had the weekend free.

"Everyone thinks I'm neglecting you," Mina had complained. "So please redeem me and come out tonight."

They were meeting at a martini bar in Itaewon, the main foreigner district near Yongsan, the largest US military base. She was to meet Mina at the subway station near her apartment and they would take the subway together with Jason, who lived a stop away in Hongdae.

On the subway, Mina and Allison squeezed into the last two empty seats, Jason standing in front of them. She could feel the passengers' eyes on them. Usually when people stared it was at Mina and her coltish beauty, but this time they were staring at Allison. "It's your eyes," Mina whispered, as if she'd been reading Allison's mind. Her light blue eyes, all the more noticeable with her auburn hair. They were so light, though, compared to her hair that they looked almost unnatural, like she wore colored contacts, or colored her hair. They were more arresting or striking than attractive—just a shade too light, opaque for the rest of her face. Bonnie's eyes.

Jason had met them directly from his lab at the university. Compared to last Saturday when he'd met her at the airport, Jason's face was drained of color and the corners of his eyes seemed to sink with fatigue. When she thanked him on the subway and then again at the martini bar for picking her up, he merely nodded, saying it was his pleasure, that it was no problem. Allison thought that she should do something for him, something that might restore the color to his face. She wasn't sure what, but she set her mind to it, hoping she'd come up with something by the next time she saw him.

The bar was in the basement of a four-story brick building off the main Itaewon drag. Filmy black scarves draped from the ceilings and curtained sections of the bar. Dim lights dotted the low slung tables and red velvet chairs and couches formed miniature living rooms. Mina ordered cocktails for everyone, and soon after the drinks arrived, the waiter reappeared with a large hookah pipe. Apple-flavored tobacco. The hookah was passed around and everyone took a hit except for Allison and Jason, who smoked his Korean cigarettes. She was sandwiched between Gary and Jason, and she passed the hookah from one to the other. The air smelled like apples and woodsmoke. With the low lights, red furniture, black diaphanous curtains, the persistent beat of the techno music, Allison felt like she'd stepped into an opium den.

Unlike last time, they did not have dinner together, and the group seemed more interested in cocktails and the hookah pipe than in ordering any food. They'd all probably eaten earlier, Allison thought, except for her. She'd been counting on, in fact looking forward to, the grilled meat she'd had her first night. She finished her first lemon drop martini and ordered another. She relaxed against the sofa, the cushions deep and soft, wondering what Ray would think if she told him she'd been to this place. Would she be more alluring to him, exotic, enticing? She imagined herself naked on the sofa, holding her lemon cocktail, and sending a photo to Ray. On the back she'd write: *You think you know me. But I know you.* She'd tucked his list of confessions between the empty pages of her passport. She'd ignored her father's message to call him, had not checked her email since she left. She wondered if Merry knew she was gone.

She felt pleasantly almost-drunk, ready for sleep, while the rest seemed to be getting started. The hookah had disappeared and they'd reverted to their Korean cigarettes in packs of varying colors and sizes. She'd seen the brands lined up at the kiosks and convenience stores, at least twenty, plus the American brands like Marlboro and Parliament. Almost all for less than two fifty a pack. At first Allison could barely endure the smoky bars, the ashy smell and foggy air. She could not remember the last time she'd been in a smoke-filled anything, but she soon became accustomed to the lighting of matches, the way the cigarettes punctuated conversations, allowing for pauses, emphasis, questions. She accepted them as necessary for this world of late-night conversation and camaraderie, a substitute for the bowl of chips in front of the TV and the predictable gambits that shaped her life at home, talk of food consumed, TV shows seen, petty gossip of home or work.

She declined a third drink. The others had just ordered another round, but she was feeling woozy from drinking on an empty stomach. She imagined her makeshift fold-out bed in Mina's living room, how cocooned she felt in those blankets, wishing she could transport herself there.

Looking up from her cell phone, Kayla announced that a South Korean warship had just been sunk near North Korea. Forty people were missing and there were rumors that North Korea had sunk it.

"Of course they did," Gary said. "Who else would? Japan?"

"The won is totally going to crash," Kayla said.

"Should we leave?" Allison said.

"Where to?" Mina said.

"I meant Korea. Shouldn't we leave?"

They laughed then, except for Jason.

"Welcome to Korea," Gary said. "And meet the crazy uncle in the attic—North Korea."

"A boat sinking is a bit more serious," Jason said. "This is the first time since the Korean War."

"But they don't know for sure it was the North," Mina said. "I'm with Kayla. The currency is going to dive. And I was hoping to go to Hong Kong this summer."

"Months away," Sam said. "It'll blow over by then."

She could not understand why the others were so casual about the news. Wayne had told her how unstable the region was, how to this day the North/South border was the most heavily fortified in the world. How the two countries were still technically at war. How Seoul was only forty miles from the North Korean border. Allison felt she needed to go back to the apartment. She knew Wayne would call as soon as he heard about the ship, and she wanted to know more before he did. She also thought it would be a good idea to pack her bag and get her passport, in case they had to evacuate the next day.

Jason was relaying a story of his US visa woes. Even though he'd been in the States already for three years, he'd been denied entry a few years ago because of a typographical error, and he'd had to wait the semester out until the problem had been resolved, forfeiting the classes he'd been scheduled to teach as part of his fellowship, delaying his research on robots. She wanted to ask if he thought that a little more security might be warranted in the wake of 9/11, that sometimes mistakes happened but wasn't it worth it for the greater safety of the country? But she said nothing, unable to find an entry into the rapid-fire conversation, which had jumped from the sinking ship to Jason's visa to the US's eventual and certain collapse to fascism in Britain to the upcoming World Cup in South Africa then back to what would happen to the won.

She excused herself to the bathroom to gather her thoughts, plan her escape. She splashed her face with water, applied some lipstick, dotting some on her cheeks to brighten them. She looked a bit clownish, but there was color now in her face. She stepped out of the bathroom to find Gary waiting outside.

"You doing okay?" he asked.

"I'm a little tired. I was thinking about going home."

He considered her for a second, as if he were trying to decide what role to cast her in a play he was directing. Even under the dark lights his face looked ruddy, splotched. He had small eyes that were almost as light as hers, a round, featureless face and soft, broad body. "I'm ready to go, too," he said. "All this gloom and doom talk gets old. I'll see you home."

She thanked him and returned to the table to retrieve her jacket and purse while he waited outside. She signaled to Mina that she was leaving and said her goodbyes to everyone else. She was walking up the steps and almost to the street, when she felt Mina's hand on her shoulder.

"You sure you'll be okay?"

"Why not? Gary will see me home."

Mina's hand lingered. It was a strange reversal, Mina worried about her, and Allison couldn't fathom why. Despite her panic, she knew Seoul was a safe city even with a boat sinking, everyone had told her that, and Gary was escorting her anyway, so why the worry? Mina pursed her lips and let her hand fall, telling Allison she'd see her in the morning.

As soon as they got in the taxi, Gary asked her how long was she planning to stay and what did she do back in the States.

"I'm here for three more weeks," Allison said. In one sense the past week felt long, like she'd lived another life, but in another, the week had slipped by, almost dreamlike in its fluidity. "I'm between jobs. But I was a technical writer until a month ago."

"How do you like it? Living in the States. Especially now that it's all gone to hell."

"It's not as bad as you think. My parents are there. Northern Virginia is a bit crazy with all the traffic, but it's home. And even in a recession there are good jobs in DC. Thanks to the government."

Gary nodded. "Not so many where I'm from in Canada. Saskatchewan. That's why I'm here. I miss home, but I need to make some cash."

"So you like it?"

"At first it was awesome. The girls are so pretty, the work easy, the bars open late. What's not to like, eh? But then I'd get a girlfriend and there'd be all these problems—the language barrier, relationship expectations and all that, and the work started getting boring. Every day singing songs and asking kids what's your name and how old are you and what's your favorite color, it can drive you fucking mad. So now the only thing I like is the bars, which I spend too much time and money on."

She wanted to tell him to stop going to bars so often then, but even to her that sounded so obvious as to not merit mentioning.

"The other thing I like is soccer," Gary said. "You should come to one of our games. We play on Sundays."

"Sounds fun." Not fun really, Allison thought, as much as something to do.

"Give me your number and I'll text you the info."

"You already gave me yours, last week, remember?"

"Right," Gary said. "Then you can text me." The taxi pulled up to the street near Mina's house. She gave Gary a ten thousand won note, which more than covered the fare, and he hugged her briefly before she exited the car.

Once in bed, Allison was suddenly wide awake. Her buzz had worn off, and she was convincing herself not to read too much into Gary's sudden friendliness. Even if he were interested in her, she couldn't decide if she was attracted to him. She wasn't repulsed by him, but she couldn't get beyond that, couldn't probe her desires to see if there was any kind of feeling for him. She'd had crushes before, but her attraction—love—obsession—for Ray had been singular enough to overwhelm other possibilities. She simply had little time to harbor secret infatuations between her marriage, the pregnancies and miscarriages, and her fixation.

Here in Korea, though, she was free from those tethers. She didn't have to face Ray every day, feed her hunger for him as she always had. She'd believed that seeing Ray, being with him at the office, was what got her through the miscarriages and her divorce. She needed him to be in her life, even if it was just as her boss, a sometime friend. She'd take the scraps of time with him if that was all he offered. Yet now she wondered if her longing for Ray all those years—fourteen!—was not deep but unrequited love as she'd always believed but an excuse for her not to move forward in her own life. For as soon as she'd cut herself off from him and come to Korea, she had to conjure what she'd seen in him, why he'd meant so much to her, why she couldn't for so long let go.

There were reasons. He was achingly handsome, if in a conventionally bland way. There was no one part of him that was particularly striking. It was more that his features fit together like pieces in a puzzle, resulting in a pleasing symmetrical whole. It wasn't his handsomeness, though, that had made her fall in love with him. It was his solicitousness. When he looked at her, she felt he was really *looking* at her, that if she were tired or sick he could tell right away. He remembered things, her birthday, her parents' names, that her favorite fruit was strawberries, that her favorite movie was *Casablanca*.

That was how their brief, tepid affair had started; *Casablanca* was showing one night at a Humphrey Bogart retrospective. Ray's date had cancelled and he offered to accompany Allison since he had nothing better to do. Those were his exact words: *nothing better to do*. They'd gone for a drink afterward, and, Allison realized now, more out of pity or boredom than desire, he'd kissed her by her car in the parking garage. She'd driven in that day instead of taking the subway just so she could see the movie. She returned his embrace vehemently, shrouding him with her hands and mouth, and she'd quickly unlocked the car, leading him to the back seat.

She was certain they could have been better together, and she'd always hoped they could try again some day, even with other marriages, children. But the marriages were not the obstacles she'd thought they were; his affairs with Mina and the others proved that. Once she read his list, her pitiful hope, so thin and strained, was finally wrested from her, as it should have been long before.

When Mina entered the apartment, Allison called out to her. Mina made her way to the fold-out sofa Allison was lying on, blanket tucked under her chin. Allison scooted toward the wall so Mina could sit beside her.

"Good. You're here," Mina said.

"Why wouldn't I be?"

"You may be here to check up on me, but I'm responsible for you. If something happened, Dad would never forgive me."

"What could happen? Except for North Korea bombing us over this whole sinking ship issue, which no one except me seems worried about."

"Just be careful. You're too trusting." Mina smelled of cigarettes and apple musk.

"That's true," Allison said. She'd trusted Ray and Mina to not break her heart, and they'd not cared at all about her. There was a brief silence. Outside a dog barked and a truck chugged past on the street below.

"You trust Dad too much," Mina said, her voice suddenly soft.

"Why shouldn't I?"

Mina shook her head, her hair hiding her face. "He's lying. I remember her, my mom. I'm sure of it."

"What do you remember?"

"Being tied to her back while she cooked and cleaned, resting my head on her shoulder. Sleeping on a *yo* with her, her skin damp, her arm flung across me so I couldn't escape."

Allison pulled the curtain of her sister's hair away, damp from her sudden tears, and placed her hand on Mina's bony shoulder.

"He doesn't want me to find her, but I will." Mina was crying harder now, making short raspy noises with her chest. "And then I'll find out everything."

"What do you mean?" Allison squeezed her hand.

Mina sniffed and raised her eyes. Because of the street lights, the room was never dark, only shifting tones of gray. Under the cast of the muted outside light, Mina's skin looked mottled, her eyes wet. She opened her mouth, ready, Allison suspected, to tell her everything.

"Don't worry. I won't say anything," Allison said.

Mina pulled her hand away, shook her head. "You would." She brushed Allison's cheek, tenderly, as Bonnie had when Allison was younger. And then she bid Allison good night.

CHAPTER 6

Lenny was wrong. Wayne lasted two months. The days were fine. He worked in military intelligence, with the linguists and all the other smart people, although how he got there he wasn't sure. Because of his security clearance, he was treated with a bit more respect than the regular GIs. During the day he developed film shot from planes of the Korean border. Long, wide images of trees and empty patches, far away shapes that could have been a Rorschach of his dreams. Tennessee from God's eye. But it was North Korea and the North Koreans would take an axe to him if they had the chance. His job was to examine the photos, look for anything suspicious, for little dots convening, moving toward the DMZ. He felt the importance of his job, and that was enough to get him through the days. But the sheen soon wore off, as Wayne realized that the possibility of finding suspicious troop movement was as likely as finding life on another planet. Because if they were really worried about it, Wayne figured, they wouldn't have put an enlisted GI on the task. With each successive day of developing film and finding nothing, not even a stray soldier lost or AWOL, he saw his job was more make-work than anything else. He kept those thoughts to himself, for they felt like a betrayal to the military, and by extension to America itself. He tried to see himself as part of a seamless operation that had to work together to protect South Korea from communism instead of a cog in a machine that in all truth could run just fine without him.

Even so, he could get through the days pretty easily. The nights were the problem. His buddies were in the Ville or at their hooches, and the barracks were scattered with solitary, withdrawn men Wayne suspected were homosexuals or terrified virgins. He'd spend the evenings on his bunk reading the Bible, the one he got for high school graduation from his mama, the King James Version, the real thing. He meant to read it from beginning to end, but he often flipped ahead to the New Testament and the red passages that were Jesus' words, hoping for inspiration, for strength. At night he reminded himself to not think too ill of his fellow GIs. *Judge not, that ye be not judged. For with what judgment ye judge, ye shall be judged: and with what measure ye mete, it shall be measured to you again.*

During the times that God could not console him, he'd write long letters to Bonnie, recalling their childhood (she'd grown up two farms over), when they started dating in high school, the first time they had sex. They'd both been virgins and it had been too fast, but he remembered the way she opened her mouth and made that tiny sound, an oh of wonder or surprise or pain. He'd start his letters with "Remember when…" and then he'd detail that day in church when their families had sat next to each other and he'd made pretenses to push his leg against hers. Or that first year they'd been married when they had sex almost every day in their cramped apartment and Bonnie still couldn't get pregnant.

He wrote her every night, but she only wrote him once a week, short hasty letters. She didn't have the time to think of the past she said, there was only now, this exhaustion and her muddled mind. She missed him when she could, she wrote. He missed her all the time. He missed her body, forever changed after Allison had been born, with its ribbons of purpled rivers across her abdomen and inner thighs. He missed her sleeping beside him, her damp brown hair stuck to her neck. He missed the fried eggs and grits she made most mornings, how she gave him the first cup of coffee from the percolator. He missed that she knew when he was out of shaving cream and that she let him listen to his country oldies station in the truck. He missed her most when his buddies talked so casually of their *yobosayos* who cooked them rice and brought *kimchi* and slept with them on a blanket called a *yo* in their hooches. He was lonely and he was twenty-two and in the end he could not abide the teachings of the Lord because the flesh was weak. He prayed for God to show him mercy.

One Saturday, he decided to take the Korean bus—what they

called the *kimchi* bus—to the city of Pyeongtaek twenty kilometers away. He was bored. By the time the bus picked him up, he could barely squeeze on. He was taller than the Koreans pressed into him, one head under each armpit, garlic and *kimchi* and *soju* thick in the air, with the cracked windows bringing in gusts of sharp manure. He could not twist in either direction, and he breathed in shallow sips as the driver careened through the narrow streets, turning corners so fast that Wayne felt the bus tip slightly to the side. Someone in the back embraced a pig, others held large bundles of *kimchi* and rice and garlic and soybean paste. With each sway of the bus, the Koreans crushed into him. Wayne struggled to swallow back his own urge to retch. When he reached Pyeongtaek he found the nearest alley and vomited the cereal he'd had that morning. He never took the *kimchi* bus again. Instead he paid the three dollars for the taxi into town.

By the end of the first month, Wayne was smoking dope bought by his friends' *yobosayos* from the Korean pharmacy, which the GIs weren't allowed to enter. The stuff was weak, low grade compared to what people grew back home, but it was all there was. He'd roll and smoke joints at night in one of his buddies' hooches while they were out in the Ville. Back in his bunk he'd listen to the Armed Forces radio play all the good music he grew up with, fixing his eyes on the Bible, trying to get past Genesis. That lasted a few more weeks until his buddies got tired of his using their hooches and *yobosayos* to get his stuff. "Get your own shit, you cheap lazy motherfucker," one of them said. And so one Friday he went out with them to Duffy's, intent on doing just that.

Instead he ended up at a skivvy show. He'd chosen a girl at Duffy's, and was trying to explain to her that he just wanted her to buy weed for him, that he didn't need anything else, but her English was minimal and she kept putting her hand on his cock, which had been painfully hard since he'd seen her. She wore one of those VD cards around her neck, announcing the date of her last check up, certifying she was clean. "No sex," he kept saying as she rubbed his crotch. He'd been masturbating every night, thinking of Bonnie and her breasts just after Allison had been born, puffed up like a stretched balloon, and how one night when she was sleeping he'd put his mouth to one and sucked on the sweet, warm milk. She'd put her hand on his head, like he was a baby, but didn't stir, and he'd continued until he'd had his fill and could fall back asleep. He thought of that many nights, and also imagined having sex with Betsy Lynn Stewart, who he'd gone out with in tenth grade before Bonnie, hers the only other breasts he'd been allowed to touch. After he masturbated he asked God to forgive him for thinking of another woman besides Bonnie. But now with the girl sitting on his lap, rubbing him with her thighs, he had to leave the bar before he did some real sinning. He stood abruptly, tipping the chair back, running out of Duffy's just as he had the first time, the girl from the bar following him. He wondered if he should try one more time for the weed. A few of his friends emerged from Duffy's with arms around the girls they'd paid for the night.

"Come on, buddy. We're going to a skivvy show."

The girl grabbed his hand, leading him along with the others to a side street, down the steps of a nondescript building marked by black Korean letters. They walked into a room that looked like a makeshift movie theater, with a tiny projector in the back and a pull-down screen like those used for showing slide shows back home. The seats were folding metal chairs in neat, spacious rows. A Korean man emerged, Mr. Jung, as thin as Mr. Lee at Duffy's, wearing a black suit that would not be enough to keep the chill out, as the room was barely heated. They each paid him two dollars. Wayne half expected Mr. Jung to return with popcorn and Cokes, but he didn't. Wayne kept his coat on, a thick down parka, and he and the girl, "call me Iris," she'd finally whispered, took the last row. She held her hand out in front of his chest. "One dollar," she said. He fished in his wallet and gave her a dollar. "You get me weed?" he asked. "Okay," she said, tucking the folded note into the waistband of her hose. She wore a short checked skirt and he wondered if her legs were blue under the stockings, for he could not guess how she withstood the cold in so little clothing. Instead of popcorn, Mr. Jung passed out joints, which he then lit for them ceremoniously.

"This is some special shit, Wayne," Sam said. Then the lights turned out and the movie began.

Although the film was grainy with splatters and skips, poorly produced and edited, there was no doubt that Wayne was watching a homemade porn flick. He had looked at *Playboy* in high school a few times, and he'd even seen an X-rated movie one night in Nashville. But this movie, which featured a man having sex with two women, was different. He felt like he was watching someone's real life, sordid as it was. The girls moaned artificially at regular intervals. Bonnie's breathing was never regular like that, and she only called out every now and then. But the sex on the screen was real and he was transfixed. He was barely aware of his own body, his penis erect again, nor did he notice Iris moving from her chair and unzipping his pants. He noticed only a warm sensation below, but his mind was not attached to his body, and it felt like one of the wet dreams he had when he was younger. There was something different in the joint he was smoking, too. He felt that he was levitating. When he looked down and saw Iris giving him the blow job he patted her head and he thought of Bonnie touching him when he'd been at her breast and somehow that made it good and all right, that he was still okay with God somehow, that He understood how hard things were, that Wayne was doing his best.

CHAPTER 7

Considering Allison had a rusted frying pan, a warped sauce pan, and a two-burner gas range to work with, dinner had turned out fine. The mashed potatoes were lumpier than she liked, but she'd only had a fork to mash them with, and her upper arms still burned from the labor. The chicken breasts had fried up evenly, with bits of ham and cheese bubbling from the middle. The gravy was a bit salty from bouillon, but served its purpose. She was cutting the bread, a reasonably crusty baguette from the bakery down the street, when the doorbell chimed "Home Sweet Home" in a high-pitched tinkle. At the door, Jason, dressed in a charcoal suit and blue tie, held a bottle of wine in one hand, his briefcase in the other.

"Mina should be home soon," Allison said, leading him to the living room. She'd cleared the coffee table of the round glass ashtray, magazines, hair clips, and lighters, wiped it clean, and set it with the three plates Mina had, colorless plastic that Mina said had come with the apartment. She lit a candle and stuck it into an empty wine bottle. The salad was already on the table, as were the few basic cheeses she'd been able to find. Allison went to the kitchen and returned with some of the cut bread and three juice glasses. "We might as well have some bread and cheese *anju* while we wait." She handed him a corkscrew she'd found in the silverware drawer.

"You've already learned Korean customs well," Jason said, smiling.

"Anything that has to do with food." Allison sat down on one of the cushions she'd strewn around the table, and Jason sat opposite her. He opened the bottle easily and poured the wine into their glasses.

They toasted and drank.

"I should have brought white wine, but I didn't know what you were cooking, so I brought one of my favorites from when I was in California, a merlot," Jason said.

Allison took a sip. "It's good."

"I went to Napa a few times, Sonoma. So much great wine." He closed his eyes and pressed his lips together. "But here not so much. Too expensive, too snobby. Koreans don't even know what they like. If it's expensive they think it's good."

"I hope you didn't pay too much for this bottle."

Jason shrugged. "You didn't have to do this, but thank you."

"I did. You've helped me so much, been so kind to me."

"A lot of Americans helped me when I first came there. My spoken English was not great. As you know, the culture is so different. I was confused so much of the time. But many kind people helped me. So I want to return the favor."

"*Kamshaminida*," Allison said. Thank you.

"*Cheonmaneyo*," Jason answered. You're welcome.

"So tell me about this ship," Allison said. "Did North Korea do it?" She'd talked to Wayne and Bonnie and reassured them that everything was okay, seemed okay.

"Time will tell," Jason said. "Maybe."

They'd gone through half the bottle and most of the cheese when Allison decided they couldn't wait for Mina any longer. They'd both texted and called her, but her phone was turned off. It could be anything: working late, a sudden private lesson, a guy she'd met, or she may have just plain forgotten and gone out with friends instead. The gravy was beginning to congeal and the crust on the chicken cordon bleu was hardening. Allison re-warmed the food and served their plates. Jason had refilled their glasses; the bottle was almost empty. They clinked glasses again—Koreans toasted many times in an evening, Allison had learned—and they dug in, both famished.

"I haven't had this kind of home-cooked Western food in a long time," Jason said. His fingers were delicate, but he was a hearty eater. "I'll cook for you next time, so you can experience home-cooked Korean food."

"You can cook?"

Jason nodded and swallowed. "I had to learn, living in LA by myself."

"You had Mina," she said, watching to see if he would look away, or redden.

"It wasn't that kind of friendship," he said.

"How come you never got married?" As soon as she'd said it, she knew she'd been rude, gotten too personal, too quickly.

"How come you never married?" he asked.

"Didn't Mina tell you? I was."

"Me, too," Jason said.

"I'm sorry," she said.

"It's okay," he said. "It's a long story. What about you?"

"Five miscarriages, which the doctors could never find a cause for. And we didn't love each other enough to stay together without children. We divorced about a year ago." She'd never said it like that before—the last ten years of her life reduced to four sad sentences. Her sadness caught in her throat for a moment before resettling into the black hollow between her breasts.

Jason had been sopping up the last of the gravy with a crust of the baguette, but he paused when she talked. She didn't know what to make of his silence, again wondering if she'd been rude, revealing too much of herself, been specific when she should have been vague.

"Ice cream?" she offered. "I would have baked a cake, but there's no oven."

"We usually just buy them," he said. "I'm okay, thanks." He finished his glass of wine and stood, brushing the crumbs off his pants.

"Don't go," she said.

"I'm not. My marriage story is similar to yours. But different. I want to tell you about it. But I need more wine. I'll be back in five minutes."

She rinsed the dishes in the sink, wondering if he'd return or if she'd chased him away. Ten minutes later he was back with two bottles of wine in a plastic bag.

"This stuff isn't very good. But it's all they had at the convenience store."

As if by some kind of agreement they returned to the table instead of retiring on the sofa, sitting across from each other more formally than the sofa would have allowed. Jason poured wine into their empty glasses.

He'd gotten married right before he was to start his doctorate in the States in fall 2004. His wife, who knew less English than he did, at first didn't want to come. They'd decided that she'd stay in Korea with her parents and they'd visit each other in the summers until he graduated. It sounded hard, but it wasn't an uncommon arrangement for Koreans. That lasted a year. She was bored living at home and had studied English intensively while he was away. She was ready to join him. He'd balked at first; he could barely survive on the research assistantship he'd been awarded, so he had no idea how he could support her. But Jung-eun, his wife, was a step ahead of him. She'd enrolled in the ESL program at his university to continue her English studies, obtaining a student visa as well as her parents' blessings, and, more importantly, their financial support. So she joined him that fall and adjusted to life in the States much more quickly than he'd anticipated.

Their life continued on that path for a year. Jason and Jung-eun couldn't spend a lot of time together because he was always in the lab or studying. By the end of the first year Jung-eun had completed the ESL program, her accented English now almost fluent, and she announced she was ready to get pregnant. For Jason, having a baby then seemed like a disaster of a plan. He was not home enough to be a decent father or provide Jung-eun the support she'd need. But Jung-eun was persistent. She was thirty years old and worried that time was passing her by. She'd read the studies of her fertility declining, and she knew, she said in English, that her clock was ticking. When it was time to have the baby she'd return to Korea and raise the child there with her family's support. Jason wouldn't have them "in his hair" (another phrase she said in English). He could finish his research and join them, just as the child was old enough to start remembering.

To an American, the whole plan seemed ridiculous and doomed, but in a Korean sense, it was practical and expedient. Because what use was a man really in that first year, he was in the way more than anything else, another person to comfort, to feed. The baby's grandmother, the *halmoni*, was much more useful. She could teach the young mother how to take care of the child. He could best help by finishing his PhD and returning to Korea, she told him. And Jason admitted that as much as he'd enjoyed having his wife around for that year, he also fantasized about the year before she'd arrived, the small silent apartment in grad student housing that allowed him the space to live and breathe only his research.

So he capitulated, and for that next year, his third in graduate school, they waited for her to get pregnant. Except she didn't. At the end of the year, they began to worry. He and Jung-eun flew back to Korea to meet with doctors there, both traditional and Western. She began a regimen of drinking the bitter *hanyak*, Korean medicine, while Western doctors ran fertility tests and shot her with hormones. By the end of summer, the doctors had determined it was Jason who was the problem. He was impotent, probably a result of a severe case of smallpox when he was a child. His parents admitted the doctor had warned them that he might be impotent, but they'd decided not to dwell on that warning; to think or talk of it was bad luck. They had never told him. His parents had betrayed him, and by extension, Jung-eun. To make matters worse, when he tried to return to university at the end of the summer, he was detained by immigration and couldn't return to school for the fall semester. He and Jung-eun moved in with her parents, while Jason lived with his life in limbo, not wanted in either country. When he finally was able to return to the States for the spring semester he resumed his research in earnest. Three months later, Jung-eun called him from Korea and told him she was pregnant, saying that the father didn't matter, that they could pretend the child was theirs. Only their parents knew of his impotency. Jason told her to marry the father, and they were quickly divorced. That final year, alone again, he had his breakthrough in his research, which resulted in the rapid completion of his dissertation and a job with a good university in Seoul.

"My parents are looking for another wife for me. But I don't want one," Jason said.

"I don't blame you," Allison said. "That's a sad story."

"I'm still angry at my parents for tricking me," Jason said. He'd brought his glass of wine to the window, which he'd cracked open so he could smoke.

"I think they were just in denial. Aren't you angry at your wife? She's the one who tricked you."

Jason looked out the window. "She was trying to help me save face. What else could she do?"

"Uh, stay with you?"

"It wasn't that kind of marriage. We were a good match in many ways. But a match to have a family. She would raise the children and I would provide. But we couldn't be a childless couple, like friends. What would we do?"

"Similar to me and Ted." She looked down at the thin ribbon of wine at the bottom of her glass. Her words felt thick on her tongue. "At least you know why you couldn't get pregnant. I've always wondered if it was because I didn't love Ted enough. That I didn't want to have a baby with him, and so some part of me willed those miscarriages." She'd thought the words for so long, but never said them before, out loud.

"That's foolish thinking. Old fashioned. Having a baby has nothing to do with wanting one or not. It's just biology."

Allison nodded, but she cried anyway, from facing her own suspicions or the kindness of Jason's words, or both. Jason did not approach her. He smoked, silent, at the window. She was grateful he had not embarrassed her with efforts at comfort. She wiped her tears from the corners of her eyes as soon as they appeared, and once she'd stopped, she went to the bathroom to splash her blotchy face with cold water. When she emerged, he told her he had to go. The wine was finished, the candle long burned to the nub, the night blurry. He swayed slightly as he walked to the door, slipped on his shoes and bid her goodnight. Only as Allison unfolded the sofa did she realize Mina had not come home.

CHAPTER 8

After that evening with Iris, Wayne went to the skivvy shows when he could no longer bear it. Somehow he felt better there than having sex with one of the girls, that he was still a rung or two higher on the morality ladder than his friends. The porn movie and blow job seemed more removed, a service rendered rather than a coupling. Wayne learned that Mr. Jung's joints were laced with opium he'd buy from Pusan, and the floating, detached quality they gave helped Wayne distance himself from what was happening. Soon, he no longer felt guilty. He felt God understood him, and that they'd struck some sort of deal. He knew he'd have to face what he'd done when he returned to Bonnie, that his guilt and his conscience would return, and he would deserve to suffer from it. But now he was just trying to get by. He didn't even have a real *yobosayo*, he just used whatever girl he paid for at the skivvy show to get him stuff for the next week. He wondered how long, though, before he succumbed to more, and crossed a line he'd so far managed to avoid. He still had not had intercourse with anyone but Bonnie.

After he'd been in Korea for two months, he was reading the Bible after smoking a few joints one evening when he finally finished Genesis. He'd read the Bible in high school, and enjoyed much of it, but now he read it hoping to gain some kind of understanding as to why the world had ended up the way it had. He read the first lines of Exodus: *Now these are the names of the children of Israel, which came into Egypt; every man and his household came with Jacob. Reuben, Simeon, Levi, and Judah/Issachar, Zebulun, and Benjamin/Dan, and Naphtali,*

Gad, and Asher. He was not in the mood for pages of lineages and begetting; he skipped ahead to the Song of Solomon: *Let him kiss me with the kisses of his mouth: for thy love is better than wine.*

He'd not received a letter from Bonnie in a week and a half. He wanted to call her, but it was six in the morning at home. She'd still be sleeping, angry if he woke her. He abandoned the Bible and went into the Ville.

The girl approached him just as he'd exited the gate. Her face was free of makeup and she looked closer to twelve than twenty, with her small body swallowed under a shabby brown coat.

"Hello," the girl said. "I take care of you real good."

He thought of asking her age, but she would only lie.

"Where's your card?"

"Pardon?"

He drew a box in the air, pantomiming the card and the girl shook her head. He was about to push her away and continue down to Duffy's, but then he struck on a plan that seemed so brilliant in the moment that it did not occur to him that it may have sprung from lonely desperation more than anything else.

He could have his hooch, he would have his *yobosayo*. She would cook and clean and procure his weed and valium and anything else he wanted from the pharmacy and they would trade a few this and that's in English, but he wouldn't have sex with her because she had the clap, and in that way he'd technically still be true to Bonnie. His own fear of going blind, of blisters, of the scourge, of the humiliation of being diagnosed and getting the treatment—that would keep him from touching her, he was sure of it.

So for one hundred dollars a month, a third of his salary, he got a hooch, rice, the soup and *kimchi* to go along with it, bricks to heat the floors, and a girl to keep it all together for him. He moved into his hooch as soon as he was able, relieved to be away from base, just as he'd been when he first left home. It was the first place he had that was his and his alone, except for the girl, whose name was Sunny. And she was not so much a presence as an enabler, someone who made his little space a home.

They fell into a routine. After work he'd come to the hooch and eat a meal Sunny had prepared—rice and a spicy soup with *kimchi* and other side dishes, all food he'd astonishingly come to love. He'd eat and then his buddies would come over or he'd go to one of their places where they'd smoke a few joints, which did hardly anything, and drink beer, and then he'd go home where Sunny was waiting for him.

He was pleased with his plan and proud of his willpower. While his buddies were fucking not just their *yobosayos* but any other thing they felt like, night after night, bragging of their conquests, Wayne had still done nothing but attend skivvy shows. Worse, he thought, the guys lied to themselves, pretended that the Korean girls liked what they were doing, wanted to be with them, that money was not exchanging hands, that these women were here not out of abject necessity, but because they, like the soldiers, liked having a good time. Some of the guys pretended the *yobosayos* were like real girlfriends, pretty sweet girls who fawned over their pasty asses, girls who cared not in the least about marriage or a green card, girls who were not desperate to escape. At least Wayne knew where he and Bonnie stood, that she loved him not for looks or money, but because they'd come from the same place and were meant to be together. It was as simple and as complex as that.

He told Sunny about Bonnie after the first few nights, when she wouldn't go away, instead sleeping on the bare floor near the gas range she cooked on. Later, she'd roll out the *yo* for him, shaking out the heavy duvet, crawling in next to him, throwing her arms awkwardly around his shoulders, finally moving her hand down to his crotch. The way she did it, slowly, searchingly, then just laying her hand there like it had fallen asleep, told him she didn't have much experience with those things.

He batted her hand away. "Stop," he said, "you're too young."

"My age is eighteen."

"Like hell it is." He sat up and retrieved the family photos from his rucksack. He'd tried showing the guys his photos, but they were uninterested, wanting no reminder of the world that awaited them when they returned to the States. Still, he wanted someone to understand what he'd left behind. Bonnie with her hair not as dark and straight as Sunny's, with the slightest hint of red, thicker, with natural curls she tamed with juice cans and irons. Allison with the same hair as her mother, feathery light, her round toddler's face, laughing, finger pointing at the camera.

Sunny examined each photo for a long time, felt the glossy finish with the pads of her fingers, traced Bonnie's dress that looked like some kind of modern painting with its squares of colors, Allison in her arms holding a lollipop.

"Beautiful," Sunny said over and over. It was one of the few English words she knew, but still, Wayne was sure she meant it.

"You understand now?" he asked. She nodded. He tucked the photos back in his backpack and then walked to the outhouse to relieve himself before bed. It was March but the air was still biting, like January at home. He was not used to the lingering chill, the still-bare trees, seeing his breath even now. The stars were the same as home, though, specks of light scattered, clumped randomly and ordered at the same time. He took comfort in that. When he returned, Sunny was lying under the covers of the *yo*. The floor was warm from the heated coal briquettes underneath them and he took off his clothes except for his boxers and T-shirt and crawled under the blanket and wrapped his arms around her naked and shivering body. Now that she'd seen his wife and child, that she knew he could not—would not—take her with him, a burden was released. She pressed herself against his erection. Blow jobs with girls who had VD were okay, his friends had advised him. Just don't have sex with them.

He wondered if he thought of Bonnie while Sunny gave him a blow job if it would be cheating even more than at the skivvy show. But he knew he would not think of Bonnie, and instead would keep his eyes open and on Sunny—could she possibly be eighteen?—her curtain of black hair spread on his groin like a mourner's fan.

"How long have you had VD?" he asked after she'd finished.

"I'm sorry," she said. "I don't understand."

He sat up and pried her arms off him.

"God dammit Sunny, don't lie to me. Don't try to trick me. I ain't that ignorant."

She started crying then, covered her face in her hands.

"*Omma* sick. You first time. So sorry. Don't make me go."

He watched her try to stop crying, to collect herself. She wiped her eyes and covered her mouth with her hand.

"Have you ever?" He stuck his left index finger in between the hole he'd made with his right index finger and thumb.

She shook her head. "Sorry. First time."

It made sense. Until she approached him, he'd never seen the girl before and neither had his friends, who knew every available girl from the Ville all the way to Pyeongtaek. The things she did do were as if she were reading a manual on how to operate some strange and unknown machinery. God was testing him, but what was the test? Before he'd come to Korea he'd have said that some dark evil was tempting him away from God, away from his marriage vows. But life was no longer that simple. Because, Wayne figured, if it weren't him it would be somebody else, and some of those guys could be real bastards. They yelled horrible things at the girls and smacked them around and demanded they do degrading things he would not. He would be kind and gentle. He'd only had sex with one person in his life, accepting that lot as the way it was to be, but now he was thinking maybe God had put him here and brought Sunny to him because God knew he would treat her well, would take care of her. In fact, to not have sex with her would be the worse sin, Wayne reasoned, for he'd be throwing her fate, her life, possibly, back to the godless winds. Yes, God was rewarding him for his perseverance and strength those first few months. None of his buddies had resisted this long and this far, had even tried or wanted to. He'd quit the desultory skivvy shows and fallen into a domestic quietude with Sunny, and now he'd take God's call to shield her from that horrible world. God had entrusted to him something higher than marriage vows.

If he'd taken a moment to really pray, to examine his motives, Wayne would have known he was full of shit, but he was so far from the world he'd known, the right and wrong in it, that in one way everything he thought made a kind of sense. Sunny lay beside him, eyes closed, waiting for him to decide. He leaned over, kissed her lightly, his lips damp and salty. She pulled him to her, and they made swift, yet sweet love. Afterward she slept in his arms, and he promised God he would treat her well while he was in Korea. He was already a little in love with her.

He hadn't even thought about protection. He'd heard you couldn't get a virgin pregnant, but he'd have to buy condoms the next day to take care of that. And then he fell asleep and didn't move until morning.

After that night their lives joined easily, without discussion. They were both domestically inclined, enjoying routines and schedules, the rhythms of days and weeks. Mornings he'd go on base to develop photos of barren land and forest, then he'd come home for dinner of rice and whatever soup and side dishes Sunny had prepared. They'd talk about what they'd done that day over beers and barley tea, and in this manner Sunny's English improved quickly. The US Military Police would come by and check on him—the midnight curfew was still strictly enforced. When it was dark, they would roll out the *yo*, have sex, and go to sleep. He was happy to be done with the temptations of the clubs and skivvy shows. He wrote Bonnie regularly, but without the fevered urgency of the previous months, and when she wrote back she said she was glad he was doing better and had settled in. He even read Bonnie's letters to Sunny, about how she canned tomatoes with LuAnn Wilkins, or she'd started crocheting a small blanket for Allison's baby doll, that the new pastor gave better sermons. As Sunny's English got better, she was able to tell Wayne more of her story. She'd grown up on a small farm on the other side of Pyeongtaek, and then her father, recruited by the Korean military, had died in Vietnam when she was twelve, leaving the family destitute. She moved up to Seoul to work in the Dongil Textile Company. She lived in the company dorm with the other workers, all female, working fourteen hours, seven days a week for 220 won a day, enough to buy a cup of coffee. She did piece work on a sewing machine in a space four feet high that blew dust and cotton and other particles in the air with no ventilation. With the help of some of the local churches, the women had started a union to try to improve conditions. One day in February the women went to the hall to prepare for elections, only to find the building covered in human feces. Thugs who had been hiding in the toilets jumped out and rubbed excrement over the women. About seventy women took off their clothes and stood naked in front of the riot police in protest. The company fired 124 of the women from the union for damaging their property.

Sunny said she had not been brave enough to stand naked in front of the police and did not lose her job. Yet she could no longer sleep at night, ashamed of her cowardice. At the end of February, on her one day off a month, she went home and discovered that her mother was sick. She never returned to the factory. She resolved she would do whatever she could to get her mother some *hanyak,* so she went to the front gate of Camp Humphreys and propositioned the first man she met who had a kind face. That was Wayne.

His monthly paycheck of three hundred fifty dollars stretched far.

Sunny used her pay and any extra Wayne would give her for her mother's treatment. She owned two skirts and shirts. She'd wear one set for a few days, then wash it and wear the other. She ate with him and needed little else except for her barley tea, which she drank both hot and cold. He didn't have the heart to tell her that the Chinese herbs would not help her mother, and that with her cancer untreated, which was what he assumed she had, she would die soon. Sunny's younger brother, Woo-sung, was taking care of his mother and their small plot of land, finishing up school before his mandatory three years of military service began.

Wayne was not the kind of man who craved a variety of women or experience. He preferred the comfort and solace of one woman, one body he could return to night after night, to study that one body's curves and breathing and aches and moles and scars so that years later, if called upon, he could conjure that one body from head to toe. In that sense he was faithful to Sunny.

In April she told him she was pregnant and needed money to get an abortion.

He cursed his ill luck, because except for that first time he'd always used the condoms Sunny bought at the pharmacy. Then he wondered if it was not bad luck at all, but God not-so-gently reminding him of the consequences of his actions. Later, the other GIs would laugh at him for entrusting himself to Korean condoms with their faulty rubber and expired usage dates. But he did not ask her if she'd tricked him, if she thought he might somehow marry her anyway, for he had come to know her and did not see that guile within her.

"You are not killing my baby," Wayne said.

"You will not be here," she said.

He'd only seen her cry once before, that time when he'd yelled at her and she'd told him she was a virgin and her mother was sick. He never saw her cry again, not even three years later when he took Mina away from her for good.

Only in the vaguest way did he apprehend the life he was

prescribing for her and their child, that a young woman with a *hapa*, a child who was half-Korean half-something-else, would have no chance in this world. She'd never be able to marry, would have to earn her livelihood as a prostitute or something close to it, and their child, boy or girl, would have no choice but to do the same. Their lives would forever depend on American soldiers and the fear and favors they might bestow on them. Wayne was not thinking of that. Instead, he was thinking of the baby, the miracle baby, and how he could do the right thing.

He would not give her the money for the abortion. Instead, he promised to take care of her and the baby, even after his tour was over. He would send her money every month and she wouldn't have to work. As long as she promised not to have the abortion.

She was silent. She did not believe him. And why should she? Most women here and their bastard children were abandoned by their GI fathers, no matter what had been promised in the heat of the moment. And the GIs did this because they were in a land that was not their own and they didn't think they were being watched. But Wayne knew better. He knew God's eye reached farther than this world, that He saw everything, was holding people accountable. He promised that he would take care of her and she wept through the night but by the morning her tears were exhausted, her eyes dry. She folded the *yo* they slept on and fixed him spicy tofu soup, his favorite, and rice before he went to work. They ate in silence, but he went on base knowing the baby would live.

Their lives returned to the domestic routine they'd established. But now there was talk of the baby that was growing in Sunny's small womb. Sunny started to show late in her pregnancy, and even in the final month her tight basketball-sized stomach was the only part of her body that looked different. She stopped eating anything spicy, as according to Chinese medicine, pregnant women were already "hot." She would not eat broken things or chicken because the baby's skin would be too rough. She tried to have only positive thoughts, as Koreans believed bad thoughts would affect the baby's development. She dreamed of the Korean national flower, rose of Sharon, which meant she was having a girl.

The months passed for Wayne so swiftly he'd almost forgotten he had anywhere else to go, another home or family to return to, a wife and a daughter, now three years old, who he loved and had so feverishly missed not long ago. Now they seemed shadows or ghosts of another world he may have dreamed.

In December, a few weeks before Wayne's Expiration of Term of Service date, Sunny bid Wayne goodbye and returned to her village to give birth to her child, as was the custom. Her mother had died the previous month and he had made her aunt swear to take care of Sunny and the baby. For twenty-one days after the baby was born, she was to rest and have only seaweed soup and hot liquids, since she would then be "cold." Sunny would send him a note once the baby was born, telling him the name and gender, and that would be the end of their communication. When she left, he felt the emptiness of his hooch so resolutely that he returned to his bunk on base and spent his nights there. A week before he was to leave he received a note from one of his buddies' girlfriends. Mi-na Kim, born December 20, 1978. And then Wayne's twelve-month tour was over and he was to be stationed in Fort Belvoir in Alexandria, Virginia, his family joining him in the housing on base.

CHAPTER 9

Allison found the bar easily. It was off the main street in Shinchon, a bar more for Westerners than Koreans. All the signs were written in English, and the light shone brightly on wooden benches and floors. Soccer played on the TV, and the cream-colored wall boasted a drinking contest—ten shots and your name and country got a personal plaque added to the hall of shame. If you puked, however, your country lost five points in the overall contest. Gary pointed to his name on a plaque with his country, Canada, engraved underneath.

She'd gone to last Sunday's soccer game, which was played on a dirt field an hour away by subway. Gary was already on the field when she arrived, and he seemed so occupied waiting for the ball to come to him that he didn't acknowledge her. The girls introduced themselves immediately, offering her beer and small bags of Korean-style chips they'd brought. They wanted to know everything about her, how long she'd been here, what *hogwan* she was teaching at, who was her boyfriend.

"*You're* Mina's sister," one of the girls, Liza, said. She'd introduced herself as the girlfriend of the captain of the team, a large beefy Australian named Luke. "That's one wild girl."

If these girls, with their early morning *soju*, thought Mina was wild, her sister must be in worse shape than she'd thought.

"She's shagged half the team," one of the others said.

"Bullshit," Liza said. "You're just jealous that Mike was flirting with her."

Jealous girls. Mina's life. She'd never had many close female friends, Allison recalled, only partially because of her looks. She suspected it was more because Mina acted like a stereotypical guy—she partied hard, met guys easily, found attachment encumbering. Now she wondered which had come first, the girls pushing Mina away, or the other way around. She wondered why she and Mina had never been close. They were three years apart, not a big gap, but enough while they were growing up for Allison to feel that she was embarking on the stages alone—wearing makeup, choosing the right jeans, first crushes, periods, pushy boys. Was it simply that they had no genetic tie, no blood to bring them together? But they'd grown up in the same home with the same parents, eaten the same food, gone on the same vacations— certainly a shared childhood past was enough to bring about some kind of connection?

Allison remembered now how Mina had followed her around those first few years, toddling in her hand-me-down dresses. Allison had no interest in Mina, this girl who had stolen Wayne's heart, who demanded Bonnie's attention. Yet Mina seemed to want only Allison. She ate only what Allison ate, demanded to be near her, would sit outside Allison's shut bedroom door. When the family was watching TV, if Allison got up to get a snack or go to the bathroom, she'd hear Mina's high voice: "Where's Arry? Where she go?" "She'll be back, honey," one of their parents would say, but often Allison didn't return. She'd sneak into their shared bedroom, lock the door, and play with her Barbies, ignoring Mina's plaintive knocking on the door. Mina might be their new daughter, but that didn't mean she had to be her sister. "Go away," Allison would yell, exasperated. And finally, when she turned five and went to kindergarten, Mina did. After she entered her own world where people welcomed her, she never knocked on Allison's closed door again, never followed her down the hall or asked where she was. Even when Allison was older, in high school, Mina didn't show the interest in Allison's life that her friends' younger sisters did. Allison had never really cared about Mina's diffidence because she'd been diffident, too, relieved when Mina had quit trying to get something Allison was unable to give.

What if, Allison wondered now, Mina's troubles with female friends—she always had plenty of male ones—stemmed from that sad little three-year-old following her around the house, wanting a connection? It was too late for speculation. Mina was now very much the way she was, long past her need for Allison's guidance or approval. Still, Allison resolved to encourage Mina to confide a bit more, as they'd done at the sauna.

After the soccer game, the group went out for grilled meat and drinks. Allison joined them, partaking of the *soju* and beer, and afterward Gary had walked her to the subway station—he was staying out later with the guys—and kissed her on the mouth, wet and loose.

"You're here for a few more weeks right? Come out next Friday," he mumbled. "You can stay at my place and we'll take the bus to the game together Saturday."

"Okay," she said, her voice high like a little girl's.

When Friday came, Mina told Allison she was going to take her to one of her favorite places for relaxing. In the early afternoon, they walked through the streets of Shinchon to the gates of Yonsei University, then up the steep, sloping hill on campus. The leaves were mostly bare, with a few trees revealing the beginnings of green buds warming in the sun. They walked past the campus buildings, some ivy-covered, others utilitarian blocks, until they reached the top of the hill and the edge of campus. They climbed a trail up a small mountain to a level footpath. They walked along the dirt road until they stopped at a Buddhist statue overlooking a spring. Mina took a ladle resting on a stone and dipped it in the spring, bringing the water to her mouth. She gestured for Allison to do the same. Allison, thirsty, pushing aside sanitation worries, filled the scoop and drank deliciously cold water, some of the best water she'd ever had. When they were done, they continued down the well-trod path, occasionally passing aging Koreans nimbly walking the trails or doing twists and stretches at an outdoor gym. Then they descended once again until they arrived at a clearing with temples painted in bright colors and a garden of strange stone animals. They took off their shoes and walked stocking feet into the largest temple, where Buddha, sitting, solemn, surrounded by candles, loomed over them. They sat on cushions and then Mina started prostrating. Allison didn't even know Mina was Buddhist. Wayne and Bonnie would be horrified, probably even more so than if they'd learned about her having an affair with Ray, the object of Allison's affection. Wayne still said the blessing every night before dinner, went to church on Sundays, and read the same

Bible he'd had since high school before bed. Bonnie sang in the choir and was always on some church committee. Allison had started going to church with them again when she'd moved back home, just to keep the peace, but her heart was not in it.

When Mina finished, they went back outside and then to a small shop on the temple grounds that served tea. Mina ordered five flavor tea and hot jujube tea, which they drank in a room more like a cafeteria than a tea shop. Atonal music played in the background and Allison was lulled into a warm soft place.

"I didn't know you were Buddhist."

"It just makes the most sense to me."

"Do Mom and Dad know?"

"Why should they? I'm thirty-two."

Allison looked down at her tea. Mina was right. Why was she still so attached to her parents and what they thought, especially her father? She was too old for all of that.

"The monks of this temple are allowed to marry," Mina said. "Which means, I guess that there are fewer rules to break."

"Lucky them," Allison said. "Most can't play it both ways."

"Whenever I'm upset or stressed out I come here."

"Are you upset now?"

"No, not really. I just wanted to share it with you. Try my tea." She and Allison exchanged cups. "In May, on Buddha's birthday, this place gets wild. Lanterns light up until they become their own sky. Just outside here, all the old Koreans drink *makgeolli*, eat *pajeon*, dance and get drunk. It's one of the best days in Korea." She paused, eyeing Allison. "Too bad you can't stay. I'd take you."

"I have to get back, find a job."

"You can get one here. You were an education major. They'd love you."

"I don't think I have it in me anymore."

"Think about it."

They finished their swapped teas and walked to the shop next door, which sold texts, incense, CDs, and prayer bead necklaces and bracelets. Mina picked up some skinny boxes of incense and two necklaces and brought them to the monk standing behind the register.

"Mina, do you think Dad would freak out if I bought some

incense for him?" Allison dropped an extra box of incense in with Mina's purchases.

Mina laughed. "Probably." She handed the money to the monk, who was standing still, like a statue, staring at her. A man with a deep voice was chanting, above a gong, through speakers. Mina pushed the money closer to him. He took it, returning her change with shaking hands. Mina thanked him, but he did not respond.

Outside, in the sun, Mina took out the necklaces.

"That guy was weird," Allison said.

"It was like he was afraid of me," Mina said. She looped the necklaces over each of their necks. "It doesn't mean you're a Buddhist or a heathen. It's a sister thing," she said.

They drank again from one of the springs, this one at the temple, and walked back a different way, along a road with older houses and tiny apartments until they approached a highway and took a bus back home. Then Allison got ready to meet Gary and the soccer guys, while Mina went to see Robert before he left on his next mission.

For most of Friday evening, Allison surreptitiously checked her watch, wondering when she and Gary would leave for his apartment and she would have sex for the first time since her divorce. The group ordered pizza and beers and boasted of the game they'd win on Sunday. The team was 3-3 for the season, but the Cheongju team was 1-5, a weaker team all around. The Seoul Strikers discussed plays and strategy, but mostly drank and congratulated themselves, as if they'd already won the game. Gary did not publicly touch her, but as the night wore on, she could feel the pressure of his leg on hers, his hand occasionally sliding up her thigh under the table. Once, as she emerged from the bathroom, he was standing there, lurching forward so that he fell into her, his head heavy on her shoulder.

She didn't think much about why or even if she liked him. That was immaterial. She had decided it was time that she *did* like someone besides Ted or Ray, and he seemed interested enough, and she was ready. She liked his sturdiness, his affable nature with his teammates, the way he didn't ignore her, exactly, but let her be, let her have her space. He was a heavy drinker, but most of the guys here were. The girls were friendly enough to her, quick to bring her a new drink (they'd for some reason that night agreed to drink Caesars, a Canadian Bloody Mary) when hers was empty. They talked of Sunday's game and how "the lads" might fare, of their jobs teaching English at various children's institutes, of other nights in bars dancing until the early morning, the trips taken to Thailand, the Philippines, Hong Kong between contracts. Allison had little to offer. Their world was so different from the one she knew, so she sipped her drink, listened, and waited to go home with Gary. Before long, he put his hand at the base of her back and tapped it. They stood. Gary said his farewells and confirmed plans to meet at the bus station the next afternoon. She waved to the girls, who yelled their goodbyes, smiled encouragingly at her. "I'm not his girlfriend," she'd told them adamantly, at the soccer game last Sunday, and again that night. But they knew now, girlfriend or not, where she was going. A few weeks ago she may have cared what people would think, when she thought of herself as a good girl. Now, what did it matter? She was in a foreign country, she did not know these people, and would probably never see them again.

In the taxi, Gary, his arm sloppily draped over her, gave the address to his apartment. The world outside their closed windows was a constellation of light and sound. Gary leaned in to kiss her neck, his lips wet and rubbery on her skin. She closed her eyes, let him continue until they arrived at his place. He fumbled with the keypad to his apartment until the heavy metal door swung open into darkness. He pulled her to the tiny bedroom, where his bed was unmade, where she had sex for the first time since Ted, a time she couldn't even remember.

CHAPTER 10

Back in the States with Bonnie and Allison, it wasn't long before the weight of Wayne's double life burdened him. They were living in a small house in Fort Belvoir where Wayne would finish his tour developing photos for low-level intelligence projects. On the second day of each month Wayne mailed Sunny an envelope of ten twenty-dollar bills wrapped in lined notebook paper, as she'd have no means to cash a check. He asked her to send a letter to his work address on base with the word "yes" written on it each time she received the money. With Allison now three and ready for pre-school, Wayne had agreed that Bonnie, who was tired of staying at home all day, could return to work. She found a steady job as a secretary at a law firm, which allowed them to save more money. Still, every dollar Wayne sent to Sunny and Mina was a dollar taken from Bonnie and Allison. He worked and came home and ate dinner with them, read Allison a book before her bedtime, watched TV while Bonnie did cross-stitch next to him, and then they went to sleep. While he lay in bed he thought of Sunny and Mina, wondered what his daughter looked like, which parts of her were his. He missed Sunny, too, their quiet life together, much simpler than the one he and Bonnie had constructed here, with their family obligations in Tennessee, their responsibility to be respectable, a good Christian family, a good military family. He wondered if the rash Sunny had on one of her fingers had gone away, if her stomach would have pale stretch marks like Bonnie's. He wondered if Sunny had broken her end of the deal, was cavorting with other men, and if she was, who was taking care of Mina. A few times when he sent the money he broke down, asking for photos or news, but he knew she would not send them because photos were expensive and frivolous and besides, photos would only complicate the matter.

Meanwhile, Bonnie could not get pregnant again. The doctor suggested she take a break, reminding her that the first pregnancy had been difficult, that stress might be the problem, and that at twenty-five years old, she still had time. Wayne agreed, they should wait to try again, if at all, but Bonnie thought differently.

"I don't want to change diapers when I'm thirty-five," Bonnie said. "It's not right to raise a child without a brother or a sister near their age. They just grow up spoiled and lonely. Maybe you're the problem, not me."

Wayne could not say that he was not the problem because he'd fathered an illegitimate child, so instead he endured. "You might be right honey. Maybe I'm the problem. Maybe it's better if I go back to Korea, get that hardship pay. You're feeling a lot of stress, and I don't think I'm helping. It ain't easy being a military wife, I know."

"Damn right it ain't easy," Bonnie said. She never used to swear. Bonnie had gotten bitter and sarcastic, worn down from the weight on her mind and body, and Wayne was not a comfort to her. He entered and left the house quietly, falling asleep after Bonnie, rising before she awoke so he would not have to touch her. He felt trapped and prayed to God to show him a way out.

Then one morning as Wayne was rising, the room still dark and heavy, Bonnie said, her back to him, "Go to Korea, then. Get out of here. But when you come back, I want a baby."

That was what they agreed. Wayne re-enlisted for another four years, requesting a second tour in Korea. He deliberated whether he should write Sunny or if he should just show up, see what kind of life she was leading, see if she had a steady GI or if she worked in one of the bars. But he didn't think he could bear that sight, so in the end he wrote her and told her he was returning for another year. He arrived in August 1979 in a country in even more turmoil than when he'd left. The worldwide oil crisis meant gas was more expensive, exports had dried up, the South Korean economy was sinking for the first time in decades, and Park Chung-hee, the military dictator, had established even more draconian measures to maintain power. Midnight curfews were in effect. No criticism against the government was allowed. And yet in spite of—or because of—this, labor unions were organizing and massive student and worker protests were occurring daily in the cities. Wayne returned to a country he was certain would collapse, allowing North Korea a chance to invade.

His job was similar to the one he'd had in 1977. He still developed photos but now they were not just aerial shots of North Korea, but also of their own US troops and the South Korean soldiers, the Republic of Korea Army, and of the Korean university student and union demonstrations, which were steadily increasing. In those photos, the protestors were barely visible through the thick tear gas that fogged the scene.

On the second day on base he got his pass, and Sunny was waiting for him at the gate. They stood stiffly, not even embracing. She told him she was living in Pyeongtaek with her brother who was about to begin his military service. Now that Wayne had returned, she and Mina would move back into the hooch where they would resume their arrangement.

"Where's the girl?" He was afraid to say her name.

"With my brother. Do you want to see her?"

He nodded. Said nothing else. She led him to the hooch, the same one he had two years ago, a meal of rice, *kimchi*, and beef soup prepared for him. He ate voraciously, the food a memory awakened. She sat and watched him. She looked the same as when he'd left, except a bit more wan. There was a hollowness to her cheeks that betrayed the strain of her life. Her hair was tied behind her in a loose ponytail and she wore a simple, knee-length black skirt and pale pink blouse.

"Who does she look like?" he asked.

"Like herself."

Then she told him how bad things had gotten. He ate as she talked, unsure if she were merely apprising him of the situation or if she thought he could help her. He thought of the folly of his coming back, leaving Bonnie alone again when she was already bitter, of leaving Allison, his Ally-gator, who had refused to let go of him, his girl. Yet he couldn't deny how right it felt to be back in this room eating his rice and soup with Sunny watching over him.

They made love on the *yo*. He was the one who wept and clung to her, while she was dry-eyed and resolute, a part of her holding back. Afterward he asked to see his daughter. They agreed she would bring her the next day.

When he arrived after work the next evening the girl was playing on a blanket, her dark straight hair cut into a short bob. He said her name and she looked up at him and then resumed playing with the spoons she held in each hand. Of course she would not recognize him; he did not recognize her.

"She looks Korean," he said.

"She has your nose," Sunny said. "Too sharp for Koreans."

But nobody in America would know she's mine, he thought.

That evening Wayne and Sunny were eating their rice and soup when a woman's voice yelled from outside. "*Sun-hui ya!*" Mina was already sleeping on the blanket next to the *yo*. Sunny dropped her spoon and ran to the door. "*Aigo*," she said, then quickly ushered the girl in.

She looked to be a few years older than Sunny, and not as pretty. Her eyes were closer together and she had a scar running along the side of her chin. Sunny ladled bowls of soup and rice from which the woman ate ravenously, not pausing to look up. Only after she finished and Sunny served her barley tea did she speak. She talked rapidly in short, staccato Korean, without inflection or emotion. Sunny occasionally would ask a question, and the woman would talk at length again. When she was finished, Sunny spoke to Wayne.

"In the past she work at same factory as me in Seoul. Now she work at textile factory. Conditions so horrible. A few days ago the owner shut the factory and move to America. He take all the money. The workers protest but the police beat them. They escape to church building but many police come again, more than one thousand. She escape again and come here to be juicy girl. She's tired of working for no money. She say that people all over Korea are protesting."

Wayne slept in the barracks that night so that Sunny's friend could stay in the hooch. He lay awake most of the night, worrying about the country's possible collapse. The next day, *Stars and Stripes* confirmed Sunny's friend's story. On page twenty five of the August 15, 1979 issue, the headline read, "ROK police release 169 arrested in raid."

Those were the striking textile workers. And on August 17, the main headline was "U.S. deplores police brutality in raid on ROK worker sit-in." The Korean government called the US's meddling "deplorable." Wayne thought the Koreans were too extreme on both sides, making people nervous, causing the country to fall into further instability. Each day Wayne found that he had to develop more and more photos of demonstrators choking in tear gas, being beaten by riot police the same age as the student protestors. Workers, professors, and students alike were fighting for better working conditions, for free elections. That was the world Sunny's brother, Woo-sung, would soon enter as he began his mandatory military service.

At the end of August 1979, the day before Woo-sung was to leave, Wayne took him and Sunny out for *bulgogi*. He didn't speak any English, but tried to converse with Wayne through Sunny, asking him about America (Is it true there is no racism? Is it true that Americans don't respect their elders? Is it true that everyone lives in a mansion?). He did not bring up the disgrace Wayne had brought on his sister. Instead Woo-sung said he was thankful for the help Wayne had given their family and he hoped that Wayne would take care of Sunny and Mina until he returned from military service. He asked many questions about Wayne's camera, said he planned to buy one once he got out. Wayne took a photo of Woo-sung in his uniform and Sunny standing against a storefront, both solemn-faced, as if they were aware of that moment of recording history, as if they knew there would be no reason to smile.

And then Woo-sung was gone. Wayne developed several copies of the photo and Sunny mailed a print to him. She kept one with the few other photos she had in a small lacquer box that had been her mother's, a gift from her father's family.

On October 26, 1979, while eating dinner with the head of the KCIA at a secret location on the Blue House compound, President Park Chung-hee was assassinated. Because of the initial secrecy of the event, the article did not make the *Stars and Stripes* until October 28.

The headline was "PARK SLAIN" in large, bold type. The next headline read, "KCIA chief named as killer of 6 in party shooting spree. Choi named ROK president."

The US position was clear: Any attempt by the North to exploit the situation would meet with a military response.

For the next ten days the US air defense unit was deployed along the DMZ with ammunition and missiles loaded. Martial law was declared, demonstrations were outlawed, curfews enforced. The Koreans kept quiet, hoping that a democratic constitution might emerge from the chaos. Wayne didn't say that the chances of a democracy or a nonmilitary rule were almost zero because those in power in the US and the ROK didn't want it. Instead he savored their evenings, astonished at how hard people tried to continue their lives, no matter how bad things got.

On December 7, military generals Chun Doo-hwan and Roh Tae-woo arrested the ROK Army chief of staff without the acting president's knowledge, and General Chun took over the country. In February 1980, an interim government was established and restored some rights to Koreans. On May 15, more than a hundred thousand protesters gathered at Seoul Station, demanding an end to martial law, which included establishing a free press and democratization. In response, on May 17, the Korean government expanded martial law to close universities, ban political activities, and further restrict the press. Troops were deployed to regional hotspots.

On May 18, the number of students protesting the closure of Chonnam University in Gwangju, a city on the south border of Korea, grew to more than two-thousand demonstrating at the city center. Paratroopers from the Korea Special Forces were called in to face the escalation, bayonetting and clubbing protestors and onlookers. The protests continued until May 20, when two hundred thousand citizens converged on the scene. The street violence escalated, with civilians raiding armories and forming militias to fight against the police. On May 21, the troops retreated until the US Army released the Korean troops on the North Korean border to Gwangju for reinforcements. By May 26, the Korean troops were ready to enter and take over the city. The Gwangju residents lay in the roads and tried to block the city, to no avail. The government re-took the city in ninety minutes.

Each day as Wayne developed photographs of the demonstrators bayoneted, clubbed, and shot, he confirmed what he'd suspected. The Korean people were fucked. He told Sunny things were even worse than she knew. They would not get better, not for a long time, if ever.

He told Sunny he wanted to take Mina back with him and adopt her. She would thrive in the States, have chances she would never have here, and Sunny would be better off in Korea as well. She could start over. He'd give her some money to start a business, buy a plot of land. Something. Sunny had never known anything but this life, but Mina could know something else. She told him she knew the woman at the orphanage in Pyeongtaek, and she could expedite the paperwork for some money under the table.

The Martial Law Command announced that one hundred forty-four civilians had been killed, and anyone disputing that number could be arrested. Yet Koreans still whispered that the deaths had been closer to one or two thousand. They also said that the US had not helped the Korean democratic movement, as the older generation had always believed, but had hindered it with their support of dictators and the latest military coup. They believed the US was complicit in the Gwangju uprising, behind the deployment of Korean Special Forces.

On May 30, Wayne arrived at the hooch to find Woo-sung wearing Sunny's robe, shivering in a corner. Sunny asked him to save her brother. He couldn't tell her that he didn't have that kind of power, that he couldn't save him. He was just an enlisted American soldier, but in her world that was enough. If Korea got bad enough, all he had to do was step through those camp gates and he'd be transported magically by one of those flying machines back to America, a country so rich that people left bowls of rice half eaten and had their own rooms to sleep in. He'd never told her what he'd heard both times he arrived in Korea. That if North Korea made it past Seoul, there were US soldiers whose job was to shoot to kill everyone in Special Intelligence. Including nobodies like him. But the fear in May 1980 was not of the North but the South. And so when Sunny said she would not give him Mina unless he helped her brother, he agreed, although there was nothing he could do. The boy was AWOL from the ROK Army. Wayne was afraid if he reported him to his unit commander, the Koreans would take him sooner rather than later.

He returned to the hooch a few nights later to pick up the boy. He told Sunny he'd arranged something but they'd have to leave now.

Woo-sung was no longer catatonic, but his eyes looked crazed from little sleep and waking dreams. His face was haggard, aging a dozen years since Wayne had taken the picture ten months before. Sunny spoke to Woo-sung in a firm, soft voice, while he looked wildly at Wayne, shaking his head.

"No go," he said in English. "No go back." He was no longer wearing Sunny's robe and instead wore his uniform, now frayed and faded where Sunny had scraped blood out.

"He's afraid," she said.

"Tell him it's okay. I'll take care of him."

She spoke in Korean again.

She touched Woo-sung's shoulder briefly but did not hug him. Wayne realized he'd never seen her hug anyone but him, except with him it wasn't so much a hug as a folding in, a release of bone and muscle, a collapsing of all that was holding her up.

He took the boy outside, giving him a knapsack containing a pair of jeans, two T-shirts, and two button down shirts in the smallest size he could find at the PX, his waterproof Timex, and a thick stack of won worth about 200 dollars. Underneath the clothes in the knapsack was a bag of rice. They got in a taxi and rode to Pyeongtaek. Wayne carried Woo-sung's backpack until they reached the bus station.

"No go back." Wayne hoped the boy understood there was not much else he could do to help him.

The boy took the sack with both hands, thanking him in Korean. "Me no go," Woo-sung said. To Wayne it sounded like "Mina go."

Wayne wondered how long the boy would live, if Sunny would ever see him again. A lot depended on whether the KCIA found him, and how long they'd care. It was best for everyone if the boy would simply disappear.

He went back to her that night and told her that her brother would be okay. They made passionate love while Mina slept on her own blanket beside them. *Mina go.*

Afterward they discussed the details of the bribes he would need to make to expedite the adoption. It required money. Wayne had made some extra money selling goods from the PX on the black market—cheese and TVs and deodorant and radios and razors, something he'd swore he'd never do on his first tour. If he got caught he'd be discharged, but the risk was low. He'd never known any of his friends to get busted. He'd use the extra money to bribe an orphanage that kept many of the mixed-race children abandoned by their GI fathers and Korean mothers. The orphanage was corrupt, but the paperwork would be legal, allowing Wayne to take Mina with him when he left in a month. Sunny had told him stories of families giving up children for a year to foster homes, only to return and find the home closed down, the children adopted by unknowing Westerners. At least she would know where her daughter was, that she would be in good hands.

He'd been working on Bonnie about the adoption for the past few months on the phone and in letters. The next morning he called her from the base when he went in to work.

"I don't know, Wayne," Bonnie said. Her voice was muffled under the line's static.

"You've always wanted Allison to have a sister."

"What if she doesn't fit in?"

"There's no future here. Children are dying in the streets. It's the Christian thing, Bonnie. We can save one."

"What if she doesn't love me?"

"She will." Wayne swallowed. "You're a wonderful mother."

"Don't do this to me. It's not fair."

Wayne closed his eyes. He tried not to let his voice shake. "She needs a mother. She needs you to be her mother."

Bonnie sighed. "I did pray to have a baby. Okay. I hope you and the Lord know what you're doing."

His last night with Sunny was just like his first when he'd arrived that August a year before. He wept and she remained dry-eyed. That vulnerable part of her from three years ago was gone with her mother, her brother, and now the daughter she was giving up. He'd come to love her and their secret family in a way he could not understand or explain. He guessed it had to do with the simplicity of their lives despite—or perhaps necessitated by—the political chaos and poverty around them. The rice and the soup and the side dishes and sleeping on a blanket in one room with a world gone crazy just outside…this attempt to live their lives was to Wayne somehow poetic and bold, an act of defiance that represented nothing more than a joy of living.

The day he left Sunny, Mina was not yet three and calling him *Appah*, father in Korean. He'd have to pretend not to recognize those words back in the States, he'd have to make her speak only English, teach her to call him Daddy. He gave Sunny the rest of the money he had, one thousand dollars, a fortune for her, and he told her to use it wisely, start a business, buy some land. They knew she would need a husband to do either properly, but they did not speak of it. He would not write to her again, would not send photos of Mina, for Mina was no longer hers, Mina did not exist. And as they embraced one last time, they reminded each other that there was only one way to go and that was forward, and they promised each other that no matter what happened they would never look back.

CHAPTER 11

Saturday as she boarded the bus with Gary to Cheongju for the soccer game, Allison saw Mina in the back, sipping something from a paper cup, dark sunglasses overwhelming her delicate face. She waved to Allison and gestured at the seat she'd been saving. Allison and Gary took their seats, then Gary was up, greeting the other guys on the bus with hearty shoulder slaps and arm punches. Mina offered her a cup. "Apple juice."

Allison took a sip. "With *soju*." Mina shrugged. "What are you doing here?" Allison returned the cup to Mina.

"Robert's on a mission." She patted Allison's shoulder with her free hand. "Thought we could have a little more sister time together."

"Late night," Allison said. "Right now the only time I want is sleep."

"Don't mind me." Mina turned and started chatting with the boys in the back. Allison heard a *Cheers!* and she closed her eyes. Gary returned with his own cup of *soju* apple juice, and she rested against Gary's shoulder, her head heavy from lack of sleep. She'd only known a few shoulders before Gary's. Ted's, of course, a sturdy, broad shoulder. There'd been Ray's shoulder, offered only once or twice during their brief affair, the hollow under his arm almost too large for her small head.

One day in January last year, she'd come to the office, her bones heavy with fatigue. Like a bad *Ladies' Home Journal* article, she and Ted had been up all night discussing *can this marriage be saved?* No, they'd decided that night, after tears and weariness and defeat. No, this marriage could not.

She'd arrived at work, raw, pale, aching in joints she didn't know existed. Ray had called her in, asked if she was okay, and she'd wept as if she'd never shed a tear over her ruined marriage, over all those dead babies, those unborn possibilities. Ray had fed her tissues until she collected herself.

"If you ever need a shoulder to cry on," he'd said. "I'm here."

But he had not actually offered his shoulder then, and she knew that he would not in the future, except as an empty metaphor. There'd been the shoulders of the few boys she'd dated before Ted, a bony shoulder at the movie theater, the boy's spread hand precariously close to her breast, a thick shoulder on the lawn of campus with the boy's arm awkwardly embracing her in a head lock. Some shoulders were so high that her nose was snuggled in a dank armpit. She remembered the smells, how she'd enjoyed the male sweat, musky, feral, sometimes commingled with the spice of heavy deodorant or cologne. How her neck would get a crick from leaning into a man's shoulder and her arm would fall asleep. Wayne's arm around her when she was young, snuggled on his lap as they watched his shows, reruns of *The Andy Griffith Show* and *Hee Haw*. When he laughed her body shook with his. She felt like she was in a bumpy car, and Wayne's arms were the carseat straps holding her in. She was not exactly comfortable, but she endured the bumps and shakes just so that she could stay in his lap.

Gary's shoulder was adequate, the right height, but he kept shifting in his seat, and when he did she'd get a sudden whiff of his armpit, smelling slightly like sour milk. She was never able to settle in and really relax.

It was her first trip outside of Seoul, and she was surprised by how far the city went, for hours it seemed, but then when it did end, the land became a succession of rice paddies and mountains, tiny villages and towns almost visible from the highway, and then another miniature city with tall apartment buildings and department stores would shoot out of the ground, a world unto its own. She'd taken the window seat because that's what Mina had saved for her. Mina, who was still sitting behind her, with her legs biting into the seat and her torso twisting and stretching every few minutes. Still, she was trying to shut Mina out because right now she was happy to have a man's arm around her, happy to feel raw and electric after sex, happy she was moving on. Last night with Gary had been like the scenery outside her window on the bus to Cheongju. There were hills, and azaleas, and forsythias, and cherry blossoms, just like back home. Korea was about the same size as Virginia, with four seasons: fiery falls, short explosions of spring, hot muggy summers, bitter winters. But still, something was askew that Allison could not pinpoint, the way a dream was familiar and yet unknown, almost forgotten. That had been last night with Gary. Sex, she remembered thinking, this is what sex with a stranger is like, with a body unknown. She remembered the. fumbling and the awkwardness and working out the pacing and sensitive spots. She remembered smells. Gary's was slightly sour and alcoholic, yet not unpleasant. But the other stuff, the constant changing of positions like he was auditioning her for a part in a movie, all the flipping and standing and sitting and squatting, that was new to her and she wasn't sure what she thought of it.

She must have dozed off, because the next thing she knew the bus was pulling into a station. Her head was pressed against the cool glass, a little drop of drool had collected on the corner of her mouth, and Gary's seat was empty. He'd moved to the back of the bus, where the guys, having abandoned the spiked apple juice, were drinking Cass beer out of tall cans. Mina's forehead rested on the back of Allison's seat, her hair trailing two loose braids. Why had she come, Allison wondered. She'd wanted this trip with Gary to be her own, without worrying about Mina or Mina worrying about her. But here she was, following her around just like when she was three and had just arrived from Korea, except that Mina knew the world they were in and Allison did not.

From the station they took several taxis to the *yogwan*, a Korean-style hotel, where they deposited their bags in Luke and Liza's room. The other rooms weren't ready, so the owner had agreed they could leave their bags in the one room, and then move them to their individual rooms when they returned later that night. The room had eggshell-blue linoleum, patterned blue wallpaper, and a double bed with a thick comforter with satin patches in bright primary colors. Allison peered into the bathroom, which held a shower hose mounted in between the toilet and sink, just like at Mina's apartment, and also the ubiquitous plastic slippers at the bathroom door. She couldn't put her finger on it, but there was something seedy about the place. It was clean enough, but it felt old and used. Maybe it was the half-full bottles of men's aftershave and lotion beside the aged TV, which had a slot for videos. She jumped ahead to later that evening, perhaps a few hours from now after dinner, when she and Gary would be in a room similar to this, repeating what they'd done last night. Or maybe he'd survey the room and change the menu, a new setting, a new configuration. Maybe sex for him was like a skating competition, a set of moves to be rearranged, reordered to fit the occasion. Peering into the bathroom, Allison felt a set of arms wrap around her, a chin on her shoulder, and a whisper in her ear, "we're sharing a room, right?"

Allison loosened the hands around her waist. "I'm sleeping with Gary."

A sigh in her ear. "Ally, why?"

"Why not?"

"Be careful."

"I'm tired of being careful."

"Okay, then." Mina backed away.

They all went out for *dalkgalbi,* the spicy chicken dish the region was famous for. They sat six to a round table, cramped in tiny plastic chairs of different colors like a Crayola box. Allison sat next to Gary. Mina took a seat at the other table. On each table, hunks of chicken, slivers of cabbage, and *tteok,* a simple rice cake, all covered in red pepper sauce, sizzled in a circular pan. The remaining space was crammed with large bottles of beer and *soju,* tiny metal ashtrays lined with damp squares of paper towels, plastic dishes stacked with lettuce leaves, thick slices of garlic, fermented soybean paste, known as *doenjang.* Once the chicken was cooked, Allison followed the others, scooping the mixture on an open leaf, topping it with a sliver of garlic dipped in *doenjang.* She rolled the lettuce leaf, stuffing the concoction, spicy and tangy, but not as greasy as the grilled meat, in her mouth. After the *dalkgalbi* was almost finished, the server scooped rice onto the pan and cooked it with sesame oil, red pepper paste, and the leftover chicken bits. Allison was already full, but couldn't resist a few mouthfuls of the crunchy fried rice.

She'd stopped counting the beers and glasses of *soju* she'd had by the time they left for the expat bar a few blocks away, a place recommended by the Cheongju soccer team. It was just past ten, still early, and they were able to find a large enough table to crowd around. Some of the teammates who didn't drink, like the practicing Muslim Moroccans and the New Zealand triathlon trainer, had returned to the *yogwan*, but there were still twelve of them, girls included, ready to see the night through.

The rival team commandeered its own table, drank a few rounds of shots, then disappeared without much fuss some time after midnight. Allison, feeling the dull ache of desire and fatigue, wondered when Gary might want to return to the room with her and try out the bed. He seemed more intent on drinking with his friends, so she sat patiently and quietly on top of a beer keg next to Mina. Allison poured beer from a pitcher into Mina's glass.

"Are we fighting?" Mina said.

"I don't want to," Allison said.

"You've been through so much with Ted and all that. You deserve more."

"I can have fun, like you," Allison said.

Mina was silent for a few moments. The bar was playing a mix of eighties and nineties music. "Then have fun with me on the dance floor." She drained her beer, grabbed Allison's hand and led her across the room. Mina took Allison's hands and danced with her like two little sisters might have, as if Mina was trying to start from the beginning with Allison, as if they could be sisters who had danced to U2 or Bruce Springsteen or Michael Jackson as little girls, twirling in front of their parents on the living room floor.

Some of the other girls joined them, and after a few more songs, Allison, suddenly feeling woozy, went back to her beer-keg seat. Sitting in Mina's too-high bar stool was a guy she recognized from the night before, a pudgy Brit named Adam whose hair was styled in a high, glistening pompadour she'd only seen in the old Elvis movies Wayne liked to watch. She asked him what position he played, and he said none, that he had no interest in sports and had come for the party and to cheer on the team. He was more interested, though, in giving her, or rather her country, advice, "from one former colonialist to another."

"It's not so bad, not being number one," he said. "We've had a pretty good run of it, although it seems we're in a bit of a crisis again. Once you get over the shock of not running the world, of having to listen to other countries, to even kiss their ass, the way we've kissed yours, once you get over that, it's a relief really, not being involved in so many bloody messes. You'll see, soon enough."

"I don't think that soon," Allison said.

"Really?" Adam smoothed the sides of his hair. "We'll see about that, dear."

"We will." Even though Wayne had retired from the military and she had lived in the DC area for much of her life, politics did not interest Allison very much. Ever since she could remember, she'd witnessed the slow moving, misguided bureaucracy that made up the US military, and by extension the federal government. She was thankful for it, for it had provided Wayne, a poor enlisted man from the mountains of Tennessee, a distinguished military career, and after that, consistent, well-paid work with one of the contractors that had prospered under the Bush administration. That same government had provided her a job, as well, with another contractor. Stability, health insurance, a pension. Like Wayne, she'd been thankful for a job, for security, without worrying too much who was in power or what they were doing.

But Adam would not let up. He told her that China's emergence as a world power was inevitable as was America's decline, that Americans like her had no clue, could not see what the future held for them, how their way of life was doomed.

Finally Allison cut him off. "What does it matter what I think? If change is inevitable. If we're doomed, as you say. What do you care?"

"Just remember. I was right," Adam said, his chin thrust out.

She excused herself to the bathroom. She sat on the toilet, resting her head on the paper holder, eyes closed. The intensity of the past few weeks fell upon her suddenly, and she wondered if she could find the *yogwan* herself, for at that moment what she wanted more than anything else was sleep.

She awoke to a quick rap on the door. "Allison, you okay?"

"I'm fine." She flushed the toilet and opened the door.

Mina was at the sink, splashing water on her face. "Good, 'cause the band's starting. It's time to dance again."

It was three a.m. Allison wasn't sure what had happened in the blur of time, how much had been spent propped up on the beer keg listening to Adam, how much in the bathroom, and how much just watching the world swirl around her. She was revived for the moment, though, and the band, a motley group of Canadians, sang covers they'd cobbled together, crowd pleasers from groups like the Rolling Stones, Nirvana, Green Day, and No Doubt. She danced with Mina and the other girls in the thin strip of flooring cleared in front of the band. Except for her earlier foray with Mina, she'd not danced since college, and she noticed her movements, if they'd ever been appropriate, were depressingly out of date. She was more jerk and foot patterns, while the other girls moved their upper bodies like rubber bands. Allison was too much leg and not enough hip. Gary was watching her, and as the song finished he waved for her to come back to him. He wrapped his arm around her waist, pulling her onto his lap. She half nuzzled, half slept on his shoulder, and then his knee started bouncing her and she thought she was young again on Wayne's knee, but then she was being lifted up and something rose in her mouth, and she opened her eyes to the room spinning. Gary stood up, started dancing in his seat. The band was playing "Smells Like Teen Spirit." Allison stumbled into the bathroom, bent her head over the toilet, and waited to throw up. But nothing happened. She stayed until the nausea dissipated, and then at the sink splashed her face as Mina had. When she stepped back into the bar, Gary's seat was empty. She saw him on the dance floor with Mina, her hair unbraided now, loose on his shoulder as she leaned forward to whisper something in his ear.

Allison went up the floor, pulled Mina by the hair. "Not this time," she said. Mina slapped at her hand.

"Goddamn Allison, that hurts."

"Why do you always take what I have when you can get anything you want?" Her face felt clammy and damp. Gary put his arm on Allison's.

"It's okay. Let's just go back." Gary's face was red, his eyes tiny bloodshot splits. Mina was biting her lip, tears squeezed from her eyes.

"That's what you think?" Mina said. "Really?"

"Not think. Know," Allison said.

Gary moved closer to her, rubbed his head on her neck, nuzzled her hair. "Time to go."

When they arrived back at the *yogwan* it was not quite five. The game was in six hours. Gary's arm fell heavy on her, more for support than ardor. They were the last to retrieve their bags from Luke's and Liza's place. They circled the floor, looking for an open room, but all the rooms were taken, though there was supposed to have been one reserved for them. Meanwhile, Adam, whose room was next to Mina's, announced to the hall he was taking a bath. A few minutes later what sounded like very bad opera singing spilled into the hallway. Mina padded out of the room just as Allison and Gary walked past her door.

"Adam's singing so loud I can't sleep. I'm not stalking you, I promise." Mina slumped on the floor next to her door. She'd changed into an oversized T-shirt that hit her mid-thigh.

"We can't find our room," Gary said.

Mina said nothing, but pushed herself up and walked down the stairs. The manager appeared from the stairwell in sweatpants, plastic sandals, and hair spiked from sleeping. Mina said he'd told her there were enough rooms on the floor for everyone, and there should be a room for Allison and Gary. The manager went around to each room knocking and yelling in Korean loud enough to rouse the soccer team, which had just collectively passed out. Above the running bath water, Adam had segued from opera to show tunes. Gary had sunk to the floor, his head between his knees, and Allison was ready to join him. Then the manager knocked on a door and someone answered in fluent Korean. The owner knocked louder, yelled something, and a woman's voice, sharp and rapid, replied. The door opened, and a Korean man slipped on a jacket while a woman checked her face in the room's mirror. They scurried out and down the stairs. The manager followed them, hurling a string of insults, Allison was certain, as he chased them out of the building.

"What was that about?" Adam was in the hall with a tiny white towel that barely met the circumference of his flabby waist and another one wrapped around his pompadour. A puddle of footprints trailed back to his room.

"She's a prostitute," Mina said. "The guy figured there'd be an open room he could use for free instead of paying for one. Since no one was in the room at this time of night, he figured the room wasn't occupied."

"Brilliant," Gary moaned. He pushed himself up from the floor.

"You have no idea what kind of life she has," Mina said.

"I'll care in the morning." Gary stumbled into the room and fell on to the bed, fully clothed, legs spread in a wide V.

"Can I go to sleep now?" Mina looked at Adam.

"Bit knackered myself," Adam said, and they disappeared into their rooms.

Allison took one of the blankets folded in the closet and laid on the patch of bed that Gary wasn't sleeping on. She was too tired to think about what had just gone on in that room, not even cleaned, and what might be under the bed, on the floor. That would come later, and whenever she recalled that evening, she shivered with the shame of it all. But that night she pulled her jeans off and fell asleep, too exhausted to care.

The next morning the Seoul Strikers, most either still drunk or horribly hung over, suffered a resounding defeat. In their bitterness, they began to suspect they'd been set up, that the Cheongju team had not shown them the expat bar out of hospitality, as they'd claimed, but as way to trap them into debilitating inebriation and certain loss. On the bus home, they tried to sleep off their hangovers. Gary's head alternated between Allison's lap and shoulder. He had only played half the game; the other half he lay on the sidelines in the grass like an animal, taking sips of the juice and water Allison proffered when he felt he could keep something down. Mina had not even shown up for the game. When Allison and Gary boarded the bus Mina, having claimed three seats in the back row, was already asleep, her backpack serving as a pillow. She and Allison had not spoken to each other since the bar. Allison still felt like avoiding her.

As the bus pulled into the station, Gary roused her. "Want to come back to my place? Finish the weekend?"

Allison looked at Mina still sleeping in the back. She should do the responsible thing and wait and talk with Mina, tell her all she knew, try to find out why she was always trying to take what Allison wanted. But she could do that tomorrow, and it would serve Mina right, show her that some guys did choose her, that she too could have fun. She squeezed his hand, grabbed her backpack, and got off the bus without even saying goodbye.

Monday morning she awoke, her head heavy and tired, but was unable to fall back asleep. Gary slept, immobile, sprawled so that he took up most of the bed. She wondered if she would see him again. She wasn't obsessed with Gary, and that was a relief. Last night they'd had hungover sex, both of them exhausted, spent. Would they be able to have sex not drunk or hungover? Or did this represent the range of possibilities? She was naked except for the prayer necklace Mina had given her, which she fingered absently, suddenly wanting to put something on. She plucked a smelly T-shirt from the floor and threw it over her head.

She was awake, she realized, because of what Gary had told her last night, after they'd had sex. Allison had said something about Mina hitting on Gary at the bar, and Gary had snorted.

"Hardly. She's always warning me to treat you well, like you're some fragile flower or innocent virgin. Christ, she won't let it go. I'm not that bad, am I?" And then he'd fallen asleep.

How many times had Allison misjudged Mina? She really didn't know. If Mina had been there, the day of the abortion, or even after, then maybe she wouldn't have stayed at that office because of Ray, maybe she'd have had the courage to make better, more hopeful choices. If Mina had told her about her affair with Ray, why she'd done it even though she knew Allison loved him, maybe Allison could begin to understand, forgive. If only they'd been closer.

Allison sat up in the bed. She wanted to tell Mina everything. Of her discovery about Mina and Ray, and the thing she'd told no one, about the aborted fetus. She'd tell Mina of her jealousy, petty, small-minded as it was, how she felt it was not a secret that their dad loved Mina best. She would tell Mina all this and let the chips fall because she was tired of the alternative. She was tired of the tight knot she always felt, of the gnawing beast in her stomach eating her from the inside out. Allison wanted a sister, and she wanted to show Mina that she was worthy of her trust. She would tell Mina her secrets in hopes that Mina would tell Allison hers. And then, after all their secrets were laid bare, she would help Mina find her mother.

She left Gary without saying goodbye. She knew he wouldn't mind; he might even be relieved. She was strangely awake and alert. She wasn't sure how she'd say the things she wanted to say, but she knew she wanted to say them without hesitation or delay. She wanted Mina's forgiveness, and she wanted to forgive Mina. They could start there.

It was mid-morning when she climbed the stairs to the apartment on the second floor. Had it only been a little over two weeks ago that she'd climbed those same stairs with Jason, that first time? She fumbled the code to the apartment, half hoping Mina would run to open the door, got the digits right the second time, and set her bag down in the hallway. Even before she saw the note, two lines written in Korean, and the envelope addressed to her, before she saw the door to Mina's room open, the hangers bare, before she saw the ashtray empty and clean, she felt it, the absence of her sister, the emptiness of the air, the hollow in her bones, the same feeling she'd had after the baby had been sucked out of her. She opened the envelope and inside was a photo, the colors a bit washed out, a crisp white border on the edges. A picture of a young woman who looked like Mina from another time. Mina if she'd grown up in the Korea Wayne had described. Beside her was a boy in a uniform, who looked too young to be in one, but was, a face he was trying to keep serious. On the back of the photo was one word in Mina's handwriting in Korean. Allison sounded out the word: *Omma.* By now she knew the word well.

CHAPTER 12

N*ot quite.*

That's what her instructor, Mr. Kim, said when Mina told him she was Korean. She was fourteen, and had earned her blue belt in Tae Kwon Do a few weeks earlier. She'd just done well sparring against a boy two years older and thirty pounds heavier than she was. Mr. Kim, usually parsimonious with praise, said she had a powerful *gi* energy, which could be used for good if harnessed correctly, but if not, could lead to many broken things.

Mina had become more curious about her Korean heritage, something she knew little of. Since she'd been adopted eleven years before, she'd wanted nothing more than to fit in with the world around her, which was suburban and white. She wanted to forget she was adopted, forget that Korea, that poor pathetic country that had abandoned her, existed. She wanted to have pink white skin like her sister, to not be so skinny, like a refugee. She wanted to be able to drink milk without getting indigestion the way the rest of her family could. She wanted someone to look at her and say, "that's just like your father," or "you have your mother's eyes," like they did with Allison. She didn't want people to look at her with pity, like she was a stray cat salvaged from the dump. So she sang in the church choir louder than the others, she raised her hand to answer the questions about God and Jesus first in Sunday school, where Korea did not exist, and Mina was glad not to be reminded of it. She helped her mother tear lettuce, butter bread, peel potatoes for dinner. She dressed her blonde Barbies in short poofy skirts exposing their long pale legs and clingy tops outlining the perfect inverted C-curve of their plastic breasts. She wanted to be sure her parents would not regret their decision to take her on, and so she devoted herself to doing everything better than Allison, who was quiet and sullen and watched a lot of TV. Mina made their parents laugh more often, had more friends, won more prizes, displayed more talents than her sister, and yet she always wondered if it was enough to overcome the truth. She was a fraud, a fake, an imposter, someone discarded from a different land, race, and culture, a person who didn't belong.

Then one day in the sixth grade, Mina smacked Jennifer Jenkins, who called her a chink in the cafeteria. Mina called her a spic, although she wasn't sure what a spic was or if Jennifer was one, and then they'd started fighting. "Go home," Jennifer said. "We don't want you here." Mina was smaller than Jennifer, but she'd thrown the girl to the floor, pinning her arms with her bony knees so that she could smack her without recourse. "I'm Korean," she said. "What am I?" Jennifer didn't answer. She slapped her. "I'm not a chink. What am I?" "Korean," Jennifer said. "Same difference." She didn't hear the screaming, hers, Jennifer's, or the gathering crowd's, nor did she know how long she hit Jennifer, a girl with freckles and brown pigtails and green eyes, until she was pulled away by two teachers and taken to the principal's office.

She sat in a too-tall chair, her feet unable to touch the ground, while the adults, her teacher, Jennifer's mother, her own parents, and the principal whispered behind the closed office door. She swung her legs, forced herself to uncurl her fists, thinking, *Don't send me back*. But where was back? When Jennifer had told her to go home, Mina had been confused at first until she realized Jennifer didn't mean home *here*, but *back there*. *There* was a place with not enough food, children in tattered clothing begging in the streets, a place that smelled like human feces and where men in uniforms shot anyone who disagreed with the government. The place Americans Saved From Communism, the place her dad saved her from.

And after all these years of being even more than a good girl, of being the best girl, she'd finally made a mistake. She'd blown her cover. She was no American girl but a Korean orphan who'd fought for scraps of food, fought for a piece of a torn blanket in a room crowded with those just like her, fought to be chosen to be taken away.

Except. That wasn't what she remembered. What she remembered was this: A woman with long dark hair Mina could curl her fists around. Slung on this same woman's back, wrapped in a quilt, resting her head on the woman's shoulder as she filled a pail with water. Sitting on a blanket on the warm floor as the woman fed her thimble-sized balls of rice. Singing, she remembered that, too, and sleeping with the woman through the night.

Was that an orphanage? Where were the other children? Was that woman her mother? Over the years she'd tried to push away her questions and memories, like lost frames in a film. She had no idea what to do with them, where to put them, how to make sense of them. She couldn't ask her parents. Either they wouldn't believe her, didn't know, or wouldn't tell her the truth. The truth. What was that? The truth was this was her family. They loved her, except for maybe Allison, who was just jealous. And she loved them, even Allison, especially Allison. She wanted to stay here, to be part of this family. She didn't want to go back, wherever back was.

The secretary called her into the office, where her parents, her teacher, and Jennifer's mother sat opposite Principal Procter. She waited for them to question her, yell at her, call her terrible things. She was ready to apologize, even if she wasn't sure what she was apologizing for. But they didn't ask her anything. Instead she kept her head bowed, felt everyone's eyes on her. Finally her teacher spoke.

"Mina, we understand why you were angry."

She looked up then and saw Mrs. James and even Jennifer's mother looking at her with kindness. Or was it pity? "I'm sorry," she whispered. Tears squeezed out of the corners of her eyes. She wiped the palm of her hand across her nose. Mrs. James nodded. "Have you heard of Tae Kwon Do, the Korean martial arts?"

"Korea?" she whispered.

"Mr. Kim has classes here Tuesday and Thursday nights. We thought it would be a good idea for you join his class."

So that was it? They wanted her to take some kind of kung fu classes after school? Her hands began to shake, but she held them tight. She wanted to say no, say they were just like Jennifer, that they thought she was something that she was not, but she looked at her father and her mother, and her mother nodded slightly, and Mina realized they'd struck some kind of deal, and if she didn't say yes to this, then the alternative would be much worse.

She began Tae Kwon Do the next week, surprised by how much she liked it from the first day. She was a good student, learning the Korean counting system quickly, absorbing Mr. Kim's lessons on the Korean way. She had agility and focus, a combination necessary to do well in the art. She performed her punches and kicks cleanly, practiced in her bedroom at home until her voice was hoarse from counting, and progressed through the lower level belts with ease.

While she enjoyed and excelled at the physical part, what she loved most was when Mr. Kim would talk about the Korean Tae Kwon Do masters and their devotion to "the way." When she heard those stories, for the first time she thought that her Korean-ness might be something she could be proud of. By the time Mina started eighth grade, she no longer wanted to pretend to be white. If anyone asked her, she said she was Korean.

And so that day when she was fourteen and Mr. Kim remarked that her *gi* was powerful, Mina had replied, that's because I'm Korean. She'd thought it would please him, her open identification with her race, this moment of solidarity with him, but he'd only smiled wryly and said those words, *not quite.*

She'd thought at the time that he meant she wasn't all Korean because of her Western upbringing, her Caucasian family. Later, she wondered.

Mina continued to lead a double life as a good American girl. By her junior year, she was a cheerleader with a football player boyfriend, good grades, student council, top-tier-college bound. A group of Korean girls started attending her high school, real Koreans with Korean parents, immigrants who spoke English with thick accents. Except for their race, the girls had nothing in common with Mina. They were insular. They ate in a tiny neat group at lunch, closed off to open spaces or extra chairs. The girls were either plain faced with glasses and bad skin or heavily made up, suggesting evil Asian clowns. They were failing abysmally to fit into any kind of social group, but Mina couldn't tell if they were trying or if they even cared.

Mina's friends were for the most part white, from well-off families who had money for college. They got shiny new Hondas or used

BMWs for their sixteenth birthdays. Only Mina's family was barely middle class, living in a small, older ranch home, unable to pay for college or a car, new or used. But Mina was pretty, thin, charismatic, smart (but not scary Asian smart, otherwise she'd be sitting with the nerds, where Asians of all stripes were well represented), exotic (she knew they said that behind her back), which trumped her handicaps. She belonged with them.

Even as Mina stayed with the coveted "in group" of kids who had hung out at the same lunch table for as long as she could remember, she secretly watched the Korean girls eating in their corner at the other end of the cafeteria. She'd walk by on the pretense of buying a Coke or chips from the machine near them, just to hear their scraps of Korean, or watch them place their food in the middle of the table so they could share everything: the pile of French fries, the slice of pizza cut into bite-sized bits, the iceberg lettuce drenched in French dressing. They ate so that the food did not touch their lips, as if they wore some invisible lipstick they did not want smeared. They spoke rapid fire Korean, interrupting each other, squealing and laughing with a gusto they never had in class. Mina wanted to find out about the lives they'd left behind, but she hesitated. If she approached them, people might think she belonged there, and not with the popular crowd. They'd wonder about her allegiances. And the Korean girls, what did they think of her, if they did at all? They probably envied her, this girl who could speak fluent English without any accent, this cheerleader who dated a football player (his name was Max), this American dream personified. So maybe they'd be flattered if she approached them and introduced herself. But then what? She couldn't exactly invite them "in" to her crowd—the world didn't work that way. She could only avail herself as some recompense, a last resort if they had any questions or problems or if someone ever bothered them. Maybe that was enough.

Yet as the weeks passed, she couldn't let her desire to sit with the girls go. What did she care if her friends thought she was weird? Being popular was something she'd taken for granted, as someone who had been attractive and charming all her life could. She told herself that she could live without them, and besides, she doubted anything would come from having one lunch with the Korean girls. In fact, she might appear generous and kindhearted, connecting with "her people." One day, she took her French fries and Coke (her usual lunch) and asked the Korean girls if she could sit with them. They'd been talking—babbling in Korean—and stopped immediately when she approached, their forks paused in mid air.

"Okay," one of the girls squeaked. There was much commotion and shifting of chairs to accommodate her. Mina offered her fries to the pile, but they refused her, telling her no, to please take some of theirs. The girls were quiet. Mina was not accustomed to silence, so she asked them where they were from in Korea.

"Apgujeong," one of the girls said. She wore thick eyeliner and her eyebrows had been plucked and redrawn into inverted checkmarks. She tottered around the halls in high heels, wearing designer labels that no one at school cared about.

"Where's that?" Mina asked.

The table of girls giggled. A few put their hands over their mouths.

"In Seoul," the girl said.

"I'm adopted, so I don't know where I'm from, but I think I'm from Seoul—or near it," Mina said.

Collectively the girls sucked in their breath, and then the one who had said she was from Apgujeong, the leader, Mina decided, said, "That explains things."

"What things?"

The girl shrugged. "You don't know where Apgujeong is. And you don't look pure Korean. You look like a mutt."

Mina stared at her fries. She'd poured too much ketchup on them; they were soggy. She wasn't sure if the girl was being rude or just direct or if there was a cultural problem. She decided to continue. "Well, I'd like to visit some day."

"If you do, make sure you go to Itaewon. You might find your mother there."

The girls giggled. One gasped. Another looked at her plate.

Again Mina was confused. Perhaps this was a place that held information about adopted Koreans. "Well, I just wanted to introduce myself. If you ever need some help."

"We don't need you," the Apgujeong girl said. They still had not told Mina their names.

The one looking at her plate was now saying something in

Korean, "*Dessuh, dessuh.*" Years later Mina learned that the word meant "enough." She was one of the plainer ones, wearing a hair clip with a butterfly affixed to it. "Thank you for your concern. It's nice of you to think of us." Her English was almost without accent. The other girls ate from the piles of French fries silently. Mina stood.

"Okay then. Well. Bye then."

"Bye," the girls echoed. They were chatting in Korean before she was a table away.

She thought she was done with them, or that they were done with her. She hadn't been snubbed like that, in a way she couldn't pinpoint but could feel, ever. Except when she'd first arrived and Allison would be mean to her in small ways—taking her dolls or her cookies or pinching the inside of her arm. Don't tell on me, Allison would whisper, or else they'll send you back. And she never did. She believed her.

That night at Tae Kwon Do practice she asked Mr. Kim about Apgujeong and Itaewon.

"We say Apgujeong is the Beverly Hills of Korea. Many famous rich people live there. Not typical Korean. Itaewon, well, that is the foreigner area, near the US military base."

Mina figured one day she might understand what the girl meant, but for now she decided to forget them. The next week, though, as Mina was waiting for Max to pick her up from cheerleading practice, the girls showed up, bunched together in a Mercedes convertible. The one from Apgujeong was behind the wheel.

"Do you need a ride?" There was a tiny sliver of a space for her in the middle of the back seat.

Mina hesitated. Behind them Max was driving up in his SUV. She ran up to Max and told him she was getting a ride with them. He studied the car crammed with girls who looked like Mina, but not.

"You sure you'll be all right?" He kissed her briefly on the lips. He was a good boyfriend, Max, tall and well-built, conscientious, with neat sandy blonde hair and green eyes. His family had moved to Springfield from Memphis a few years before, and he was unfailingly polite. A good southern boy, her father had said, approvingly. Mina could not complain.

"They're just girls," Mina said, laughing. "Hey, I think I'll let them know about Jim's party. Okay?" She kissed him back.

"I don't see why not," Max said, touching her neck. Then she was off, squeezing into the tiny space in the back. She gave them directions to her house and then told them about Jim's party. They were noncommittal about the party, but finally told her their names. A girl in the front kept fiddling with the radio, dissatisfied with whatever station the dial landed on. They dropped Mina off at her house, she thanked them, and they sped off.

She didn't see the girls again until the party that Saturday. Three of them had come, Ji-young, the Apgujeong girl, Eun-hee, and Hye-jin. Only the girl with the bangs and butterfly clip who had said *dessuh, dessuh* at the lunch table was absent. Mina introduced them to a few of her friends, the ones she knew would be nice to them. But the Korean girls had nothing to say and seemed incapable of engaging in even basic social banter. Soon, they drifted toward the living room, which had been cleared for dancing. Mina forgot about them until she saw them later, huddled together, silent, expressionless, watching her as she danced with her friends and Max. Later, just before midnight, Ji-young approached her and said they were going home.

"It's kind of a boring party," Ji-young said. "Compared to the ones at home."

Mina saw it then, the girl was pissed off. With her expensive clothes that tried too hard, her accented English, the jewel encrusted pocketbook she carried in the crook of her arm—nothing about her fit here, even if it had in Apgujeong.

She thought that was the last she'd see of them, but later that night, after Max had dropped her off, the doors of the Mercedes parked across the street opened as she was about to let herself into the house. Ji-young stood at the edge of the yard, holding a bottle of something, champagne Mina guessed, with the other two girls flanking her. Mina walked down the gentle slope of their front yard until she met them.

"What's up?" she said.

Ji-young crashed the bottle on Mina's head. She fell onto the grass, gasping, her scalp warm and tingling. Sweet drops of champagne trickled into her mouth. The other girls were crying now, grabbing Ji-young's arm, but she stood over Mina, holding the cracked bottle.

"You think you're hot shit with your golden boy and your cheerleader outfit. Well, guess what, in Korea you're nothing. Your dad was a GI, your mom some low-class Korean whore who worked on Hooker Hill. You're not even a real Korean, just a mutt. A *honyol*." Ji-young was panting. "A *tuigi* devil child." Mina thought the girl might kill her.

Mina didn't move. The air smelled like decaying flowers. A salty taste of iron filled her mouth. She mumbled the Tae Kwon Do philosophy Mr. Kim had made her memorize four years ago when she'd first started. "I shall be a champion of justice and freedom. I shall build a better and peaceful world." Ji-young was bent over her, her mouth twitching into a smile. She held the broken bottle in her hand, raised like a lantern showing her the way. The girls each grabbed one of Ji-young's armpits and pulled her back as they whispered to her in Korean. Mina stood up, dazed. The porch light was still shining, her key in the door. She was now past curfew; Dad would be angry. She took a step toward the house. Her face was sticky, yet her body felt warm, flowing. Ji-young jumped from the girls' hold, with her hands open like claws. Mina threw a kick into Ji-young's solar plexus, sending her to the ground. She folded inward, gasping for air. Mina wanted to finish her off, just as she'd tried to finish Jennifer off in the sixth grade, but she stopped because of Mr. Kim and her oath.

"You better be gone before my father comes out. He'll kill you," Mina said. The two girls dragged Ji-young back to the car. She heard cries, a plaintive wail. She was inside then, and she heard more screaming, and the blood was covering her eyes, but she was safe now, and she allowed herself to fall into her mother's arms.

Not quite.

She told her parents some white girls from school had done it, jealous of her dating Max and of the attention their boyfriends gave her. She protected the Korean girls because she wondered if they might be right, that she was a mutt. Later in LA she learned the word *honyol* meant mixed Korean blood, a derogatory term until more recently, and that *tuigi* was so bad it was rarely used anymore. She'd study her face in the mirror, secretly compare it to the other Korean girls, who now stayed far from her, and she couldn't help but see for the first time the differences. Her eyes were dark, Asian almonds, although she did have what Koreans called a double-eyelid, a fold above her eye not as common among Asians. Her nose was prominent, not large, but sharper than the other Korean girls. And there was something about her face shape, her jaw, thin and pronounced, that looked Western.

She'd always imagined her real parents as poor. That's how Korea was, her father had told her, poorer than even the hollers in Tennessee, with only rice for food and shit for fertilizer. Her parents had been in love, yes, perhaps even married, but unable to feed her. Or, later, she'd imagined that her mother had probably been single, an unwed mother, forced to give Mina up against her will. Either way, her parents, or her mother at least, were good people who had given her up reluctantly, for her own benefit. She'd never thought her mother might be a prostitute, that her mother didn't want her. She asked her father about Hooker Hill one night at dinner. He stopped chewing and stared at her.

"Where'd you hear about that?"

Mina shrugged. Allison smirked and shoved peas in her mouth. "Don't know. Just that it's some place in Itaewon."

"It's a sinful place. You don't need to know nothing more than that." He resumed chewing and asked her mother to pass the peas.

By the time she'd graduated from high school, Mina had cobbled together the most likely story, the one the Korean girls told her. Her biological father was some GI, her mother a Korean who'd worked on Hooker Hill. She was taken to an orphanage, where her parents, Wayne and Bonnie, had adopted her. But what about her memories of sleeping on the young woman's back, of playing with pots and pans on a blanket? A woman's hands feeding her rice. Someone she called *Omma*. One day she would find the truth.

CHAPTER 13

Allison called Gary first. After a few rings, his cell phone switched to a Korean pop song which switched to a recorded message, then a beep. She left a message for him to call her as soon as he could. She knew that calling him not thirty minutes after she'd left his place made her look dramatic, clingy, but she hoped he had enough sense to know her better and listen to her message when he woke up.

She scrolled through the few contacts on her phone. She couldn't call Wayne yet, alarming him when there might not be cause, when Mina might show up the next day, wondering what the fuss had been. She tried Mina's cell, but that also plugged her directly to voice mail. She left a message, begging Mina to call her.

The only number left was Jason. He answered after a few rings, in English.

"Mina's gone." Her throat was tight.

"Where are you?"

"In the apartment. She left a note in Korean."

"Can you read it to me?"

"I'll try. It says, '*jja ji ma.*'"

"I'm coming."

While she waited for Jason, she washed her dirty clothes and took a shower, letting the slow stream of water warm her as much as possible. She turned on Mina's computer and checked her email. Nothing.

She lay on her couch bed without folding it out and closed her eyes. She could smell Mina on the cushion, and a kind of dark muskiness that reminded her of sex. She breathed slowly, focusing on alleviating the tiredness that had accumulated at the front of her head. The photo remained with the note, unexamined. Allison was not ready. Not yet.

The next thing she knew Jason was shaking her awake. The note and photo were on the glass coffee table. He opened a window and lit a cigarette.

"You should remember to lock the door," he said.

"What's the note say?" Allison brought her knees to her chest. Jason was wearing khakis and a polo shirt, like some prep school boy from the East coast.

"Not to look for her."

"Why did she go?" The same question her family had been asking since Mina graduated from high school.

"She found something about her mother."

Allison examined the photo, tapping the corner, a blur of an edge of a young woman, with bones like Mina's. The woman was standing beside a young man who looked like a boy except that he wore a uniform. At first glance Allison thought they were a young husband and wife, a photo to commemorate the couple before he went to military service. In this photo the woman looked like Mina, could easily be her mother, and the man, the man had the same bones as the woman, the high cheekbones, the long neck that flattered him less. It drew attention to his large head, which looked like it was being held up by a Popsicle stick. From the way they were standing, not touching, but comfortable, familial, Allison decided they were not husband and wife, but brother and sister.

"Really?"

Jason studied her. "What do you think?"

"I don't know. But I was going to tell her I would do whatever I could to help."

Jason finished his cigarette and closed the window. "Robert's helping her."

She scooted over on the couch, patting the space beside her. "You don't trust him."

He sat at one end of the couch, knees together, shoulders drawn in, taking as little space as possible. "There's more room," Allison said. She touched his knee, and his legs slightly opened. She fingered the edge of the photo. Who had taken it? "She said I trust Dad too much."

Jason removed his glasses, cleaned them with the corner of his shirt. "She had suspicions. But no proof. She must have it now."

Allison stepped off the sofa and stood in front of him. His slimness made him appear younger than he was. She was tempted to crush his bones until he told her everything. Instead she got on her knees, encircled her arms around the slim calves, placed her head on his lap. She heard his breathing quicken. "Damn it Jason," she whispered. "She might be in trouble, and if something happens to her because you won't tell me what you know, you'll have to live with that the rest of your life."

Silence, except for his breathing, shallow, rapid. She held his legs together, let her head weigh heavy on his slender thighs.

"She thought your dad was her real father," he said. "That her mother was maybe some kind of room salon girl or prostitute or something."

Allison closed her eyes, pressed her lips together so she wouldn't say something she'd regret. Like, that Mina was a delusional liar. Their dad would never do that. She counted her breaths. A hand, awkwardly, tentatively stroked her hair. "But Mina is Korean," Allison said.

"Half. Can't you tell?"

She couldn't. Mina was just Mina. Mimi. Adopted from an orphanage in Korea. Saved from a life of misery and squalor. Besides, she couldn't imagine her dad cheating on her mother. It wasn't so much that they were crazy in love as it was she couldn't see them with anyone else. They were so intertwined that she couldn't fathom how they'd extricate themselves except in death. Then she remembered a night when one of Wayne's old buddies from Korea was in town and had come for dinner. He and Wayne were laughing over some shared joke, a name dropped that needed no explanation, and an allusion to another, and then there was a look from Wayne, and the man changed the subject.

"If Mina's looking for something about Dad, she's probably at Camp Humphreys."

"She already went there with Robert. Found nothing. Too many GIs with the same story."

"I have to go there."

Jason shook his head. "It's like finding a haystack in a needle."

Allison didn't correct him. His confused expression seemed apt. She rooted through her suitcase and pulled out a pair of jeans and sweat pants, a few tops and underwear and stuffed them into her backpack. Mina *was* her needle, the thorn in her side that she now saw she couldn't live without. Who she could be a real sister to if the world would give her that chance. She continued to pack, throwing in her toothbrush, shampoo, not that it really mattered, not that those things couldn't be bought anywhere on any street in Korea, but she packed them anyway. When she looked up she saw Jason was leaning forward, hands clasped, a small grin on his face.

"How are you getting there?"

"Bus. I've taken a bus before. It's not complicated. Just go to the terminal and buy a ticket."

"Which bus terminal are you going to? Express Bus or South?"

"I'll ask the taxi driver."

Jason smiled. "What if he doesn't speak English??"

"Oh. I've got a guidebook somewhere." Allison cast about the room, trying to remember where she'd last seen the book. "Okay then. Which terminal should I go to?"

"Perhaps a train is better."

"Jason, damn it, I don't have time for this. She's getting farther away as we speak."

"I'm just teasing. Don't worry. I'm going with you."

"Of course you are." Allison zipped her backpack and slung it on her shoulder. She picked up the photo and waved it at him like a flag.

They arrived at Pyeongtaek in less than two hours. On the train he told her he used to go there once every month or so because it had the best country music bar in Korea.

"Did Mina ever come with you?"

"No way," Jason said. "She hates country music. What about you?"

"Dad likes the older stuff. I've never listened to it much," Allison said. "But I can try."

Jason smiled faintly. She didn't know if he was amused or mocking her. He told her that Yongsan, the main Army base in Seoul, was slowly being disbanded, and the US personnel were being moved to Camp Humphreys to eventually accommodate a population of forty-five thousand personnel, including families. "You want to know where your taxes go?" Jason said. "Inside base it's a paradise. Twenty-five square miles. Sidewalks for walking and bike riding. A children's water park, Olympic outdoor pool, an indoor pool, bowling alley, gyms, movie theater. The American dream is better on a base in Korea than in the States now." He laughed.

"How do you know that?"

"It's no secret. Some Koreans are upset that Americans here get a lifestyle we can't have, with their big houses and lawns. But it's good to bring the families over, otherwise there's too much prostitution, which is already a big problem here."

"Everywhere, I guess," Allison said. "Anyway, it sounds completely different than when my Dad was here."

From Pyeongtaek they took a bus to Anjung-ri, where Camp Humphreys was located. The main street was lined with empty bars and shopkeepers hawking cheap T-shirts, duffle bags, suitcases. A few hotels jutted out from the sidewalks, with neon lights advertising clean rooms in English. Jason led her to the end of the street away from the base.

"This is where I stay," Jason said. "It has a jacuzzi. Forty five thousand won a night."

"Forty bucks? That's not bad." She looked up at the narrow building. The outside facade was composed of columns and swirls that vaguely resembled a plastic castle. "Could we share a room? Much cheaper."

Jason shielded his eyes and looked at the building. "It's a love hotel. The atmosphere can be strange."

"What's strange about a hotel? Or love for that matter." She picked up her backpack, which she'd let fall on the street. "We're wasting time."

At check in, the man gave Allison a small plastic zip bag with shampoo and face lotion, two toothbrushes, Q-tips, cotton pads, a ponytail band, a body sponge, and two condoms. The room was dominated by a round bed and a mirror on the ceiling. Two terry cloth robes hung on a wooden peg on the wall. Next to the flat screen TV was a basket of half-full bottles of men's aftershave, women's moisturizer and cologne, and three white towels rolled to the width of her fist, bound with a band of paper printed with the hotel's name. She thought of that hotel she'd stayed in with Gary, how dingy it seemed in comparison, and yet it had been designed for the same purpose: illicit sex. Gary had been with her only a day ago, but he was already gone from her, someone even her body could not remember. He'd never called her back when she needed him. She sat on a white mattress pad. Jason opened the closet and removed a shiny polyester comforter, brightly patterned in thin rectangles.

"You okay with this?" Jason said.

"Sure." She almost asked him what he meant—you okay with us sharing the room, or you okay with us having sex here, because surely that was what would happen, that in some way it seemed the world had conspired for it to happen from the day he picked her up at the airport. That's what she thought now, at least, and if her sister weren't missing she might have pulled him to the bed then and there and begun nibbling on his smooth neck. Would sleeping with two different men in two days make her a slut? Did she care? The idea appealed. Ray and Ted would never believe it. Her lust, though, was more of a dull throb compared to her more urgent desire to find Mina.

Jason was standing by the door. "So what's next?"

Allison stood. "I guess we go to these hostess bars. Show them the photo. See if they knew my dad or the woman or boy in the picture. If they've seen Mina."

The bars along the street had open windows and empty seats. The first one they went to was on the second floor. A large sign on the wall as they'd walked upstairs informed the GIs that they could not offer to pay for sex with the girls or to spend a day with them, that prostitution was illegal. Inside, a few GIs drank mugs of draft beer by the open window and played pool with the bar girls, who were Filipino, not Korean. Some were skinny, some lusciously curvy, not far from fat, all wearing the same clothes, short skirts, unsteady high heels, low-cut tops. They seemed to know the GIs well. Allison had heard that the drinks were outrageously priced at these places—fifteen or twenty dollars for a cocktail to pay for the girls' time, but this place didn't seem to operate that way. They ordered two beers from one of the girls. From her window, Allison watched a blond woman push a stroller back and forth a few feet away from the base's front gate. After the girl returned with their drinks, she sat on the stool next to Allison, playing with her cell phone, which was accessorized with pink Hello Kitty hearts. Once she tired of her phone, the girl, whose name tag said Gigi, called to the baby in the stroller from the open window. She took photos of the baby with her phone, then cooed and waved. One of the girls playing pool called to her, and she slowly got up and joined the table for a game of doubles.

"Explain to me what's going on," Allison said.

"Korea's rich now. Girls come here to work for us."

"I thought they were prostitutes, but maybe not?"

Jason shrugged. "Ask these women. They own the place."

Two older Korean women sat at an empty table toward the back of the bar. Allison had not noticed them before. They sported short curly perms, patterned baggy pants, clashing shirts, and thick-soled rubber shoes. They were short, stocky, and definitely unsexy, almost asexual. They looked like the women she'd seen selling fruit on the street or fish in the market or Korean dumplings from a food stall. They were women who would push Allison out of the way to get the last seat on the subway, who would haggle with the vendors over the price of rice or vegetables. *Ajummas.* And now they were watching Allison watch them. Allison waved. One of the women got up and started toward them, stopping and chatting with a girl behind the bar who was pouring colorless chips into an empty bowl. The woman made her way to them and set the bowl down in front of Allison.

"Everything okay?" the woman asked.

"Oh yes." She glanced at Jason's almost-empty glass. "Two more beers please."

The woman nodded curtly and went back up to the bar. She returned with the beers.

"I don't live here," Allison said. "I'm just visiting. From the States."

The woman nodded. She glanced at Jason and then spoke in Korean to him. He said something back, and the woman nodded.

"She wanted to know if we're a couple," Jason said.

"And you told her?"

"Just friends," he said.

"Has a girl named Mina come in recently?" Allison said. "With a black GI?"

The *ajumma* shook her head.

Allison took out her wallet and removed a crinkled photo of Wayne in his uniform shortly before he retired, a photo she had tucked away there and never looked at again. "Do you recognize him? He was here in 1977, 1979, and 1980."

The woman stared for a moment, held the photo far away, shook her head. "No recognize. They all look same."

Allison showed the woman the photo of Mina's mother and the boy. "What about them?"

The woman looked out onto the street. She spoke again to Jason in Korean, this time at length. He nodded, holding the sweaty mug of beer but not lifting it. When the *ajumma* finished, Allison thanked her for talking to them before she returned to the table with the other woman.

"She owns this place with the other *ajumma*," Jason said. "She was born right before the Korean War. Her mother was a Comfort Woman, a forced prostitute for the Japanese soldiers during World War II. Then she was a prostitute for the GIs, and this woman became one, too, what else was there for her? She saved her money and finally bought her own place. She says it's different now, that the girls who work here don't have sex with the GIs, they just play pool and keep them company. She says the money's dried up, that if she didn't own the place she'd have nothing. That she can barely feed and clothe the girls she's taken on."

"Do you believe her?"

"No prostitutes near a US Army base?"

Allison nodded. "She wouldn't talk, even if she recognized them."

"Probably not. There's a place down the street this *ajumma* told me about. The same woman's owned it since the late seventies. If anyone would speak about your dad or Mina's mom, it would be her."

The streets were still empty after five o'clock. Allison had thought the bars would be packed with drunken GIs, but the soldiers were few and far between, and the ones who were out were well-behaved models of restraint. The next bar was no different from the first, except that three older *ajummas* sat at a table and there seemed to be even more bored Filipino workers. A country song blared from the speakers.

"Alan Jackson. One of the best," Jason said.

"I'm not the biggest country music fan," she said.

"You will be." He grinned and lit a cigarette. One of the *ajummas* came up to them. This was because they assumed they were a couple, so the Filipino girls had no real interest in them, Jason explained.

"How about *soju* pitcher?" the woman suggested.

"What are the flavors?" Allison said.

"Excuse me?" The woman tapped her permed head. "English makes my head hurt."

"Korean makes my head hurt too," Allison said. "What color *soju*?"

"Ahh. Orange, cherry, green."

"Cherry's good," Allison said.

The woman left.

"Why doesn't she look at you?" Allison said.

"Many reasons," Jason said.

The woman returned with the pitcher, Kool-Aid cherry red, holding two straws.

"Please stay," Allison said. "I want to talk to you."

"What about?" the woman said.

"I'm just looking for someone who may have known my father. Did you work here any time between 1977 and 1980?"

The woman shook her head. "Not here." Then she shuffled away and talked to the two other women. One rose, unable to straighten her hunched back, and shuffled over. She looked different from the other *ajummas*—her hair was more gray than black and she didn't curl it. Instead, it lay thin and flat on her skull, a smooth helmet of silver.

"Are you with the MP?" the woman asked. Military Police.

Allison shook her head. "My father was here during that time. I'm trying to find someone who knew him." She took out the photo, and showed it to the owner. She shook her head, batted the photo away.

"Too many, especially at that time. All same."

"What about this person. Does she look like someone you know?" Allison turned on her digital camera and flipped to one of the photos she'd taken of Mina in Korea. She zoomed in to Mina's face, her smile wide for the camera, the background sparkling from the street lights.

The woman pulled the camera closer. "*Sae sang hae*," she whispered.

"I don't know her. She is *hapa*?" Her lips pursed.

"Yes. She's my sister. I think this woman is her mother."

The woman took the photo Allison gave her, held it at arm's length, and squinted. She gave the photo back, shaking her head. "I know nothing," she said, and scurried away.

"Bullshit," Allison said. She sipped the *soju* cocktail through her straw.

"She won't tell you," Jason said. "Too much trouble."

"But she knows something." Allison's throat tightened. "It's true."

Jason was quiet. He put out his cigarette, and then wrapped his arm around her.

Allison considered the possibility that her decision to help Mina was thirty years too late.

CHAPTER 14

It was after Ji-young hit her with the bottle that Mina started sleeping around. If her mother had been a prostitute, Mina reasoned, perhaps she should see what the fuss was about. She lost her virginity to Max a few weeks after the party—she'd had to initiate; he'd been content waiting until Senior Prom. That summer she cheated on Max with a lifeguard at the pool, and that fall he went to college and they called it quits. Her senior year in high school, she started hanging around the dorms and college apartments near George Mason. Once, Mina was with a group of students sharing cigarettes outside a building Allison was walking into, head down, alone. Allison didn't even see her. That's my sister, Mina told them, and they laughed at the idea. Sometimes on weekends she'd drive into DC and hook up with guys there so that the girls at school wouldn't know. She led a double life, the old good girl Mina at school and home, and the new bad Mina, who smoked and drank and had sex with men she hardly knew, leaving them before they left her, when she was out.

After she graduated from high school, she moved into a group house in Adams Morgan, worked as a waitress, and enrolled in a few random courses at George Mason to satisfy her parents. Before, there'd been talk of medical school or law school. Now she told them she needed time to figure out what she wanted to do. She had a string of boyfriends whose hearts she inevitably broke, but it was only after her affair with Ray the summer she worked in Allison's office that she decided to move to LA.

To Mina, Allison's life was depressing. She held a stagnant job in a sterile office where she fawned over wimpy Ray, spending nights at home watching TV with her emotionless husband. Mina resented Allison's squandering of all she'd been given: biological parents, a husband, an identity. She had an affair with Ray just to confirm what she suspected: that Ray was a dick, and a very bad person for Allison to be hung up on. She'd planned to tell Allison about the affair, hoping that would end Allison's infatuation with Ray, but then one morning when Mina had shown up to work wearing the same clothes she'd worn the day before, Allison had pulled her aside, telling her if she wanted to be a slut that was her business, but not to advertise it at work. A month later, when Mina moved to LA, she didn't even tell Allison she was gone.

After only a few days in Koreatown, Mina knew she'd found her tribe. There were so many mixed-race Asians living there that she became one of many. Some looked more Korean, like her, others were half-black, half-Korean, others looked more Caucasian, with light hair and eyes and long, thin faces. Many had grown up in LA, others had moved there for reasons similar to hers. Some were in college, others were involved with the movie industry and its periphery, many worked in bars and restaurants, others dealt drugs or fell into gangs. Her parents called, worried about her. They thought she was reckless and impulsive to give up college and family for a string of waitressing and temp jobs among strangers. But that was compared to Allison, Mina would tell them over the phone. That's because she's both of you and that's what you're used to.

Here in LA she was capable and balanced compared to how she'd felt in DC, loose, at odds, out of control. She was managing on her own, paying rent, no longer having sex with dubious men. She started learning Korean from her friends—informal, with lots of slang. Her parents became two people who loved her and who paid for her plane ticket to see them every Christmas so they could make sure she was okay. Each holiday it seemed Allison was recovering from another miscarriage, baking cookies and making stuffing with a forced cheerfulness that was painful to watch. Mina never invited her family to visit her and they never offered to come.

After a few years in LA, Mina began taking psychology classes at a community college. She thought she might become a counselor to mixed-raced children like her, help them find a place in a world they would never fully belong to. She would have been fine continuing her studies, earning her degree, living in LA, if it weren't for the dreams. The more Korean she learned, the more she'd dream of—she was sure of it now—her mother. Sometimes she'd wake murmuring *Omma*. After she finished her BA, her dreams intensified. A woman with long black hair was carrying her on her back, Mina holding on as tight as she could, slipping, eventually falling in a dusty road, her mother walking on without coming back for her. Mina was convinced she was haunted by her mother's spirit. She wondered what to do. Her friends told her the obvious, just go to Korea. Try to find her. Jason will help you.

She'd met Jason her last year in LA. He was one of her few friends who had been born and raised in Korea. He came to the coffee shop she waitressed in several times a week. He'd always order the same thing, coffee, black, and an egg salad sandwich. He'd eat slowly, staying at the table long after he finished, nursing the cup of lukewarm coffee she'd offer to refill for him. He quietly refused. Instead he lingered, stepping outside from time to time to smoke from a pack of cigarettes whose label she didn't recognize, a Korean brand. She knew when men had crushes on her, and Jason was not one of those men. Because of that she soon began sitting outside with him during her break. Together they smoked his Time cigarettes, and she let him talk. He stayed at the café because he hated going home to an empty room, he told her. They became unlikely friends, him the awkward doctoral student, she the gregarious girl with friends from everywhere. After a few months, he told her that he felt like he was her older brother, her *oppa*, and with that came responsibility. He would watch out for her in this crazy town, he told her. She didn't remind him that she'd lived in LA for almost eight years, much longer than he had, and that if anyone needed protection it was him. His gesture was noble, this Korean man with his wire-rimmed glasses and egg sandwiches. He'd wait for her until her shift was over and they'd walk across the street and eat donuts before she went out with her friends and he returned to the lab where he often worked through the night.

She had found the photograph the last time she was at her parents' for Christmas. She claimed a headache when the rest went to the Christmas church service, not caring that no one believed her. She'd seen the album many times, but not the shoebox of loose photographs beside it on a shelf in Wayne's closet. The book contained photos Wayne had preserved under strips of plastic, arranged to tell the narrative he wanted to convey. The hooches, shacks that Koreans lived in with tin roofs and dirt floors. His friends in their uniforms, arms around each other, pleasantly drunk, the rice paddies and streets empty of cars. The Koreans had a midnight curfew, he told her, they were terrified of the police and the KCIA. People disappeared. Dusty images, cherry trees blossoming, carts pulled by men, him in the snowy mountains with his buddies, men who for the most part had not aged well. She could barely match the pudgy, ruddy friends who came over for dinner with the lean, cocky boys in the photos.

Once she'd asked him about the box, and he'd told her there was nothing in there she wanted to see. As she sat on the closet floor, sorting through the loose photos of blurred scenery, duplicates, poorly cropped images, she thought he might have been telling the truth. Then, toward the bottom of the box, she found a photo of a boy and young woman who looked almost like her. Mina took the photo, telling no one, deciding what to do next.

Before Jason returned to Korea, she told him about the incident with the Korean girls in high school. She pulled back her hair to show him the cut on her scalp from the bottle—twelve stitches—and the slight scar that remained. He turned visibly pale, shaking his head, eyes closed.

"I am very sorry that happened to you. She is not a typical Korean."

"I know," Mina said. "She was pretty unstable." She licked her finger, dabbed the confectioner's sugar from the wax paper on the table. "But I kind of understand now. I mean, her whole world had been flipped over. Class, race, everything. And there must have been some trouble with her family."

"Maybe," Jason said. "Still, please don't have a bad impression of us."

She showed him the photo then, the first person she'd shared it with. He studied it, then handed it back to her.

"I want to find her."

"Maybe the past is the past," he said.

"What do you think?"

"Maybe they gave him the photo when they adopted you."

"Or maybe he knew her," Mina said.

He shook his head. "Maybe it's not important."

"Maybe help me?"

"I will show you around. It's your country, too."

In October 2009, she left LA for Seoul, and Jason kept his word. After he met her at the airport, he took her to a *soju* bar that night in Shinchon, where they ate squid *pajeon*, chicken feet, and tofu *kimchi* while downing shots of *soju*—the first time she'd ever drank with him—until the sun came up.

After that Christmas, she didn't mention Korea to her parents again until she'd arrived in Seoul. Just as she believed when she was young that her family would send her back to Korea if she misbehaved, she was irrationally afraid that her father would have her stopped from leaving the States. Her passport was as good as anyone else's, a US citizen free to come and go, as long as she didn't overstay her three-month visa in Korea.

"We're keeping North Korea from attacking their ass, and they want us out," Wayne always said whenever he read of the anti-American protests in Korea in *Stars and Stripes*. By the time she'd arrived in Seoul, Mina knew better than to believe Wayne. Seoul was more modern than any city she'd seen before, a neon metropolis taller and wider than LA, stretching forever in all directions. After her first week, she stopped counting the Starbucks and Burger Kings and Dunkin' Donuts that populated the streets. She didn't bother telling Wayne that the city was safer than any place in the States, that the transportation system and infrastructure were light years ahead of anything in DC. She just called him one night, said she was in Seoul, that she was fine, that the city was treating her well, and to not worry.

Jason helped her find a place to live and work under the table tutoring privately and teaching at a children's institute, giving her more than enough money to live on. She made friends quickly, as she always did, and fell in and out of a few easy romances. Soon after she arrived, she went to Camp Humphreys, where Wayne had been stationed, but the place, so changed since Wayne had been there, offered nothing for her. The *ajummas* wouldn't talk to her. The GIs told her they could not help her. She wasn't sure if her mother had even lived there. She renewed her visa, stayed on. One late night she went out with her friends in Itaewon. Near three in the morning, Mina stumbled out of a Russian disco and told her friends that she was going to Hooker Hill to find her mother. She didn't expect to see her mother working as a juicy girl, but she thought that maybe her mother had become an owner of one of the bars, as sometimes happened. She wasn't even sure her mother had worked on Hooker Hill, but Mina was convinced that if she saw her mother, she'd know. They'd recognize each other immediately as a mother and daughter must.

The hostess bars were sadder than she'd imagined. Most were empty, desperate places. Women of various ages in short shorts, tube tops, and high heels lounged in the doorways or sat on stools reserved for patrons who had not arrived. Garish fluorescent lights lit the bars, which had open doors and women beckoning. Hooker Hill had once ruled Itaewon, when American GIs dominated the neighborhood. Now the streets were crowded with Koreans going to martini bars and smoking hookahs, lining up on the street for Turkish kebabs and waiting in line at French and Italian restaurants that spilled onto the sidewalks. There were Pakistanis and Indians and Africans and broad-shouldered Australians, but none were in these tiny bars on Hooker Hill. Mina felt silly, drunk. She'd been foolish to think she'd find her mother here. She didn't even know her mother's name.

It was then she met Robert. He was as tall and thin as a basketball player, with smooth, cocoa skin. He was one of the most beautiful men she'd ever seen, and she'd seen many. She began seeing him once or twice a month, whenever he came to town.

For all Mina knew, he might have other women as well, which could have kept him away or busy, but she doubted his life had the time or space to accommodate more than one woman. He was in Intel and couldn't talk much about what he did, except that he'd be gone on missions for days or even weeks at a time. Their arrangement worked for her; she could spend time with her friends, meet other guys if she wanted, which she usually didn't, because with Robert she was dating someone beautiful and remote, someone like herself.

Each time he returned, the first day was the hardest. It was like he'd forgotten speech, saying little, although he never had problems having sex with her. His body was long, an endless river, his skin without blemish. His eyes were large and round, his jaw firm. She didn't mind that he was quiet; she'd tired of always talking anyway. Instead they'd lie in her bed and he'd read *Stars and Stripes* while she'd watch Korean dramas to improve her fluency. He'd eat cans of Vienna sausages heated on the gas range, and she'd drink cups of green tea. After the first day, he'd speak vaguely of his mission, spending days in the woods, living off the land, slipping across to the North Korean side. It was the most domestic she'd ever been.

He was from Trinidad, and had gone to the States, first working as a cab driver and then joining the US Army to expedite his citizenship. When they weren't watching TV he'd play songs popular in Trinidad on her computer, music heavy with percussion, a hybrid of calypso and reggae. He told her he had a child back in Trinidad, a daughter, who had just turned seven. She told him about her family in the States, her adoption, how she'd come to Korea to find her mother, but now believed her efforts were futile. She showed him the photo.

"Why don't you ask your dad?" Robert said.

"He won't tell me."

Robert turned the page of his newspaper, creasing it along the fold. "There's other ways, then."

"Can you help me?" she asked.

He looked down at the floor, shook his head slowly, for emphasis.

"I'll help *you*," she said.

He jerked his head up, startled. So, Mina thought, there was something. She wondered how deep that something was, but it didn't really matter to her then, she'd help him do anything if he could find her mother.

That was the night she called home. She'd gone out with some friends to a club in Hongdae, hoping to score some ecstasy so she'd feel better. Instead she drank double vodka tonics, paid for by various men in the club. She had a good time for the first few hours, dancing with her friends. Then she got drunk and morose. She found an empty chair on the second floor. It was plush and soft and comforted her in a way that embarrassed her.

When she woke the club was empty and dark. Outside, under a bright morning sky, garbage spilled out of trashcans and vomit the color of *kimchi* dotted the damp streets. Most of the shopkeepers would not open for a few more hours. She stopped at a Family Mart and bought a bottle of *soju*. She drank the *soju* straight from the bottle like a wino or a barbaric Westerner, without consideration for custom or convention. Her ears were ringing; her head felt damp and spongy, her cheeks were sticky from the tears that were finally falling. She'd held them back the whole evening.

It was a little past eight, an hour after dinner in Virginia. She imagined Wayne in his recliner, feet kicked out, his one after-dinner beer in its sweat sleeve, TV turned to the History Channel. Her mother would be on the sofa, legs tucked under, a decaf iced-tea beading on the end table, the latest Nicholas Sparks or Jodi Picoult novel open on her lap. And Allison, she would be there now, too, already changed into the sweatpants she slept in, pretending to enjoy Wayne's shows. After her divorce, she'd moved back home—about the same time Mina had moved to Seoul. As far as Mina could tell, Allison seemed even more remote and contained, her small world shrunken that much more.

Mina wasn't sure why she was calling or what she would say, only that she was still as much drunk as sober, and she thought she might be able to gauge something—sincerity or guile in their voices, some tenor of deception that she'd never detected before. After the fourth ring the answering machine picked up. When she spoke, her voice was a watery whisper.

"Are you my father?" She closed her eyes, took another swig from the *soju* bottle. A motor scooter flew past her. She heard someone turn on a gas stove, the clatter of pots and pans for some family's breakfast.

She was sobbing now, she choked on the words. "Are you my father?"

Wayne picked up the phone.

"Mina? Of course I'm your father."

She tried to catch her voice, to say something to him, to ask him why, but she couldn't talk. Wayne's voice was far away, full of concern or fear, begging her to come back. She heard her mother, too, and Mina wondered what she knew. Mina hung up and turned off the phone. She laid her head on the plastic Family Mart table and slept until someone wakened her with a hand on her shoulder.

Allison arrived a few weeks later, different somehow. Sometimes Mina would secretly stare at her sister, wonder if they were indeed related by blood. She couldn't see any resemblance, since Allison with her auburn hair and light blue eyes looked much more like Bonnie than Wayne, who had dark brown eyes and hair. They might share Wayne's small sharp nose, his strong jaw, but Mina wasn't sure. Their differences in appearance and temperament far outweighed any similarities. That they might be biological sisters seemed foreign to Mina, improbable, remote.

She wanted to share with Allison her suspicions that Wayne was her real father, that the woman in the photo was her mother. That for some reason he had taken the baby—Mina—with him back to the States. Allison didn't even know Mina wasn't full-blooded Korean. She almost told her when they'd gone to the sauna and the temple together, when they been like sisters more than at any other time in their lives. She imagined Allison helping her find her mother, confronting Wayne, for once taking Mina's side. But she could not see Allison choosing her over Wayne. And besides, Mina thought, why say anything until she had proof?

And then, Allison got angry and didn't come home. Mina hoped they could clear up the misunderstanding, if there was one. That night, Robert called. He had a few days off and was in Seoul. He came over and they had sex on the sofa Allison now slept on, neither really worrying if the neighbors could see her arched back, his naked silhouette through the open window, and then they went out for a late dinner at an overpriced Italian restaurant. Only after they'd finished their meal did he tell her he wanted to take her somewhere the next morning. She nodded, raising the almost-empty glass to her trembling lips. She took out a cigarette and fumbled with the lighter. She rarely smoked in front of Robert, but this time he didn't chastise her. She knew not to ask where he was taking her. But she wondered what he'd found: a grave, an aging prostitute, a woman lined and broken living on the streets, a woman, her mother, abandoned? Or perhaps Robert had discovered that Wayne was not her father, after all. Maybe it was one of his friends, as they had also theorized, or just another GI. Her father could still be anyone, really.

Late Saturday morning they took the subway to Ilsan, a modern, affluent suburb outside Seoul that Mina had never been to. Once they got out of the subway station, Robert led her past the center of the town, which was organized around a man-made lake. They walked along a wide, tree-lined sidewalk to a group of houses that seemed to belong in North America or Europe. The neighborhood was called Beverly Ville, after Beverly Hills, and a sign announcing such was prominent at the entrance to the community. The houses were modest by upper-middle-class American standards, sized-down Tudors, colonials, and sleek moderns with well-manicured postage stamp yards and knee-high fences. But in Korea, with real estate at a premium, these houses, she guessed, were worth millions. Robert stopped in front of a house indistinguishable from the others. Two stories, with a front porch and tiny balcony jutting out from the second floor. The yard was groomed, with trimmed bushes and patches of flowers arranged in careful patterns and groupings that Mina could not appreciate. Robert took her across the street and they stood on the sidewalk. She wondered if he was lost, but she said nothing. Robert flicked his wrist, glanced at the time. "It's ten o'clock," he said, as if Mina would know what he meant.

The front door opened. A woman in slim black pants, hair just past her shoulders, a large leather purse crooked on her arm, emerged. Garage doors opened and she stepped into a shiny sedan, a Lexus, a car that would cost more than double its price in the States. Robert did not need to say anything. The woman was all those missing parts of Mina, like the photo, but more startling in person, parts she thought had been invented by some God just for her. Those parts were on this woman—the tall, thin body that carried itself with more grace than Mina's, broad cheeks, a long, swan-like neck, full lips. All those bits of her that had floated unattached, curiosities, they all fit now in intent and origin. It was as if Mina had snapped into place. The woman drove onto the street so that she was almost parallel to Mina. She seemed not to notice them, intent instead on the road in front of her. A few blocks later, she turned left, disappearing from view. Mina started to run after the car, but Robert held her with both arms so that she could not go.

CHAPTER 15

The country bar was filling up by the time Allison and Jason wandered in. They were two *soju* kettles and a Thai dinner into the evening, but they were not ready to go home. The DJ waved at Jason, then one of the waitresses ran up to them, giggling.

"Long time no see," she said in English.

"I've been busy," Jason said, looking at Allison. That was the first time she really felt it. The stomach flip-sink, that thing she'd only felt before with Ray. It was his eyes piercing through his smudged lenses that got to her. Their fierce intelligence. How calm and composed he was. She was about to reach for his hand, just to feel it, when he smiled and looked away.

"This is the best country bar in Korea, better than most in the States." And then he began singing. Garth Brooks, something about the dance, she recognized that one. Then others, names she didn't know, names he'd tell her, listen, he said, they tell such great stories.

To her they were kind of hokey, clichéd, even. But he was so earnest as he sang and later danced to them. He twirled her around the dance floor, two-stepped with her while she tried to keep up. When she finally sat down, he asked other girls to dance, girls more skilled, more expert than she was. Despite all he'd told her about his marriage, she recalled even the first time she'd met him how easy he'd made it for her, how he'd somehow decided that life would be something he went with instead of something he'd given up on like she had. That was what she'd done when things ended with Ray. When she got the abortion. She'd given up but not let go.

When he sat back down he was still not sweaty. He continued singing.

"You need a hat," she said.

"I have one. And boots. But I didn't have a chance to go back home and get them. You were in such a rush."

"You knew the *ajummas* wouldn't talk," she said.

"Sometimes the experiential way is best."

"Is that from your robot research?"

He nodded, singing, *All my exes live in Texas.*

"Can the robots help me find Mina?" She felt dumb even asking it, it sounded so ridiculous.

"Good question," Jason said. "I'm thinking about it."

Her mistake then was to drink another *soju* kettle and pull out her camera. She skipped to the photos she'd taken of Mina, so precious few, but in each one she looked for signs of Wayne, or of herself. Something had happened here more than thirty years ago, but she still didn't know what. Jason was on the dance floor again; now was her time to find out more. She was out of the country bar and walking down the street, back to the *ajumma* who had told her nothing, but, she suspected, knew something.

The *soju* bar was not so empty now, and Allison kept falling into people, and they kept bumping into her. A few guys called out to her, but she could say nothing to rebuke them, she was too drunk to be upset. Where was the *ajumma*? The bar girls were busy now, holding colored drinks, laughing too hard at jokes Allison couldn't understand. She touched the soft shoulder of one of the girls. Her smile was frozen, her shirt looked uncomfortably tight. The remains of her gloss glittered in patches on her lips.

"Where's the owner? I have to talk to her."

The girl's smile fell and she turned away from Allison. She called to another girl in a language that must have been Tagalog. She saw they were going to make her leave, so she ducked and stayed low into the crowds until she made it to the door to a back room.

The *ajumma* was there, sitting on the floor, legs crossed, smoking a cigarette.

Allison sank to the floor. She was afraid she might throw up, afraid she'd be unable to ask for what she came for. "My sister is lost.

I'm lost. Tell me."

The woman shook her head. "I never met your sister."

"But her mother. You know her."

She calmly smoked her cigarette. Allison thought of Jason, and wondered if he knew that she'd left. "Why don't you ask your father?"

"He knows, doesn't he?" Two girls had grabbed Allison by the elbows and were leading her out. "He knows, he knows, he knows," Allison repeated in a slurred voice.

Jason was on the street, his shirt untucked, calling her name. He took her back to the room. They didn't speak. He didn't touch her. Even when they fell asleep during the darkest part of the night, even the next morning, when they awoke, they said nothing, did not reach for each other. They lived in that silence until Jason got up and went to the bathroom.

"The jacuzzi's broken," he said. All Allison could do was laugh.

CHAPTER 16

Mina's apartment was the same as when Allison had left the day before for Camp Humphreys, clean and scrubbed, musty and humid. Jason dropped her backpack in Mina's bedroom since there was no reason for her to sleep on the couch now. She sat on the bed, while Jason hovered at the door.

"My flight's in two weeks. I have to find her before I leave."

"We can do our best."

"Will you stay? You can have the couch."

"If you want."

"I want." She folded her legs. "I got together with Gary this past weekend."

"I know." He was looking at the floor.

"I was tired of Ted being the last, you know?"

"Good night, Allison." The words were sweet, slow. She thought he might come over and kiss her, chastely perhaps, on the cheek. Instead he turned and walked into the dark living room. She heard the window open. She imagined he was having one last cigarette, exhaling out the screen, poking his finger through the bars as he sometimes did, tapping ash into an empty tuna can. The window squeaked closed, the sofa squeaked open. She wanted to bring him back with her to bed or crawl into that tiny sofa and sleep with him. But it was not the right moment, she knew. They needed more time.

Allison woke up at six, showered, then waited for Jason to wake up, but she heard nothing from the living room. She'd conjured Mina's mother in a dream just before waking. Mina was living with her mother, they were watering plants in an English garden, both wearing muddy Keds without laces. When Allison arrived, they greeted her as if they'd been waiting for her, invited her in for tea and rice cakes.

Jason was still sleeping, a thin blanket wrapped around his legs, a white T-shirt covering his torso. He was breathing hard, deep in sleep, and she thought *leave him be, wherever he is*. He'd missed two days of work to help her. She touched Jason's hair above his ears, cut short, stubbly, and then ran her fingers over the thick, longer top. He stirred slightly, opened his eyes, and placed his hands on hers.

"I'm starving," Allison said. She moved her hand to his shoulder.

"McDonald's?" he asked slowly, words still coming to him.

"*Soon du bu*. Mina and I ate it the day I got lost. The day she found me."

He squeezed her hand. "I'll be ready in ten minutes."

The *soon du bu* restaurant was open twenty-four hours, and busy with people getting ready for work or finishing up a long night. Allison stuffed herself on the spicy soup, grilled fish, and vegetable dishes. She gave half her rice to Jason, who seemed to enjoy that most of all. As they left the restaurant, he turned toward the subway station. Allison grabbed his hand.

"Thanks, Jason."

"You should call your parents."

"I will." She knew he had to get to work, but she didn't want to let him go. It was early April, still cold and windy, and the faint hints of green on the trees were weeks away from budding. "It was a one-time thing, with Gary."

He pulled his hand away, took off his glasses and cleaned them in the street. "Mina and I never did anything."

"Oh." She had let go of his arm. "I didn't think so. Not really."

"Call your parents." He put his glasses on and disappeared into a crowd of college students on their way to the university from the subway station. She wondered when she'd see him again.

Allison returned to the apartment and checked her email, hoping that maybe Mina had responded to the frantic messages Allison had sent. Nothing from Mina, a breezy email from Bonnie detailing the work she'd been doing in the garden, an email from Ray, subject: IMPT.

Ray could make sure there were repercussions, like not writing her a recommendation letter, making it difficult to get a job in their industry. If she didn't find Mina before her flight, she'd have to decide if she would stay longer, dip into her savings. She opened the email.

"I'm writing to you not as your boss, but as a friend. Come back," Ray began. He told her he may have taken her for granted, that the entire office was upset by her sudden disappearance. He would forgive her lack of professionalism, "leaving them in the lurch," and in fact, he wrote, he'd look into that three percent raise for her, if she came back soon. He'd taken the liberty of keeping her on the payroll, using her vacation days for her disappearance because she'd been so loyal and deserved some down time. Come back soon and all would be forgiven, everyone missed her, "I miss you," he wrote.

Before, that would have been all it would take, his casual yet effective sign off. She would have returned to editing manuals and technical papers down the hall from Ray, listening to Norah Jones and Sarah McLachlan on Pandora, refilling cup after cup of Tension Tamer tea, going for soup and salad at Applebee's or Panera or Chili's with the girls on Thursdays, gossiping about the latest *Idol* or *Dancing with the Stars*, sneaking in online virtual tours of homes she couldn't afford, even now with the housing downturn, not alone. Her life had not been one of unhappiness, a life not unlike most people she knew. Yet now, Allison couldn't imagine herself anywhere else but this apartment in this city whose language she didn't know, a city where men wore suits and women dressed up for no reason except to look good, a city not far from the border of their broken country, a city of bullet trains, neon nights, sunken ships.

She did not answer his email. She did not call her parents. Instead, she filled the electric kettle with hot water and made a cup of barley tea. Then she started calling anyone whose number she had who knew Mina.

Her friends had not seen her, nor had her *hogwan* heard from her. She'd been teaching illegally on a tourist visa so the *hogwan* could not report her to immigration, which made Mina that much more elusive. Gary's phone went straight to voice mail. She wondered if he even listened to her two messages, both asking for his help to find Mina. She couldn't remember even feeling attracted to him, couldn't remember what the fuss had been about. So that was what it felt like, she thought, a one-night stand. As if it had never happened. She wondered if that's what Ray had felt with her, with the others: nothing.

For the next two weeks, she did not see Jason, though they talked on the phone. He was busy with work, he said, the robots were undergoing final tests. Robots in the shape of penguins and ducks and other animals the children could pet and talk to, robots who could teach them the ABCs and colors. Mina's job, but without the hassle of hiring foreigners. He may have been busy, but he was also avoiding her, Allison knew, just as she was avoiding talking to Bonnie, confronting Wayne, responding to Ray. She answered her parents' frequent emails and voice messages with vague replies and assurances. *Everything is fine. Mina is busy. Talk soon.* But nothing was fine.

The morning before she was scheduled to return home, Allison called her parents. Wayne picked up on the first ring. Gun shots and a deep-voiced commentator droned in the background.

"What's her name?" Allison said, her voice cracking despite herself. She traced the shapes of the photo in her lap.

"Ally?" Wayne said, loud into the receiver. "What's going on?"

"Mina's mother, what's her name?" Allison heard the other line pick up.

"Wayne, turn off the TV." The gun shots stopped.

"Mina's disappeared. She's looking for her mother."

"My baby," Bonnie said.

"Bonnie's her mother."

"Stop it, Dad. She left me a photo of a woman who looks just like her."

"She won't find her," Wayne said.

"How do you know?" Allison said.

"We're coming to Seoul," Bonnie said.

"Don't. I've cancelled my ticket. I'm staying," Allison said. She was only one month into her three-month tourist visa. "I can find her. I just need her mother's name and a little more time."

"I'm calling the Embassy in Seoul," Wayne said.

"She's been working illegally. They could put her in jail." Allison knew that wasn't true, that Mina would just have to pay a fine and leave the country, but she wasn't ready to get the Embassy involved. "Her name, Dad."

"Damn it Wayne, if you know something, then tell her," Bonnie said.

Allison waited in silence broken only by Wayne's heavy breathing on the other end.

"She went by Sunny," he said, finally, his voice choked. "But her real name was Lim Sun-hui."

CHAPTER 17

Until the end of April, Mina's life was a shiny ribbon unspooling from a center she hoped she'd never get to. She'd wake up in her studio in Ilsan, have a cigarette, and then walk around the lake before the retired Koreans crowded the five-kilometer track, edging her out of the path she'd cut. She'd reduced her life to basic needs, and the morning walk was one of them. The running and cycling paths, the tiny islands, the pagodas, the wood bridges, the landscaped gardens—all brought her a kind of peace. She'd never been a regular exerciser before, but those mornings she enjoyed walking the five kilometers, her sneakers soft on the green cork trail, the lake chilly and implacable under the morning sky. Whether it was raining, or the sun was out, or the clouds converged in an impenetrable blanket, she walked the trail. She used that time to reflect on the day before, on her time with Mrs. Lim—her mother—and the two teenage children, a son and a daughter, to whom she taught English in the afternoons, between piano lessons and math classes at the institute a few blocks away.

Before the children arrived home from school, Mrs. Lim would have her own English lesson with Mina, who Mrs. Lim seemed to not recognize at all. Mina had chopped her hair into a pixie and wore small, red-framed glasses to minimize their physical similarities. Her goal was to get to know Mrs. Lim better, and then decide how to broach the rest. For now, Mina was happy with her world: coffee and English conversation with Mrs. Lim for an hour, then more rigorous, less creative English lessons with her children, who Mina could never really believe were her half-siblings. She never saw Mrs. Lim's husband,

Mr. Choi. He worked long hours and late nights managing the real estate properties he'd bought and developed over the years.

He was a self-made man. Mina had taught Mrs. Lim the expression. They were very poor when they'd first met, Mrs. Lim said, both without fathers. His father had been arrested in the sixties on suspicions of being part of the democracy movement, and he'd never been seen again. Her father had died in Vietnam when she was twelve years old. Koreans were heavily recruited to help the Americans fight, and were put on the front lines in the most dangerous positions. But there was no time to feel sorry back then, Mrs. Lim had told her in her simple English, for more people were suffering then than not. Their case, she told Mina, was nothing special.

Mrs. Lim had a little money saved, though, when she married Mr. Choi, and they bought a tiny property out in the farming country, near Daegu. After a few years, as her husband had predicted, they were offered a large sum of money by a land developer who wanted to build a high rise apartment complex on their soil; the area was slated to become an affluent suburb near the new highway. Mr. Choi took that money and invested in more property. After a few years, *he'd* become the developer buying tracts of land from farmers who could not afford to say no.

Savvy. That was another word Mina taught her. Even if Mr. Choi did not have a college degree, he was savvy.

"He has Midas touch," Mrs. Lim said.

Her English, while broken, had little accent—unlike other adult Koreans Mina had met, Mrs. Lim could pronounce her l's and r's and her p's and f's. She didn't add another beat to words like Koreans often did, and she used the letter "v" properly, instead of puffing the sound out as a double syllable: vuhwee. Her vocabulary and grammar were basic. She rarely used anything but the present tense, and instead used markers to indicate time. *Tomorrow I go shopping. Yesterday I go to beauty salon.*

Her life seemed to have more in common with the fifties fantasy housewife than a modern woman. She even had a maid—"cooking I love, cleaning I hate," Mrs. Lim had confessed, and her children were gone most of the time—either in school or at the after-school *hogwan* classes. Mr. Choi often did not come home until after eight, sometimes later, and then as soon as her children had come home from their math classes they retired to their rooms to study more. Mrs. Lim had an abundance of time and little responsibility as long as the household ran smoothly. She watered the plants herself even though a gardener came every few weeks to manage the yard, and she still did the shopping and the daily finances. She monitored her children's test scores, an indicator of their potential future ranking on the national college entrance examination. She made sure they were in the right institute classes, that their uniforms were clean, that they did not spend too much of their precious free time on the computer.

"Don't you wish you had more to do?" Mina asked one day after two weeks of English conversation.

Mrs. Lim shook her head resolutely. "Can I tell you a secret?" She leaned forward and grabbed Mina's hand. Mrs. Lim's frail fingers crushed Mina's knuckles.

"Always," Mina said. Her coffee, in a delicate china cup, was almost finished, tepid. The refrigerator growled menacingly in the kitchen. Was Mrs. Lim going to confess what Mina suspected, that she'd been one of those room salon girls who had sex with GIs for good money, and that during that time she'd had a baby she'd given away? And what would she say when Mina confessed her own secret, that she was the very baby Mrs. Lim had birthed almost thirty-three years ago?

"I'm a bit ashamed but I enjoy my time alone," Mrs. Lim said. "I'm so free. I'm happy doing nothing special. Just being. I'm not boring at all."

Mina let her breath out, freed her hand from Mrs. Lim's death grip. "Bored."

"Pardon?"

"You said boring. You mean bored."

Mrs. Lim nodded. "Ah yes. Yes. Bored. My mistake."

The moment had passed, but Mina could not let it slip away yet. She took one of the tiny butter cookies Mrs. Lim had put on a plate, bought in the bakery at the basement of Lotte Department store.

"I think I understand," Mina said. "I imagine before, when you were poor, your life was not so comfortable. That's why you enjoy your free time now."

"Yes, yes, yes," Mrs. Lim said. "I never think about that before, but that is a good reason."

"And having a husband and two children, is it some kind of burden?" Mina said the sentence in English, but she thought of the Korean word for burden, *budam,* when she said it.

"I don't know about burden. Maybe duty," she said. She stood, taking her cup and saucer to the kitchen.

What about your duty to me? Mina stared at her half-eaten cookie. But she dared not say anything. Even if their time together was just an hour a day during the week, it was a luxury she'd not imagined when she wasn't sure if she'd even find her mother.

The time teaching English to Mrs. Lim's two children, Mina's half brother and sister, on the other hand, was her burden. She wanted to have some kind of affinity, a connection she'd not had with Allison, until recently. Had she remained in Korea looking for her? Or had she returned to the States now? She'd left the photo with Allison, in case something happened, proof that she was not crazy. Even with the photo, she was certain Allison would not find her, that she, like Mrs. Lim, had discovered a way to have a secret life, free from worry or bother. She was not sure if she wanted to even talk to Wayne and Bonnie again, at least not until she had some kind of idea of what had happened. One day, she would have to return to Robert, who was waiting for her, patiently, to fulfill her end of the bargain.

It wasn't that Mrs. Lim's children were rude or uncooperative; they seemed devoid of any will or emotion beyond the world of study. Mina could not say that they were unhappy, because that would mean she'd have to attribute feelings to them, when she wasn't sure if they had any. Their English vocabulary and grammar were far more advanced than Mrs. Lim's, but they had no desire to communicate, and therefore no passion for language. One evening Mina gave up and began speaking Korean with them, something Mrs. Lim had expressly forbade her to do. She told them that the tables were turned and they could teach Mina Korean that evening, could teach her whatever they wanted.

The oldest child, the son, shook his head. "I can't," he said in English. "I have to study. No time for play." His sister cast her eyes down to her open English textbook, that evening's passage already marked up in pencil, with translations and explanations jotted in Korean. Mina sighed and resumed the lesson, which was a reading about the fermentation process of *kimchi.*

She wondered what would have happened if she'd grown up in this family. With their million-dollar house, a rich workaholic father and domesticated mother, closer to an imaginary American TV show than her own life had been. Cogs in a machine, the members with their own desultory but necessary duties, the Choi family worked smoothly. Would she have been as submissive as the girl, whose school uniform and ubiquitous shiny butterfly barrette reminded her of one of the plain, quiet girls from her high school? And how, if her mother had been a juicy girl, a bar girl if not a prostitute, how had she gone from there to here? There was only one answer to that question—the family did not know about her past. Just as Bonnie and Allison did not. If she told the truth, both families might collapse, perhaps never to recover. But she needed to know if Wayne was in fact her father, what her mother's circumstances had been. Mina schemed to find a way to learn.

Except for her quest, Mina's days were blissfully detached from her previous life. She no longer went out on the weekends, for fear someone she knew would see her. Instead she watched Korean TV in her studio, downloaded American movies and TV shows on her computer, illegally, as everyone did here without fear of recrimination. She rose early in the mornings, lingered by the lake after her walk. She sat in the grass or near a garden and watched the grandmothers strolling with their friends, modern housewives pushing their baby carriages, men cruising by on their bicycles, slick in their bright matching shorts and shirts like yellow and black bumblebees. During that time she felt she'd awakened to the same morning, that the day ahead of her would be predictably bucolic, a tape replayed each day.

She asked Mrs. Lim if she ever went to Lake Park and she said no, although the family used to go on Sundays when the kids were younger. When Mina asked her why she didn't go, she said, "I know too many people. They bother me."

By the beginning of the fourth week, Mrs. Lim had confessed that she was certain her husband was having an affair. Or not an affair, exactly. He was staying out late in those terrible bars, throwing his money around on booze and women.

Mina was careful. "Don't you think those women don't have much choice?" Mrs. Lim shook her head. "Believe me. They have choices. They just want easy way out."

"I'm sorry to hear that. About your husband."

Mrs. Lim shrugged. "It's common. It's okay. More time for me." They were drinking green tea that day. Mrs. Lim had shown Mina how to measure the leaves, how to make sure the water was at the proper temperature before pouring it into the pot. After a few minutes, she then poured the tea in another pot before she half-filled the tiny celadon cups from which they took delicate, measured sips. The tea tasted like mown grass, but Mina thought it impolite to say so. They ate puffy rice cakes that tasted slightly sweet but mostly bland. Mrs. Lim continued, "I am satisfied with my life."

And regarding her, this serene woman who looked as if life had barely touched her, as if it were a shadow she sought to elude for as long as possible, Mina knew that Mrs. Lim spoke the truth. That she did not ache for her lost daughter, and had in fact tucked her away years ago, so that she was just a shadow of a shadow. Mina decided then to not say anything to Mrs. Lim, but instead to continue her relationship as her English tutor for as long as Mrs. Lim allowed, even if it were for the rest of her life. She needed to be with her in a way she'd not needed to be with anyone before, not her parents, not boys, not Robert. If she had her hour with Mrs. Lim then her day was right; she only needed the small talk, the cups of coffee, a pot of tea, her secret recognition: those are my ears, my eyes, my neck.

Mina worked hard not to betray herself. She kept her hair short. She'd introduced herself by her childhood name, Mimi, kept the details of her family obscure, saying she'd been adopted in LA by an older couple. Mrs. Lim treated her kindly, as a foreign visitor, as a teacher to her children, a paid companion who would not gossip or judge her. You see what people tell you to see, Mina thought. After all, Mina had not seen her own Caucasian features until they'd been pointed out to her. She figured as long as she kept her own gestures in check, the sudden wrist flick, the wry half smile that mirrored Mrs. Lim's, as long as she kept her hair style strange and short like a Westerner's and wore glasses, Mina was certain Mrs. Lim would never recognize her daughter.

And she might not have, except that one morning, instead of having tea or coffee, Mrs. Lim invited Mina to the sauna. She went once a week, one of her only "old school indulgences" (another phrase

Mina had taught her), usually with a few other women from the neighborhood. Mrs. Lim said, "You can't go to sauna alone. That is saddest thing."

She didn't tell Mrs. Lim, but she often watched her go to the sauna. The sauna was across the street from Mina's studio, and around ten on Fridays, Mrs. Lim drove by in her black Lexus, heading toward the parking garage. Sometimes there was a woman in the passenger seat, but often she was alone. Mrs. Lim had admitted to Mina that the ladies who accompanied her were not really her friends, just wives of other prosperous husbands; she needed to socialize with them at least once a week to maintain proper relations. Mrs. Lim said she had no close friends, but she liked that, she lacked the energy such a friendship would require. Mina, too, rarely had any close friends.

"What about your sister?" Mrs. Lim had asked. "Are you close to her?"

"We were starting to become closer," Mina said, absently touching the prayer beads on her neck. If she hadn't disappeared, felt compelled to find her mother, then perhaps they would have continued their tentative steps toward something more.

They left for the sauna at half past nine that Friday. The sauna was new, with glistening tiles and white towels, baggy T-shirts and shorts for the unisex rooms and saunas known as the *jjim jil bang* that did not yet reek of bleach. They went to the *jjim jil bang* first because Mrs. Lim wanted to try the traditional mud dome. Mina grabbed two of the burlap blankets stacked next to the furnace entrance and followed Mrs. Lim inside. Half a dozen bodies were covered in burlap, more closely resembling mounds of dirt than people. Against one part of the mud dome, stacked eggs were hard-boiling themselves under the heat. Mina covered her head with the burlap bag, took small measured breaths that hurt her throat, burned her chest. Within thirty seconds she was dripping sweat, her heart accelerating to the speed of a hummingbird's wings. Still, she couldn't be the first to leave. She wanted to show Mrs. Lim she was worthy, a real Korean, not a wimpy Westerner. Next to her, Mrs. Lim sat still as stone, covered in her blankets, silent, unlike the other women who occasionally sighed or muttered against the heat. The dome seemed to hum, and Mina wondered why she was here, why any of them were here, in this mud-plastered room with a heat she'd never encountered, when they didn't have to be. Her head dripping sweat, her T-shirt and baggy shorts soaked, Mina wondered if this was how hot the desert was, the way the sand turned to glass and the air became waves. She wondered if Mrs. Lim was a mirage, an image she'd conjured in her desperation. When the air began to spin, when she could no longer breathe without daggers entering her chest, she left the mud room, her feet burning through her socks.

She gulped several paper cones of water from the cooler before she felt disappointed in herself. Ashamed. Mrs. Lim's daughter would have stayed with her mother, even until death. Mina was not worthy.

Mrs. Lim emerged from the dome, slowly, without haste. Mina poured cold water from the cooler and handed her a paper cup. She took tiny measured sips, her skin dewy and glistening. "You stay in for long time," Mrs. Lim said.

Mina shook her head. She was being patronized. She did well for someone who was not Korean. Not one of them. She was glad her face was sweaty so that any tears she shed were not noticeable.

They went downstairs to the women's sauna, and there Mina finally had to remove her glasses. They walked in with their toiletry bags full of shampoo, body wash, special lotions, and scrubs. Mrs. Lim bought two containers of strawberry yogurt for them to slather on their faces and a special hair mask. They soaped up quickly, rinsing in the shower before heading to the crystal sauna for more opening of the pores, softening of the skin. They soaked in pools of warm green tea water, and then poured buckets of cold water over their bodies to bring their skin's temperature down. In the salt sauna they rubbed large grains of salt on their legs and arms to loosen dead skin before the real scrub. Mina looked at her mother's body and saw how hers would be in twenty years: still slim and long-waisted, bony, with jutting hips and sharp knees and flat perky breasts with large dark nipples. Mina heard a woman ask Mrs. Lim if they were sisters. Mrs. Lim laughed and said no, that was impossible, that Mina was an American visiting. The woman laughed and said they looked so much alike. Mina saw what the woman saw. Their hair was wrapped up in towels, their hungry bodies the same in build, their necks swanlike, their mouths full. But Mrs. Lim didn't even notice. She could not see. Mina was disappointed and grateful all at once.

They finally went to their stations to scrub the dead skin off their bodies. Mina took her yellow scrub pad and began working on her ankles until shreds of dead skin rolled into brown rings, like she used to see collect on American boys' necks. She and Mrs. Lim were quiet for a while, doing the work of making their bodies clean. Finally Mrs. Lim asked Mina to scrub her back. Mina squirted Mrs. Lim's back with the hose, then started at the top of the shoulders and worked her way down.

"Is the pressure okay?" she asked.

"Oh it's perfect. You a good back scrubber."

"I have experience scrubbing my sister's back," Mina said. Which was true, even if it was only once.

"I used to go with my mother. She always scrub me head to toe."

Mina wanted to ask more about Mrs. Lim's mother—had she also worked in the room salon long ago, like the older *ajummas* she'd encountered? That was how this happened. Korean girls were kidnapped or sold to Japanese soldiers who took them to Japanese bases to sexually serve the soldiers. After the war they'd return, pariahs to their families and communities, and they'd slip into prostitution with the American GIs, the only world they knew. But it would be rude to ask such a thing, and she could think of no polite way to bring up the subject. "Do you have any brothers or sisters?" Mina finally asked.

Mrs. Lim paused, shook her head. "I had a brother."

Mina stopped scrubbing. Mrs. Lim never used the past tense. "Had?"

"He die long time ago." Mina waited for Mrs. Lim to continue. "Korean life is very difficult for a long time. Many hardship. Everybody fear. Government very cruel." She dragged the word cruel out so two distinct syllables hung in the air.

"I'm really sorry, Mrs. Lim. You must miss him."

Her neck bobbed rapidly. "Scrub harder, please."

She rinsed her mother's back, the ribs and backbone visible through her skin.

"My turn. I scrub you," Mrs. Lim said.

Mina turned and closed her eyes. Mrs. Lim had a firm touch, brisker than Allison's, more purposeful, not as lingering. She imagined growing up with this touch, those hands that had wrapped her in a blanket, that would have scrubbed her in pails of water at home, would have fed her and clothed her in the same manner, with a brisk tenderness that did not linger. Then she felt the scrubber and Mrs. Lim's pressure increase on her lower back. She was scrubbing in the same spot, rubbing Mina's skin raw. She bit her lip, for now the pressure was aggressive, burning, but she didn't want to give in the way she had at the mud sauna. Mrs. Lim was muttering in Korean, and then the scrubbing stopped. She grabbed Mina's shoulder and turned her around.

She gasped as soon as Mina met her face. She reached out and touched Mina's cheekbones, her neck. "Mi-na?" she whispered. "*Ottekee?*" How?

Then Mina remembered the tiny half moon of moles—the dolphin—at the base of her back. From when she was born.

"*Mian hamnida,*" Mina said. I'm sorry. But she wasn't, not really. She was relieved the secret was out, that now they could move forward.

"You must go away," Mrs. Lim said in Korean. "I promised your father I would never see you again."

"It doesn't matter, now," Mina said.

Mrs. Lim shook her head and continued in Korean. "I said goodbye thirty years ago. I have another life now. I cannot see you." She collected her items, the lotions and soaps and conditioners, and put them in her plastic case.

Mina tried to take the items back out, so desperate she was to keep her there. "I won't tell anyone. I promise. Please let me see you again."

"Not possible," Mrs. Lim said in English, standing. There were still flecks of a dried skin patch that had not rinsed away. "Don't come to my house again."

"*Omma,*" Mina said, a long, low wail.

Mrs. Lim paused, but did not look back at Mina, shrunken on the plastic stool. "I am not your *Omma.* That is your American mother. Please forget me." And then she disappeared into the changing room.

Mina thought about chasing her, begging her as she changed and even as she walked to her car. Sometimes, she'd learned, Koreans didn't mean no, they just wanted someone to grovel a bit before they said yes. But this was not that time. Mina knew the havoc she could wreak if Mrs.

Lim's family ever found out about her. Mrs. Lim could lose everything, her house, her status, her children, her freedom. What would she do then? Mina sat on the stool crying. That quickly, she couldn't believe it was over. And then, she thought, why not beg? This was her mother. Mina deserved more. She left the sauna, quickly changed, ran the three flights of stairs to the parking garage just as Mrs. Lim's black sedan was exiting. Mina tapped on the window, and then hurled herself on the hood. Later, she would think how ridiculous she was, that she'd obviously been watching too many Korean melodramas during the day. But Mrs. Lim drove onward, until Mina rolled off the hood and onto the sidewalk.

That afternoon when it was time to tutor the children, Mina rang the bell to Mrs. Lim's house. No one answered. The lights were off. Mina imagined them huddled in some dark room, perhaps in one of her children's tiny bedrooms with the striped bedding and matching wallpaper. She rang the doorbell again, realizing they were not huddled anywhere, that they were in the car with their mother, driving steadily, taking a trip somewhere they'd never been before. Anywhere but here, where Mina stood.

CHAPTER 18

By the beginning of May, Jason had found Lim Sun-hui's home in Beverly Ville. He'd gone there one evening on his own, before he said anything to Allison, to make sure it was really her. Standing across the street, he watched through the unobstructed window in the living room. She stood frozen, framed by the lamp light like a statue or an animal hoping to avoid detection. She was wearing a simple, fitted T-shirt and slim black pants. She had a swan's neck, long slim torso, hair that fell like a sheet, cut long and straight. In the dim light she was a calmer, more composed version of Mina's future self. She looked briefly into the street where Jason was watching her, as if she felt his presence, and then turned off the light.

"Then what?" Allison sat across from him at Angel-In-Us coffee shop in Shinchon. Jason's watery Americano was cold. All that remained of her cappuccino were the small bits of foam resting at the bottom of the paper cup.

"Her children, a boy and a girl, were upstairs studying in their bedrooms. Their desk lights were on. Their backs were to the bedroom windows. She stopped in each room, touched them on the shoulder, and then left. I didn't see her again."

"Can we go see her now?"

"Tomorrow, when her kids are at school." Jason placed his cup inside Allison's and tossed both in the trash. They walked back to the apartment side by side, silent, not quite touching.

S he'd never been to Ilsan before, had no reason to, so she was surprised when the bus let them off at a large outdoor walking mall, with Nike and Starbucks and The Body Shop and Korean stores with names like The Face Shop and N 2 U that sold makeup and Gap-inspired casual wear. Past the stores were the outdoor meat places. The remnants of the previous late night's festivities littered the doorways and sidewalks: large glass bottles of beer and *soju* piled high, the garbage sorted into paper and plastic, the leftover wet food tied in orange bags. The rows of closed restaurants made a sad post-party ghost town, smelling of congealed grease and rotting vegetables. But then they approached the lake, and the world opened again.

The lake and its surroundings were manmade, but the scene was hopelessly bucolic. Mothers with strollers sat on the grass, older people pedaled bicycles along the trail, a few runners jogged at relaxed paces, friends held hands as they walked over bridges, through knolls, small pagodas, and rock gardens. Azaleas were in full bloom, as were magnolias and crepe myrtles. The leaves on the other bushes and trees were budding a yellow-mint-green.

"She lives here?" Allison asked. She'd still been expecting Mina's mother to be poor, a housekeeper or some other type of servant for people who inhabited this world.

"Not here exactly. About fifteen minutes' walk."

They walked from the lake and mall until they were in more familiar territory: Korean signs and shops stacked vertically and horizontally, wide roads thick with traffic, busy men wearing suits, school girls strolling in their skirted uniforms. The air smelled vaguely of car exhaust and grease.

They arrived at the neighborhood, which was unlike any Allison had seen in Korea. "The American Dream," Jason said.

"Like an amusement park."

They walked a few blocks until they stopped in front of a blond brick structure, compact by American living standards but large and spacious by Korean ones. A brick and wood fence, knee-high, just for show, ringed the small property.

"She lives here?" Allison said again. She still could not shake her image of the poor wan girl in the photo standing next to her even paler brother.

"Please, Allison, don't be disappointed."

She turned toward him, his face, as it often was to her, unreadable, impassive, a mask. He was holding her arm, the way a guide might, as if he were about to take her to a place she did not know.

"Okay," was all she said, but she was thinking, disappointed with what? Was he telling her to not get her hopes up regarding Mina? That was unacceptable.

Allison unlatched the tiny gate, which seemed to be built more for a doll's house than a real one, and walked to the door. She rang the bell. She felt Jason behind her, the space between them a tiny wedge of air. A woman yelled in Korean from inside. Jason yelled something back. Silence. He said something again.

"What's going on?"

"She doesn't know us. Doesn't want to answer."

"I'm not leaving until I talk to her."

"Do you have the photo?"

Allison pulled from her purse a tiny manila envelope and opened the clasp. Jason yelled something again, and finally Allison heard slippered steps, locks clicking, the door cracking a sliver, just enough for Allison to slot the photo inside.

After a minute, the door opened and Allison saw for the first time the woman who was no doubt Mina's mother. Her eyes and mouth and neck were the same as Mina's. The same as in the photo. Still. She was wearing simple, well-cut clothes Allison imagined were expensive. She dressed like Merry. Wordlessly, the woman led them to the living room, stylish and modern with a leather sofa, wood and chrome lamps and tables. On the wall was a large framed photo of Lim Sun-hui, and no doubt, her husband and two children, young adolescents, looking as stoic as Lim Sun-hui did in the photo with her brother from thirty years ago. The life she'd made.

She gestured for them to sit down, disappeared into the kitchen, returning with glasses of ice water. She sat in a plump velvet chair opposite them, swallowed for a moment in the cushions and pillows until she pushed herself upright.

"What do you want?" she asked in English. She held the photo in her right hand, clasped the edges with her thumb and index finger.

"I'm looking for my sister. Mina."

The woman's face slackened. She brought the photo to her mouth. The room suddenly seemed to drain of color, to wash itself of everything except for the light outside squeezing through slats and curtains. "I don't know anything."

Allison didn't move. She grabbed Jason's hand when she felt him shift slightly toward the door. "No," she whispered. "Not yet."

Then the woman resumed talking, now in rapid Korean, her voice higher pitched as she continued, until she stopped and brought the photo to her eyes.

"Her brother disappeared a long time ago. He's dead. This is the only photo she has of him. She had a copy, but she lost it," Jason said.

"She can keep it," Allison said. She walked over and placed her hands on the woman's, cold and shaking. "You lost your brother. I don't want to lose my sister. Tell me."

Mrs. Lim set the photo on the coffee table. "She teach my children English," she said. "For many weeks I don't know she is Mi-na." Then she switched to Korean.

"She hid her identity, but about a week ago Mrs. Lim discovered the truth. She told her to go away and not come back. She doesn't know where she went."

"Why?"

"Look around," Jason said. "She has a family. A life. If they discover her past, she could lose everything."

Lim Sun-hui was nodding now. "Wayne promise me. No contact again. My family cannot know."

"Wayne's her father," Allison said softly. So this was it, what Jason had been trying to tell her, what Mina had suspected, what Allison should have known as soon as she'd seen the photo. He'd had an affair with this woman. "He took that photo."

Lim Sun-hui nodded. "So long ago. So sad time for Korea."

"And my mom? Does she know about this?"

"I don't think so," she said. "It is our secret."

Allison stood. "You better hope I find her. Because if I don't then I'll tell your family everything."

Jason gripped her arm, guiding her to the door. "We'll find her," he said. Then he said something to Lim Sun-hui in Korean as she followed them to the door.

They had walked a few houses toward the bus station when Allison sat on the sidewalk and started crying. She leaned against a white picket fence surrounding a yellow house. A small dog barked from the front patio. Jason patted her back. "We'll find her," he said again, as if his saying it would make it true. Allison swallowed. The sun was still strong on the street, which was so quiet and empty she thought of all the foreclosed homes in the States, abandoned, uninhabited.

CHAPTER 19

Nights when she couldn't sleep, Allison worried the prayer bead necklace Mina had given her, imagining Mina fingering hers at the same time. She prayed to anyone she thought might be listening, asking for second chances, to make things right. During the days she wandered the streets of Mina's old haunts, searching for traces of her sister, trying to make sense of her own broken world.

Men and their lies. Wayne and Ray. Her devotion to them. How could Ray, she wondered, lead a double life so effortlessly? Ray had written her again, this time in a more official capacity, warning her of the consequences of abandoning her job without notice. Unless she said something, Ray would continue to lead a double life until he tired of it, until he could no longer be bothered, and then he'd return to Merry, the girls, to reap the benefits of family in his aging years. Because he was handsome and charming. Because he'd always gotten his way. Because he believed he deserved a life without consequence or pain. Because he was entitled to it.

Entitled. He really believed he was entitled to Merry and those golden-haired daughters, to a steady job, *and* to his darker side, a side so predictable, in retrospect, (how had she not seen it, Allison wondered, how had she not seen everything?), and pathetic that it wasn't worth more than a throwaway scrap of paper to him.

He'd been entitled to Allison. To a brief, uninspired affair because there was nothing else to do, and then he expected her to stay on, working for him and his own advancement at the expense of hers because he knew, he always knew, how much she loved him. If he'd cared about her at all, he would have sent her away when he saw that, forced her to get on with her life. And then, because he was also entitled to it, he fucked her sister.

Her sister. Had anything changed now that they were bound not only by family but by blood? Did that make Allison more responsible for her? She hoped not. She hoped she had embraced Mina as her sister that day after she'd left Gary's house, the very day Mina had disappeared. Their shared blood didn't really matter, after all the rest.

The worst part with Ray was that she'd allowed it. Whatever he'd done to her, she'd done to herself, and more. He'd not forced her to stay. She'd tied herself to him, her loyalty misaligned, misspent.

Except. Wayne had lied, too. Their family was built on that house of lies, just like Ray's. Did Bonnie really not know? Did she turn a blind eye? Did Merry know anything? Did she lie awake at night and wonder? Perhaps they preferred not knowing, staying in the shadows. Would Allison have done any of it differently herself?

She didn't know. But these men could not escape the consequences of such entitlement. She would not allow it. She might ruin lives, Merry's, the two little girls', Ray's, Bonnie's, Wayne's. She didn't care. At least they'd be facing the truth of their worlds.

She still had Merry's email from when she'd invited Allison to the July Fourth barbeque last year. Her first without Ted. *Hope you can make it! Feel free to bring a date* ☺ *xoMerry*. She was a smiley face and xo kind of woman. Allison had gone to the party because the invite had offered her a way out of the church barbeque her parents were going to. Some nice single fathers there, Bonnie had said. At least she'd not have to deal with that at Ray's and Merry's.

Not far from the pool in the back of their house, Ray was manning the grill of veggie burgers, chicken breasts, a few bratwurst for the remaining unapologetic red meat eaters in the group. The ones who didn't care about animals' quality of life, who bought fruit with pesticides on it. Allison had felt sorry for the girls, denied their hot dogs, nitrates and all, their tiny bodies strapped into life preservers as they paddled around the shallow end of the pool. No drowning on Merry's watch. The cooler of beer was stacked with microbrews and ultra lights, and a bottle of uncorked white wine chilled in a bucket of ice. Allison watched the others not drink whatever was in their hands.

Merry was chatting with the other mothers about schools, schools, schools. Which teacher was best for fifth grade, for seventh, which skill-sets the girls were ahead in, behind in, what after-school activities were the best. The girls were in piano and ballet at the moment, but the oldest wanted to play soccer and what the oldest one wanted so did the youngest. The problems of tweens. Merry called the girls from the pool and told them it was time to reapply their sunscreen.

Allison had arrived dateless, hoping for a few moments alone with Ray. Nothing more than a bit of conversation shared over drinks. That had become enough for her, the accidental touch of fingers as he passed her a beer from the cooler. She remembered him getting up from the bed, a towel casually wrapped around his waist, resting in the crack of his butt. She'd still be in bed, unable or unwilling to leave, to abandon the salty smell of sex, and instead she listened to him shower, quickly and efficiently. He always emerged from the bathroom already dressed.

She'd been sitting on the edge of a lounge chair, taking small sips of her beer, while Ray talked to her about Moving On. How it was Not Too Late. All that crap. But she listened and nodded and told Ray she was trying, but things Took Time. Then Merry had appeared, as if on cue, the wine spritzer she'd been carrying the whole afternoon more prop than drink, and sat next to Ray, who put his beer down and wrapped his arms around her.

"I'd like you to meet someone, Allison. A friend from work," Merry had said, and then, like a magician, she waved her wine glass and a short lumbering guy appeared, almost apologetically, from the side of the house.

His name was Merlin and he worked with computers. Ex-military, he told her, and then for the next twenty minutes he talked about how he survived his one-hour commute every morning by listening to war history audio books, how he'd like to move out of his condo in Arlington but he wasn't sure what to buy or where to go, how the dentist had charged him several thousand dollars his last visit and his teeth still felt terrible, how he used to be unstable, that was why his marriage had failed, that he'd locked himself in the bathroom with a knife and wouldn't come out, but now that he was on medication, life was as smooth as a lake, how Rogaine really did keep him from losing all his hair, and that the current season of *American Idol* was the worst, a sign the show, and pop culture in general, was deteriorating. He told her his favorite winner had been Carrie Underwood, that although he wasn't much of a country music fan himself, he could appreciate star quality when he saw it, and no one had been as good as her. Finally he stopped, breathed, sipped his Coke and looked at her.

"Thanks for sharing, Merlin," Allison said.

"I thought you'd be taller," he said.

And now in Seoul, Allison became angry for the first time at Merry, the woman she'd put on a pedestal, not only because she was beautiful and had two healthy children, but especially because she had Ray.

Merry had thought Merlin was a find for Allison. A catch. The best Allison could do. The Rays of the world were supposed to be with the Merrys, and she would help the others, the ones without all her gifts, who would not or could not have her fabulous life, by offering them the Merlins of the world.

She addressed the email to Merry and typed in Ray's confessions, memorized. Then she sent it.

B uddha's birthday was Friday and Jason had promised to go with her to the temple. She remembered Mina asking her to go for the celebration. Maybe she'll be there, waiting for me, Allison thought. Saturday was a band festival near Yongsan, and Allison hoped she might find Robert, who so far had remained elusive. Both long shots.

On May 20, the day before Buddha's birthday celebration, the South Korean government officially accused North Korea of sinking the ship with a torpedo. On the morning of the Buddha's birthday, Allison read the subject of Wayne's latest email without opening it: KOREA ABOUT TO IMPLODE: COME HOME ASAP.

The temple on Buddha's birthday was far from the calm place Mina had taken her two months before. The road leading up to the temple was lined with makeshift convenience stores and food stalls selling beer from iced coolers, bottles of *makgeolli*, ramen, acorn jelly salad, and Korean pancakes called *pajeon*. The streets were crowded with families making their way up the hill to the temple, where the ceremonies and celebrations were in full swing. Older men, dressed in fifties-style windbreakers and checkered shirts stayed behind, drinking *soju* and eating *anju*, playing games, telling stories, singing songs. Some of the men and women danced to the makeshift percussion group ringing a patch of grass. It was late afternoon, just before twilight, and everyone seemed already drunk. Allison thought, if Mina is here, this is where she'll be.

She sat with Jason on plastic chairs at a tiny table, used wooden chopsticks to cut their green onion *pajeon*, drank tiny paper cups filled with *makgeolli*. Jason told her that *makgeolli* used to be a poor man's drink, but that the manufacturers were re-branding it as a healthier version of beer because of its digestive properties and slight nutritional value. He warned her, though, that it could cause evil hangovers. As she sipped the milky liquid, she decided she preferred it to beer.

After they finished their *makgeolli*, Allison answered the calls of the dancing old men and women clapping their hands to a music sorrowful and joyful at the same time. Jason joined her, awkwardly raising his hands and legs to the drums. When the song ended they bid farewell and walked toward the temple.

"We never danced like that in my family," Jason said.

"You dance country better," Allison told him.

Up the hill at the temple, crowds surrounded the main stage. Above them, paper lanterns of dangerously bright colors hid the sky. Each lantern held a candle and a tag bearing the name of someone who had donated money. On stage women in traditional *hanbok* moved like graceful butterflies whose slightest flap of a wing changed the direction of the world. Allison lifted her head toward the lanterns, flickering under the setting sun. She touched her bead necklace as the white tags fluttered. She would donate money so she could put Mina's name on a lantern. Maybe that would bring her luck. Around her, cell phones flashed at the group of monks drumming and chanting. But among the couples and families and occasional wandering drunk, there was no Mina.

Allison got in line for the lantern donation while Jason wandered back down the hill to use the restroom. When it was her turn she faced a monk and an assistant who would write the name for her. The monk looked up when she told them to write Mina's name.

"Is she your friend?" he asked in Korean.

"Little sister," she said.

He pointed to the prayer beads around her neck. Allison nodded, fingering the necklace. He was the monk who had sold Mina the necklaces. The one with the shaking hands. "I'm looking for her. Have you seen her?"

The monk shook his head. Allison felt the people behind her, impatient, pressing forward.

"What's your family name?" he asked in Korean.

"Morehouse."

Until then the monk's face had been impassive, an empty plain. He closed his eyes. "Is your father's name Wayne?"

"Yes. How do you know?" Her Korean was rudimentary, but she'd learned some basic phrases in the past few months. He rose from the table and gestured for her to follow him. They walked away from the ceremony, past the drumming and the women in traditional dress singing songs of longing, down the road to a structure, a traditional dwelling, where he disappeared behind sliding doors. From the building, the road leading to the temple was filled with families and old people moving toward the lanterns. Allison searched for Jason, who would now be unable to find her. Where she stood was darker, with only the moon and a white bulb outside the dwelling. The monk reappeared, ghostlike, with his robes and shaved head, a spirit from another world.

When he was close he reached into his robe and pulled out a photo, holding it under the stark light. It was yellow, creased, but it was the same photo that Mina had left her, the photo of the boy and the woman, Lim Sun-hui, Mina's mother. He pointed to the boy in the photo.

"Me," he said in English.

She had found a ghost, then, a person thought dead, or he had found her, and she thought, if I can find him, then there is hope that Mina is out there, and I will see her again.

She found Jason wandering under the lanterns and brought him to the monk to translate. He told them, briefly, his story.

His name was Lim Woo-sung, but now he was a *sunim*, the title for Buddhist monks. Years ago, he said, he had done a bad thing and had tried to escape it. Now he knew there was no escaping suffering as long as one remained attached, but then he had thought he could run away from what he'd done. He'd fled to the mountains, surviving on plants and roots, the occasional pheasant, and the bag of rice he carried in his pack. He'd live in the mountains for as long as the rice lasted, then he'd enter a village and bathe in the sauna, buy another bag of rice, and return to the mountains, where time was long and elastic. He knew the money would end one day, and then he'd be forced to face his life. He considered turning himself in, but he thought it better to die in the mountains than in prison. Sometimes at night he'd hear them, Korean soldiers, American GIs chasing him, crunching through the leaves, the weight of their cargo announcing their arrival. Then he'd awaken and find himself alone.

Toward the end of his time in the mountains he took to drinking. He was tired of contemplation, tired of extending what was to soon end. He'd go into towns, no longer bothering to bathe, and buy *soju* and *makgeolli* and cigarettes and disappear back into the mountains where he'd drink and sing old folk songs that spoke of longing, sadness, separation. He stopped trapping pheasants. He drank and rinsed in streams that each day seemed closer to ice. He cursed his mother for getting sick, his father for dying in Vietnam, his sister for becoming involved with a white man, for having his baby, a *hapa* who was even more doomed than he was. Then one day the snow came and he lay down to sleep.

There were many things he could have dreamed that he did not, like how he arrived at the hooch, still in his uniform, blood turned brown, the smell of cooked rice, of his mother, cadaverous, cursing him for being born, of his father, beating him with a stick when he'd fallen asleep in the rice paddies, of the photo he still carried from the American's camera. He did not dream of what he was or what he might have become. Instead he dreamed of his sister's child, the strangeness of her when she was first born, her gold eyes that eventually turned brown. He dreamed of her sleeping on the *yo*, hand curled around a spoon, as his body shook with what he'd done. He dreamed of her visiting him, on this mountain, her eyes gold again, like when she'd first been born, like a tiger's. He dreamed this tiger woman settled her spoon over his closed lids, giving him peace. When he awoke, he was covered in blankets, and a man in a robe was rubbing his hands. The monks took care of him until he was strong enough to leave, but he knew that he would not, and instead would join the monastery and work to ease the suffering of the world as well as his own. He learned to let go of his old self, the one who had done bad things, who had been afraid to face punishment and death. Now he chanted and prayed and meditated and helped run the monastery in whatever capacity he was needed.

Twenty years passed. Then one day he saw his sister, his *nuna*. She was still slim, though more severe-looking, holding the hands of two small children. Beside her was a man in a suit taking pictures. The cherry blossoms were in bloom, they'd shed their petals in a few days, and she and the children were posing against the trees growing at the temple's entrance. They were dressed up, either coming back from church, for it was Sunday, or a wedding, perhaps. They did not see him watching them from the steps of one of the smaller buildings. They were a quiet, composed family, and, he could tell, well-off. While they were inside the temple praying he risked walking to the entrance to look at their shoes. All shined leather, barely worn, with Italian names imprinted in the insoles. Rich, he thought. Through the crack of the sliding door he watched his sister pray, her legs folded on the tiny cushion. He wondered if through her own determination and his years of practice, they had erased Wayne and Mi-na from their histories, except for moments like these, when he remembered them, more as shadows than as people. He hid again so that he could watch them disappear down the road.

"Why didn't you talk to her?" Allison asked.

"She has her life now. I have mine," Lim *sunim* said.

"She thinks you're dead."

"In some ways I am. Dead to this world," he said.

"If you want, I can bring her to you," Allison said.

The monk raised his head toward the lanterns beyond them, a bright blanket covering the sky. "If she wants," he said. He bowed his head slightly. "Now I must go."

CHAPTER 20

When they arrived the next day at the Hae Bang Chon festival in the late afternoon, the streets were already crowded, full of foreigners, mostly Westerners, but also people from Morocco and Nigeria, and Pakistan, and the Philippines. Foreigners lived here, Jason said, because the housing, next to the Yongsan Army base, required a small amount of key money for deposit compared to other areas, and was close to Itaewon. The apartments had once been rented out to US Army personnel but that market was drying up with the soldiers being moved to Camp Humphreys. Instead they were being filled by this new group of expats. A narrow street wound its way up to Namsan, a large green hill that housed Seoul Tower.

Allison almost forgot she was in Korea, felt instead that she was at some suspended world party. The neighborhood boasted stores and restaurants with names in English like Buddha's Belly, Pita Time, Philly's Sub, Standing Coffee, Jacoby's Burgers, and Pinoy Phillipino Mart. The Family Mart convenience store was crowded with expats in flowery dresses, tight T-shirts, and frayed flip-flops. The unwashed masses, as Wayne called them. Trainspotters, Jason called them, after the movie. Mina's friends.

"I came here last summer, just after I moved back," Jason said. "A friend lived here, had a barbeque party. Just a year ago there were no coffee shops, no outdoor seating, only one or two restaurants. Seoul is changing."

Allison nodded. The world was changing. Or her world at least.

A thin man, shirtless, wearing a bright red wig, danced on the edge of the sidewalk. Clumps of people holding beers spilled onto the street, which was clogged with taxis, cars, and a bus stuck in the traffic. A man with an electric guitar blared the Radiohead song "Creep" into a microphone.

"He's awful," Allison said.

"Maybe some of the other places have better bands." He led her down the stairs to the American Foreign Legion. Inside, behind the bar, a few old men, Americans who could have been her dad's friends, slowly poured beer into clear cups for the scattered customers. The room was dark and Allison felt immediately depressed. It reminded her of what was, what could have been. She turned to leave, but Jason was pushing toward a stage and people sitting at tables, listening to a girl sing about love and loss.

"Better huh?" Jason said, grabbing the last free table in the back. He went to get them something to drink.

She had to admit it was, and while the band was merely mediocre, like something she'd hear at a friend's college party, it was better than the music outside. Jason brought back two beers, foamy and chilled. When had she started drinking so early on a Saturday afternoon? She wasn't sure. She was in an alternate universe, her other life in the States on permanent pause, as if there she were still sitting on the couch, frozen, watching TV with Wayne, the moment never changing until she chose to return to it. That life felt like the proverbial dream now; this one was so much more vibrant, real, even though she had no job, no real home, no plans for tomorrow. But here, with Jason, their knees almost touching, the accents British, Irish, something else, Western African, maybe, Korean as well, she felt part of not so much a cacophony as a calling. A calling to what? That she still didn't know. *Don't give up.* That was all. Mina had to be out there somewhere. This was her world.

She didn't know when he brought a bottle of *soju* to the table, only that it seemed that Jason drank most of it in a few minutes. His face flushed, he slumped in his chair.

"Jason, are you okay?"

"I want to be free," he said. "Like them." He stood, swaying slightly, and walked up to the stage. The band was playing Patsy Cline's "Crazy." Standing behind the singer, he took off his shirt and tossed it into the audience. The crowd laughed. Allison watched, silent. He'd left his glasses on the table. The singer gave Jason the microphone.

I'm crazy for trying,
Crazy for crying,
And I'm crazy for loving you.

He was not singing to her, but to the crowd of foreigners, who Allison was afraid were laughing at him, not with him. His voice was torrid, desperate, in despair. This was not Jason, mild, sweet Jason. When the song ended, Jason met her eyes, dropped the microphone and pushed his way out of the bar. Allison grabbed his glasses and shirt and followed him outside.

The streets were even thicker with expats, the conversation a loud, insistent buzz beneath bad music. She followed Jason up the street toward the mountain, threading through the crowds, until they were clear from the party below. How quickly, she thought, it became so removed, the bad music and the people scurrying like drunken ants.

He'd stopped running now, Allison trailing him up a flight of wooden stairs to the mountain, and then collapsed on the grass and rocks, out of breath. Without word or signal, Jason grabbed her in an embrace. He was fast and hungry, running his hands over her body, rubbing her breasts, clenching her hair, his body urgent. He pulled up her shirt, slid his hand inside the band of her shorts. She did not think to stop him, this stranger who wanted her—or something—so desperately as if his life depended on it.

"Take me with you," he said, "say yes." His hand was in her shorts and he was rubbing her, more skillfully, more assured than she would have imagined, as if he had all the experience in the world, as if he'd learned that secret, the secret that none of the others had: Ray, Ted, Gary. He was with *her* body, not a body.

"Yes," Allison whispered.

"Louder," he breathed in her ear.

"Yes," Allison said, louder, her voice throaty. She shivered and he covered her gasp with his mouth. He lay on top of her, his breath matching hers, and she wondered what he would do next.

Some voices in the distance, an *ajumma's* loud, aggressive tone, arguing but not. He sat up, his chest bare, slick. Allison handed him his shirt and glasses. He looked away from her, fished in his pocket for his cigarettes. Smoked one slowly. Below the crowd was swelling. A police car drove by with a bullhorn, yelling at the crowds in Korean.

Ishould see if any of Mina's friends are here," Allison said finally. Jason nodded, stood. She touched the damp collar of his shirt. He smelled different from other men she'd known. She never smelled sweat on him, just the faintest trace of garlic and salty skin. "What just happened?"

"I lost myself," Jason said. "Forget about it. It didn't happen."

But it did happen and she would not forget it. He'd hid himself from her so well. Because she'd needed him to. They walked back into the festival and bought some *makgeolli*. A politician's open truck was stuck in traffic. Local elections were in full swing. The past few weeks Allison had watched an occasional open bed truck drive by with a man in a suit and white gloves bowing to the street. Speakers blared the candidate's praises and promises. Sometimes she'd pass a group of people wearing vests with a candidate's photo printed on them. They chanted his name and bowed as Allison walked by. Now from the speakers a man urged people in this district to vote for him. The guy with the red wig jumped on the truck bed and started dancing and yelling at the crowd. The truck crawled along; no one threw him off.

"He'd never do that in his own country, wherever he's from," Allison said. She was embarrassed by his behavior, the reckless disregard for the country he was a guest in. But no one stopped him. A police car was stuck in the thick traffic, its siren spinning. A voice spoke from a megaphone, similar to the politician's, trying to get people to clear the road. One girl threw a napkin in their direction.

"When I was at university we were afraid of the police," Jason said. "They could beat you. Kill you. But we protested, still."

"What did you protest?"

"America. We wanted freedom."

"Were you ever arrested?"

"No, just tear gas. It was a kind of bonding experience. But not too long before that, especially around the time of the Gwangju uprising, protesting was life and death. Now the police, they are some kind of joke."

She didn't know what the Gwangju uprising was, but didn't want to ask now. The music was too loud and too awful to talk. Police and politicians were shrieking messages so distorted she couldn't tell if they were in English or Korean. She wanted to go back to the hill. Instead she leaned in next to him, felt his hand at the small of her back.

Then she spotted Mina's friends, part of the group she'd gone out with that first night in Seoul. They were across the street, clumped together, standing at the edge of the one-lane traffic drinking *makgeolli*. She told Jason to wait, and she slowly pushed her way to the other side. One of the girls gave her a big hug, squealing, as if they were long-lost friends.

"Have you heard from Mina?" Allison shouted in her ear.

"Oh my God, is she still missing?" the girl said. "Maybe she's in jail."

"Why would you think that?"

The girl scrunched her eyes. Her pupils were pinpricks. "I'm sure she's fine. Probably just went on some trip with that mysterious boyfriend. She's cool."

Allison nodded. "You're full of shit."

The girl smiled, bobbed to the music. Mina would not rely on this group. They were not really friends, not people she'd go to for help. Robert she would. Jason, too. Mina relied on men to help her. Like Allison did, in different ways. In front of the convenience stores, one of the girls in the group, someone she didn't recognize, was sitting on a guy's lap in a chair, her mass of hair covering his face as she made out with him. Her loose tie-dye dress was hiked up her generous thighs. When she came up for air, Gary's pale, bloated face was underneath, smiling a rubbery smile. He raised his hand in the peace sign.

"Hey Al, long time," he said.

"Mina's gone."

"Yeah. I heard something about that."

The girl wriggled off Gary's lap and stomped off in her flip-flops. "Come back," Gary slurred. The girl stopped. Then she stepped toward Gary's outstretched hand, collapsing on the ground, laying her head on his knee, petting his leg.

"You asshole. I shouldn't have wasted myself on you. She was right about that." She stopped to catch her breath. Jason had appeared. He was drinking a beer, smoking a cigarette, just a few feet away from them.

Gary was no longer smiling. He struggled to stand but Allison pushed him back into the chair. The girl had sobered up. She was standing now, looking from Gary to Allison.

"She just didn't want me fucking both of you is all," Gary said.

Allison shoved again. Gary fell backward into a few plants that lined the convenience store's wall. "You know jack shit about my sister."

The crowd had gotten larger. A siren wailed mournfully a few stores down. Jason pulled her away just as she lifted her leg to kick Gary. Instead she only got air.

"You've proved your point," he said. "Okay?"

Allison no longer knew what she was looking for. They walked up a block to where the party tapered out, to watch the spectacle unimpeded. The politician's truck cleared the crowd, speeding past them. She wanted to go up further, to disappear with Jason behind a rock, among the trees. She felt his arms around her waist. Since that morning they'd gone from not touching each other to some kind of constant contact that she only noticed when it abated. Fingertips, legs pressed together, her head on his shoulder, his hand on her back.

She started taking photos of the clotted street, now almost impassable, filled with people from every continent, it seemed. The man with the bright red wig now wore only a sarong knotted at his bony hip, and was raising his hands to the sky. She zoomed in on the clusters of people drinking beers, squeezed in, free from the world, either Korea or their own and whatever they'd left, for that night. Then she spotted Mina, or someone like Mina, a small dot shadowed in one of the alleys. A skinny girl with long dark hair would not mean much in this crowd, but Allison recognized the shorts, some plaid cut-offs, and purple tank top with a lotus flower in the middle. Mina had one like that. Allison snapped the photo just as the dot disappeared.

"I think I saw her." Allison worked her way as fast as possible back down the hill, with Jason holding her hand.

When they arrived, there was no one wearing the plaid shorts or tank top. Allison called Mina's name, scoured the alley that led them away from the party toward another street so quiet that it would be easy to not even know the festival was happening. A man who looked Indian or Pakistani was smoking a cigarette among the drying laundry on one of the balconies of the small apartments. A few children speaking Russian tossed a ball in a driveway. She waved to the man.

"Have you seen a girl come by here? Tall, long dark hair? Korean, kind of? Plaid shorts and a purple shirt."

"No, nobody," the man said. "Except these noisy children."

Jason spoke in Korean to the children and they answered him back. "They didn't see anything either."

"I didn't imagine it." Allison turned on her camera and searched for the photo she'd just taken. But the street lights had been too bright, the sky too dark to reveal anything in the alleyway except a dark blur.

"That could be anything. A dog. A motorcycle."

"She's around here. I can feel it," Allison said. But she wasn't sure if she was feeling something or willing it, determined to make it happen, refusing to believe any other possibility.

Jason's phone rang. He looked at the number then answered it. She knew it was work. He didn't say much, except, *ne, ne, ne*—yes, yes, yes, and then something before he hung up.

"One of the robots' programs has crashed. I have to go."

"But it's Saturday night," Allison said, dumbly.

"This isn't just a job for me," Jason said.

She saw him then as when she'd first met him, thin, almost frail, with his dark glasses and the sharp eyes behind them. "I get it," she said, squeezing his hand. "But I'm going to stay, look for Mina a little longer."

"I don't know."

"I'll be fine. There are a thousand people here, nothing will happen to me. I'll take a cab. I'll call you when I get home."

He stared at her. "Why don't I just take you home?"

"It's okay, Jason. Really."

He looked up at the sky and back at her. His phone rang again.

"Go," she said. "I'm a big girl. It's Korea, not a war zone. Well, technically it's a war zone, and yes, North Korea did just recently sink a Korean ship, but you know what I mean."

He nodded. He hugged her quickly before he walked her back but didn't kiss her goodbye. She waved to him as he walked toward another street where it would be easier to hail a taxi. As soon as he disappeared, she went back into the alley and resumed calling her sister's name.

An hour later, she'd found nothing. The streets were swelling with people increasingly drunk and belligerent. The guy with the red wig had to be restrained by other revelers because he was yelling at a policeman. A pudgy guy in a tank top sang an off-key cover of Beck's "Loser." The police had parked their cars and were pushing back the crowd, which now spilled into the streets. The Westerners in particular seemed to be itching for a fight. They were getting drunker and angrier, and Allison couldn't figure why. They were in a foreign country, making more money than they could in their own, drinking beer on the street, listening to bands, and the cops were asking them to move to the sidewalk. Yet they felt righteous and indignant, as though they wanted something to protest.

She was hungry. As she walked up to the convenience store for a chicken kebab, she recognized no one. The night should have been dark but instead the sky was like perpetual dusk, with lights from the stores and streets shining brightly. A bus of Japanese tourists was caught in the traffic. They waved from their closed windows and snapped pictures of the melee, of the crazy foreigners. The garbage cans had long filled and were overflowing. She was certain she'd seen, or felt, Mina, but now she wondered if she was chasing her own shadow. Mina might not even be in Korea, especially after what happened with her mother. She could have simply disappeared. On purpose. Or not. Monday she would keep her promise to Wayne, go to the American Embassy and report Mina missing. She hoped she was not betraying Mina by doing so. If only her sister would send her a sign, tell her what she wanted her to do.

And then, gazing down at the spectacle that seemed to be building toward a riot, she saw Robert in the same spot in the alley she'd thought she'd seen Mina earlier that night. His white basketball shoes and polo shirt glowed in the alley. Even from that distance he looked clean and pressed compared to those around him. She threw her half-eaten chicken beside one of the overflowing garbage cans and pushed her way down the street. This time he did not disappear. He was not a figment of her imagination. She would walk up to him and demand he tell her what he knew. But as she approached him, she changed her mind. He was talking with someone in the shadows, another man, shorter, squat looking, and she was certain they were exchanging something. They hugged, touching fists, and the squat guy's hand slipped into Robert's pocket. She lurked around a corner and waited. The short guy turned back into the crowd, walking right past Allison. Robert lingered in the alley for a moment, watching the guy disappear. He turned his head and she was certain he was looking at her. She smiled, but he didn't acknowledge her. He was looking at something above or beyond her, she wasn't sure. Then he walked down the same alley in which she'd called Mina's name.

He turned left, up the street toward Namsan. She stayed a block behind, walking past the Indian's apartment, past the spot where the children had played, and up the street, still eerily calm and quiet with the festival only a street away. He stopped once, turning around, but she ducked behind a parked car before he saw her. They continued up the street past small apartment villas, into the older section where more Koreans lived and the English signs were minimal. Old men drank *soju* and played cards at a convenience store, Korean children chased each other in the street, a couple walked hand in hand, a *galbi* restaurant was full of drunk Koreans laughing and playfully arguing. The street smelled of pork fat, and against this idyllic backdrop she wondered what they—any of them, all of them—were doing here. Robert turned up another street and the road went almost straight up. His stride did not slow, and she struggled not to lose him, not to wheeze too loudly. Finally he stopped in front of a house, unlatching the gate. He walked to the top floor and unlocked the door.

When he'd closed the door, she opened the gate. The stairs wound up three floors to the top. The patio was dark. A light burned inside. She thought she heard a TV, voices speaking English. She put her hand on the doorknob, hoping he might have not yet locked the door, and then she felt something at her temple and then she was out.

CHAPTER 21

She awoke to lips on her skin. Cheeks. Eyelids. Soft full lips. She opened her eyes. Mina. Mina, her face wan, hair short and stringy, but Mina, alive. She didn't recognize the room. It was dark, but there was a lamp beside her. She was on a *yo* on the floor. Mina was tucked beside her, a wet cloth in her hand. Music, somewhere, in another room, on the street, she wasn't sure. Percussion, a woman's voice low, wailing.

Allison wrapped her arms around Mina, crushing her in her embrace.

"You found me," Mina said.

"What kind of sister do you think I am?" Allison said. She rubbed her temple. "What happened?"

"Robert did that. Quick stick." Mina went to the window, sliding open the panel, lighting a cigarette. "He thought you were following him."

"I was." Allison sat up. She'd found Mina, but not the Mina she'd been looking for. This Mina was listless, preoccupied, her hair was matted, her skin grey, her shoulder blades like broken wings. "I met your mother."

Mina turned. "What did she say?"

"Not much. Wayne's your dad. They made some kind of deal. He's been lying all these years."

"I don't know why she won't see me again," Mina said, her voice dull.

"I can't believe Dad cheated on Mom." And then, to her own surprise, Allison was crying. "Just like Ray cheated with you. You did it to hurt me."

"That's not why." Mina was looking out the window, although there was nothing to see but bricks from the next building over.

"I was with him first," Allison said.

"I wanted to show you what a jerk he was," Mina said. "It wasn't my best plan."

"Before he was married, I was pregnant with his baby. I never told Ray. I never told anyone," Allison said.

"What happened? Miscarriage?"

Allison shook her head. "The other," she whispered.

"Oh God, Ally," Mina said.

"Dad always loved you most," Allison said.

Mina said nothing. Then, "I'm sorry about Ray. My moral compass wasn't working so well at that point."

"Did you spank him?"

Mina laughed. "Sometimes. He liked it."

"Do you hate Dad?"

"I don't know." Mina turned from the window and sat on the floor. "Do you?"

"You have his nose. And his jaw," Allison said. "I can see that now."

Mina picked at the thread at the end of the *yo*. "Since I met her, I've been sick and I can't get better." Her voice wavered.

"Let's go home."

Mina shook her head then leaned toward the room Robert was in. "We're getting married."

Allison crawled across the bed, took her sister in her arms. "It's not too late. You don't have to do this."

"He has a daughter. She needs a mother. Want to be my bridesmaid?"

"Whatever you want."

"What I want isn't possible," she said.

"You'd be surprised." Allison was thinking of Lim Woo-sung, a ghost come to life, of lying here in bed with her sister breathing beside her.

At first Robert didn't think Allison should stay in the apartment, which only had one bedroom, but Allison refused to leave, and Robert admitted it was better that Mina was not alone when he was away, which was often. Allison was afraid that Mina would disappear again, and this time she wouldn't find her. She called Jason and told him where she was but that she would not leave the apartment unless Mina did. "At least she's okay," Jason said. "Have you told your parents?" Allison had called them and told them Mina was safe, that she'd gone on a vacation unannounced, a miscommunication, all were fine, but no, she didn't want to talk to them, not yet.

Mina slowly improved. She was eating more, not smoking as much, gaining strength. She and Allison spent their hours talking about their childhood, telling the stories that they'd never shared before. Slowly they began to see their family from each other's perspective, experiences, dreams. They talked about their father and Lim Sun-hui—what had happened between them? And Bonnie, did she really know nothing? Allison spoke of those first days after Mina had arrived from Korea, stealing Wayne's love. Mina told her the real story of the Korean girls who beat her up, the ones who first told her a fragment of the truth. They compared notes about Ray, and Allison almost regretted sending Merry the email. Almost. They talked about what kind of mother Mina would be to this girl—Shayla—she'd never met. She'd be like Bonnie in many ways, she admitted, and more. She'd not lie or pretend that she was someone she wasn't. Allison did not tell her that she'd found Lim Woo-sung. She was saving him for something bigger, another moment. Hypocrite, she thought, even now, not telling Mina.

One night they drank *soju* then pricked fingers and rubbed them together. Double-blood sisters. Still, Mina would not leave the apartment, would not step outside into a world she did not want to face, no matter how Allison tried. Slowly, Mina worked her way to forgiving Wayne. He believed the problems she'd had in the States were a shadow compared to what she would have had to endure growing up in Korea as a *honyol*. And, he believed, not only would she have lived without a future; so would Lim Sun-hui. He believed they'd have rotted together in the Ville outside the base and, right or wrong, Wayne had acted on that belief. Allison was not so forgiving.

"Dad should have told the truth," Allison said over and over, as if repeating the words would exorcise her anger. "And if Mom left him because of it, it would have served him right."

The phone call was easy. Allison got both her parents on the line and told them that Mina was getting married to a GI here on June 25, and they should come to Korea for the ceremony. Surprise her. Bonnie was ready to go, but Wayne was not.

"The country's about to implode, in case you haven't been following the headlines," Wayne said. "Can't you just get her back home where she belongs?"

"She'd say she belongs with Robert."

"It all seems so fast," Bonnie asked. "What's he like, this Robert?"

"He's from Trinidad. With a seven-year-old daughter."

"He's colored?" Bonnie asked.

"Black," Allison said.

"What about this Sunny person?" Bonnie said. "Will she be there?"

"I don't know," Allison said.

"I don't want her there. Bonnie's her mother. That woman has nothing to do with our family," Wayne said.

"Can we talk to Mina?"

"Look, if I told her you were coming, she wouldn't see you. The only way is to surprise her."

"We'll be there," Bonnie said. "I have to see my baby girl."

That was the problem, Allison thought. It wasn't that Mina had no mothers, it was that she had two.

Allison and Jason were in front of Lim Sun-hui's house in Beverly Ville. The blinds fell, blocking the windows.

"She won't talk to you," Jason said.

Allison unlatched the gate. For show only. "Yes she will." She rang the doorbell. "I know you're there!"

The neighborhood was quiet. The Koreans who lived there were rich enough to buy their way out of the mess of public life. They stayed inside or worked in large office buildings or shopped in expensive department stores. They did not sit on the streets to watch traffic or meet with neighbors or wait for the fruit and vegetable truck to roll by selling its wares. Lives were contained, hidden. Allison banged on the door.

"Your brother Lim Woo-sung is alive."

Jason grabbed her arm, pulling her away from the door. Allison wrenched free, still yelling. The door opened. Lim Sun-hui looked as wan and haggard as Mina, mirror images of the same decline. "Not possible."

"I talked to him."

She led them inside. She sat straight, rigid on the chair opposite them, wearing the same style of simply-cut clothes as before, neutral tones, linen fabric. She squeezed her hands, veined and bony, in a tight vise.

"Mina's getting married in Seoul in one week. Please come to the wedding. Then I'll take you to your brother."

"I give her away to save my brother. So that he can live. But then I never hear of him. They are both dead to me. That is only way. Now she's alive and he's alive. I don't understand." She covered her face with her hands.

"Just for one day. Then you can go back to this life, pretend it never happened. Be her mother, then you can see your brother. Your family will never know."

"He wants to see me?" Lim Sun-hui stood. "Okay. I will do it. Now please go."

Jason was quiet on their walk back to the bus stop.

"Tell me," Allison said.

"You didn't tell her your parents will be there."

"I don't care," Allison said. "Maybe I'm not such a great person, Jason. Maybe you don't want to be with me after all. Maybe I'm not who you think I am."

They were at the bus station. The buses lined up, stopping only long enough for passengers to board before whizzing away again. Downtown in forty minutes. Their bus was at the end, and Jason, saying nothing, picked up his pace so they wouldn't miss it.

CHAPTER 22

Allison met Bonnie and Wayne at Incheon Airport the day before Mina and Robert's wedding.

"This sure isn't Kimpo," Wayne said. He was in a foul mood, tired and cramped from the fourteen-and-a-half-hour flight. "That airport was a shithole."

"It's been thirty years," Allison said. "It's called progress."

"It's lovely," Bonnie said. "When do I get to see Mina?"

They retrieved their luggage, two large, hard suitcases that took two airport luggage carts, and wheeled them up to wait for the shuttle. Bonnie had, despite Allison's warnings, overpacked. They were staying at a hotel in Itaewon, not far from Mina's encampment. They'd agreed to surprise Mina that night at dinner, if Allison could get her out of the house.

That was not to happen. Allison had said she wanted to take them out to celebrate their wedding the next day, but Mina refused. Robert had pleaded with her as well, perhaps wondering if Mina would even make it to the wedding. As Allison watched him talk softly and calmly to Mina in the bed, she had to admit that he was beautiful. From the photos Mina had shown her on the computer, his daughter Shayla was the same. She was already lanky with hair that grew around her face, and she had a smile that Robert didn't, a smile open to the world. Allison had not told Robert that Mina's parents were here, or that Lim Sun-hui would be coming. In the end they agreed to take-out. Allison would get Thai from a place down the street, then she'd pick up her parents at the hotel, bringing them to Mina.

Her parents, groggy from the naps Allison had told them not to take, rode with her in a taxi up past Hae Bang Chon to Robert and Mina's apartment. Bonnie kept murmuring how crowded everything seemed to be, so busy, bustling, while Wayne remained stuck to the window, quiet.

By the time they'd climbed the stairs to the apartment, Bonnie was out of breath. "Well," she said, "I can see why everyone is so thin here."

"This looks more familiar," Wayne said. "More like how it used to be."

Allison opened the door, setting containers of Thai curries and boxes of rice and soup on the kitchen table. Wayne and Bonnie waited behind, hidden. Mina, wearing the oversized T-shirt and baggy shorts she seemed to live in, padded to the kitchen. Allison had not seen her eat that day. Her hair needed washing and was growing out in uneven chunks. Mina leaned over and sniffed. "Smells good."

Allison gestured for Mina to sit. Mina pulled out one of the rice containers and began eating with some silver chopsticks.

"We have some guests for dinner. Don't be angry."

Mina looked up, slowed her chewing. Allison opened the door. Wayne and Bonnie stood, frozen for a moment, like prizes behind a contest door.

"Mina, my baby." Bonnie lurched forward and threw her arms around Mina, who still held chopsticks in her hands. "What's happened to you?"

Mina gently pushed Bonnie away. Bonnie opened her purse and fished out a crumpled tissue to dab her eyes, carefully sopping up dark mascara.

"Why are you here?" Mina was looking at Allison.

"We came to get you." Wayne was still in the doorway, his face ashen. He stepped toward Mina and she slid her chair back.

"That's not true," Bonnie said. "We're here for your wedding. We wouldn't miss that. Allison told us. Please don't be angry, dear."

Mina stared at Allison. Allison knew Mina thought she'd betrayed her again, but she hoped in the end Mina would understand. Mina called Robert's name and he emerged from the living room.

"Robert, these are my…this is Wayne and Bonnie Morehouse."

Robert extended his hand to Wayne first then to Bonnie. To Allison he was still a man of few words. He and Mina didn't seem to talk much. He'd inform her of when he was coming or going, when a mission was coming up and how long he'd be gone, or he'd advise her what to eat to help her gain strength. When Allison had developed a cold for a few days he'd told her to cut out dairy, to rinse her mouth with salt and water, and to avoid bananas. When he was home he was either on the computer, listening to calypso and Caribbean pop music, reading *Stars and Stripes,* or watching sports on TV. Once Allison had caught him watching some eighties-style porn movie on his computer, girls with too much makeup and big hair, who looked and sounded like Melanie Griffith in *Working Girl.* "Mina knows," he said, and Allison didn't doubt it. On the positive side, the two didn't seem to fight, which was a first as far as Allison knew for Mina, and he was not full of surprises, was even tempered. He dressed well.

Allison saw Wayne hesitate before shaking Robert's hand, the movement subtle, like the air was so thick that it was keeping his hand away from Robert's. She wondered if anyone else had noticed. Bonnie was too busy putting her Kleenex away. Mina was looking at Wayne's face. Robert seemed impassive, his Army face, except for a slight twitch, almost as subtle as Wayne's hesitation, at the corner of his mouth. Bonnie shook his hand quickly, two hands over his one, a strongly accented, "So pleased to meet you. My, you are handsome." They did not say what they'd told Ted ten years ago: welcome to the family.

Allison brought out the plates—there were only three, so the couples shared, while Allison had her own. She wished Jason were here, so she could share her food with him. She wanted to feed him with her chopsticks because she wanted to observe him as he ate, giving him a chance to think about nothing except the food being offered. But he did not approve of her scheme, and she was tired of changing to get approval. *You're not a puppetmaster,* he'd told her. So she tried to focus instead on the tastes in her own mouth, the slight sweetness of the coconut, the tangy spice from the red curry. Wayne and Robert had barely said ten words, Bonnie kept trying to pry out more information about the wedding, how she could help, did Mina need a dress, flowers, shoes, etc. Wayne was watching Mina, trying to find out how much Mina knew about Sunny, but Mina was avoiding his gaze, listlessly eating tiny bits of rice.

After they'd finished eating, Allison took a bottle of *makgeolli* from the refrigerator and poured some into tiny glasses, which she passed to the table.

"I'd like to toast Robert and Mina. To their future."

Bonnie raised her glass, but her eyes were large, as if permanently surprised. "What's this?"

"A traditional Korean rice wine called *makgeolli*."

"*Makgeolli* kills!" Wayne yelled, and everyone turned to look at him. "That's what the signs said. Back then."

Robert started laughing. Then Mina and Allison joined him. Bonnie laughed, too, although it was clear she wasn't sure why. Robert drank his *makgeolli*, Mina and Allison following.

"Not dead yet," Mina said. And they laughed again. Wayne raised the glass to his lips, took a sip and smiled.

He'd barely acknowledged Allison, but after they finished their drinks, Wayne asked to speak to her privately. They walked out to the deck that provided a panorama of Seoul, glass high rises and incongruous apartment buildings, cars and traffic and neon, upward reaching with tentacles spreading outward as far as could be seen, layers of mountains far in the distance.

"Those mountains look so harmless from here," he said. "But they're a bitch to climb. All craggy and rock, unforgiving." Allison waited for him to continue. "I couldn't let her grow up here, a half-breed prostitute. That's what she would have been."

"You cheated on Mom and lied to her. To us."

"Don't tell her. Please."

"Don't you think she's figured it out by now?"

The air shifted suddenly, a breeze from nowhere. The rainy season was coming. "How much does Mina know?"

"You'll have to ask her."

"Why's she marrying that guy?"

"You're pissed because he's black."

"She can do better."

Allison was tired. She would not remind him that Bonnie could have done better as well. She would not remind him that in her own case, better had not worked out.

He pulled a rubber-banded group of envelopes from his jacket pocket. "By the way, here's your mail." And then he went inside.

That night, after Bonnie and Wayne had returned to their hotel, Robert to a friend's to stay the night before the wedding, Allison waited in the darkness for Mina's wrath. Mina had not spoken a word to her except as needed at dinner. They lay on the *yo*, Mina quiet, her breathing regular, as if she were sleeping.

"Don't be angry," Allison said.

"I can't believe you brought them here. After all we'd talked about."

"I just thought you should see them. That you might feel better."

"I'll feel better in six months when I can take Shayla and live in a cabin in the middle of Oklahoma and build a fence large enough to keep the world out."

"Good luck with that," Allison said. Mina never responded.

CHAPTER 23

L ater that night, Allison still could not fall asleep. She wondered
how the reunion would go tomorrow when Lim Sun-hui
arrived—she'd know from her parents' expressions everything she
wanted. Who knew what. No one had noticed that her three-month
tourist visa had expired a week ago and she was here on borrowed time.
She'd been afraid to leave the country to get a new visa, to leave Mina
alone for that long. Now Allison would have to leave Korea soon, face
immigration, pay thousands of dollars in fines for overstaying, possibly
be blocked from coming back in. Yet all she wanted was to come back,
to spend more time with Jason, to stay with Mina until she returned
to the States with Robert's daughter. Allison was trying to prepare for
the inevitable loss they were all hurtling toward, the disassembling of
their own hobbled lives.

She went into the living room, turning on the light. She slid the
rubber band from the stack of mail Wayne had collected for her and idly
sorted through it, mostly junk mail or reminders for bills that she had
already paid online. She stopped when she reached one letter, written
by hand in that unmistakable scrawl. Ray. Postmarked June 1. Weeks
after she'd sent the email to Merry. She thought about not opening it
so she wouldn't have to read how she'd ruined Ray's innocent children's
lives, his own pain and suffering. Yet, she felt she owed him at least a
reading. She opened the letter.

Five things I want to admit to you (this is easy):
I had sex with you so you could help me with my job.
Your sister was a better fuck than you.
Merry will forgive anything I do to avoid the humiliation of a divorce.
I knew you were obsessed with me.
Good luck getting a job in this town again. How's that for truth?

Ever since she'd decided to come to Seoul, Allison had told herself that all she wanted to know was the truth. She could not change what Wayne had done, what Mina had done, what Ray had done, but she could live out of the shadows, in the sun. Yet this was not the kind of truth she'd been expecting. She'd been searching to discover the lies others had told her, but not ones she'd told herself.

Five things:
Everything Ray says, I already knew.
The miscarriages were my punishment for not having the first baby,
*   for lying to Ray.*
I don't want to go back home. Everything there is falling apart.
I like being the puppetmaster.
I may never forgive.

CHAPTER 24

The wedding was at noon, at the Yongsan Chapel. A smattering of Robert's friends had been invited but Mina had not wanted any of her friends to come. That morning when Allison had gone to pick them up at the hotel, Bonnie had confided to Allison that she was still hoping to talk Mina out of the wedding, that Robert didn't seem like a "good match" for her daughter. Allison was sure that Wayne was planning worse—a kidnapping if he could convince Mina not to make a scene at the airport. Allison had neither encouraged nor discouraged them. She knew Mina would not change her mind, especially now. She told them she was going to meet Jason and bring him back in time to get him into the base.

Outside it had started to rain. Jason was at Seoul Station in a suit and shiny tie, stiff and formal. He was holding a large umbrella over himself and Lim Sun-hui, who was wearing a severe silk dress, dark blue, dark lipstick, which Allison had not seen on her before, spiky shoes with a loose strap in the back where her narrow ankles met the heels. Her face, accented with a film of loose powder, looked paler than usual.

Allison was beginning to understand the weight of what she'd done, what Jason had warned her of. She was irrevocably changing the course and direction of people's lives in ways they'd not wanted. Looking at Jason, she wanted to fall into him, to call everything off, to put Lim Sun-hui in a taxi back to Ilsan, to tell Bonnie and Wayne to go home, but she couldn't. This was what it had come to.

The cab ride was longer than usual, with the rain slowing the streets from downtown to Yongsan. Lim Sun-hui, her beaded clutch in her lap, crumpled and smoothed a white handkerchief. Jason sat in front.

"You two look good together," Lim Sun-hui said. "So why you fight?"

"I'm just a terrible evil person, and Jason finally figured that out."

Jason laughed, turning briefly to catch her eye. She fluttered her fingertips at him, trying to smile. She burned to be alone with him.

"You know, today is bad luck to have wedding," Lim Sun-hui said. "Why?"

"It's the sixtieth anniversary of the start of the Korean War," Jason said.

"Oh. I didn't know," Allison said. "It's just a day, right?"

No one said anything back.

They arrived at the villa with too few umbrellas. Allison ran ahead, the brief seconds of rain sticking her dress to her skin. Behind her, Jason helped Lim Sun-hui up the stairs, one arm crooked around her elbow, the other holding the umbrella over her. Her shoes and stockings were splattered with muddy water, but it was not to be helped. Allison put her hand against the metal door; her palm needed cooling.

"You promise I see my brother?" Lim Sun-hui asked.

"Soon. I promise." And then she opened the unlocked door. She heard the TV in the living room, the sounds of English, and she saw Wayne, laptop open, probably playing some war game. He didn't look up, possibly didn't even hear the door open. She stepped across the hall past the kitchen, into the bedroom. She'd folded the *yo* up that morning so that the floor was bare. Mina was sitting on a cushion, long legs spread, hair held back in randomly colored clips and barrettes, an attempt to bring some order to the chopped mess. She was wearing her dress, a cocktail-length taffeta, with tufts of white to give her shape and weight, but her feet were bare. Allison guessed she had her make up on, was waiting for Bonnie to paint her nails or some such thing. She was humming a tune that sounded Korean. Flat, melancholy tones, sounds that could pull anyone into sadness.

Bonnie yelled from the bathroom. "I can't find the clear polish."

"She's here," Allison said. She heard Lim Sun-hui take off her shoes, the closing of the umbrella, Jason's reassuring whispers.

Mina rose slowly, stopped humming. She stood, her ankles as narrow and thin as her mother's, toenails freshly painted pink. She looked past Allison to the kitchen, taking a step just as Lim Sun-hui walked in the bedroom. She still held the clutch, although the handkerchief had disappeared. Lim Sun-hui had re-applied her lipstick since the cab ride, a brownish color that, Allison thought, diminished her.

"*Omma*," Mina whispered.

And then there was a shout, or more of a wail, a guttural thing and Lim Sun-hui fell to her knees and began rocking back and forth. Mina sank with her, in her, and the two formed an inward folding flower of grief.

Jason stood in the doorway, pulling Allison to him. "This falls on you." He turned, his black socks ever-so-slightly worn at the heel. "I'll see you later."

"Don't leave me now," she said. But Jason was not looking at her. He was sliding his feet into his shoes, still laced loosely so that he never had to untie them, a common trick, he said, in countries where people didn't wear shoes indoors. When he looked up, the sides of his face were damp from the rain, his bangs flopped over, and suddenly he looked much younger than he was. He half-nodded, half-bowed to her, and then he was gone, leaving the umbrella behind.

The bathroom door opened and Bonnie entered the kitchen area. Wayne's face still glowed behind the computer screen, his fingers moving rapidly over the controls. Allison stood outside the bedroom door, like a night sentry.

"What's that noise?" Bonnie asked.

"It's Mina."

Bonnie walked to the door. "Well, let me in, she sounds awful. Has she changed her mind?" Wayne looked up from the screen. Allison watched Bonnie watch him. He rose, walking slowly, as if he knew his world was about to change.

"What's wrong?" he asked when he was halfway there.

Allison opened the bedroom door. Two women were on the floor, embracing, sobbing, jabbering in a language that no one else understood, and then Mina looked up.

"She came. My mother came."

Lim Sun-hui turned to face them, and then she fell back. "Wayne?" she said, shaking her head.

The room was quiet. Wayne stepped forward. "Sunny?" He held his hand out to her. She pushed herself off the floor and took his hand, reached up to cup his face, caress his cheek. He traced her face and shoulders, resting his hands on them.

Allison had not considered this: they had loved each other.

Later she would draw the parallels, how Sunny had loved a married man, how, removed from the world that reminded him of his own family, he could love her. How in that one small way he had tried to do right. Bonnie said nothing, allowed her hands to open. The bottle of polish fell to the floor. She held her hand out to the wall for support. Allison reached to hold her up.

"This is Mina's mother?" Bonnie asked, her voice a choke more than a sound.

Wayne dropped his arms, turned toward Bonnie. "Yes." He looked back at Lim Sun-hui, then swallowed. "And I'm Mina's father."

Bonnie was gone, tumbling down the steps, onto the street.

"I'll talk to her," Allison said. "Alone." By the time Allison had caught up with her, Bonnie was sitting on the steps outside the house, the rain dripping on her, falling off of the leaves of trees, onto her shoulders and buried head.

"Why did you have to dredge this up?" Bonnie was crying.

"Dad's the one who lied to you, not me."

"You think I'm stupid? You think I didn't know?"

"Then why did you let him get away with it?" Even now, after this, women still protecting their men, Allison thought.

"I prayed to God and he gave me another baby." Bonnie shook her head. "Was that so bad?"

"No, Momma." Allison placed her arm around her mother delicately, lightly, so that she hardly knew it was there.

Bonnie looked up at the house. "I better get back in there." She grabbed Allison's hands. Her hair was falling, her face a stream of rain and tears. "Maybe you don't know that feeling, how you want something so badly you can't think straight about it anymore."

Allison nodded. "Sure I do," she whispered.

Bonnie stood. "Come up with me?"

Allison shook her head. She listened to Bonnie walk up the stairs. Even though the air was warm, she folded her arms and shivered. She'd never felt so alone.

Jason was standing at the gate to the house, saying nothing, watching her in the rain. She walked to him, wondered how much he'd heard. Jason opened the gate for her and took her hand. He placed his other hand behind her neck and kissed her, and for a moment she was back on the rocks in the mountains, removed from the world, and she wished that for Mina too, that she and her mother could hold each other in that room forever, suspended in time, not having to move forward or go back.

Allison led the way. She held Mina's tiny hand, Mina walking just behind her. She was still in her wedding dress, which looked like it was scattered with diamonds, but they were just drops of rain, glistening under the path's lights. She'd abandoned her heels for her Keds, allowing her to nimbly negotiate the muddy path. Behind her was Robert, his hand occasionally falling at the small of her back on the steep parts of the hill, Lim Sun-hui, agile even in her narrow skirt and pointed heels, Wayne, his face wet and red from the humid air, then Bonnie, constrained in her gold-threaded suit, too hot for the already humid weather, her impractical shoes sinking into the soft ground. Jason was last, the rear guard, to make sure no one was forgotten or left behind. The skies were dark but it had stopped raining for the moment.

Once the temple opened up to them, Lim Sun-hui pushed ahead, not quite running, but moving in a clipped pace toward her brother, who was waiting for them in his monk's robe, his hands pressed together. When the rest caught up, she was facing him, mere inches away, but they did not touch. Mina stood behind Lim Sun-hui. Robert stood a few feet away, his hands neatly clasped in front of him. Allison took Bonnie's hand, and then wrapped her arms around her mother, who was surprisingly warm and sturdy.

No one spoke.

Wayne staggered toward the temple. Every movement seemed to be one of great effort and pain. His skin was blotchy, his mouth twisted as if he'd suffered a sudden stroke. When he reached the temple's steps, he crumpled.

Allison didn't know it, but Wayne was remembering the day he'd seen Woo-sung shivering in the corner, naked but for a pink-flowered silk robe that draped his shoulders, the belt untied, its ends coiled like a snake on the floor. The front of the robe hung open, revealing Woo-sung's hairless, bony chest. He remembered Sunny filling a cup with water and pouring it on Mina's back, scrubbing Mina's skin with a white, gentle, fragrant bar of soap Wayne had brought from the base. Sunny rinsed the soap off with her hands and then placed Mina on her blanket to dry in the warm air. *You help Woo-sung.*

Soon Mina would be old enough to remember these things: her mother, the small room they lived in, the crazy brother, the large man who often slept with her mother on the thin blanket that was their bed. He had to get her out before the memories held fast.

Woo-sung had been quiet, his eyes blank. He'd stopped shivering. The robe had slipped from one of his delicate shoulders, so that he looked like some genderless seductress from a forgotten era. Woo-sung would not remember this day, or the days before or after for a while. Wayne had pressed Sunny to him and thought of all the other nights they'd been together, her body warm and feverish, how few there were remaining, how much he'd miss her, even now as she sacrificed herself and their child to save her brother, a man not made for the world into which he'd been born.

"God forgive me," Wayne whispered into his hands, which stretched like a mask over his face.

Allison let go of her mother, leaving Jason silent beside her. At the temple spring she dipped a hollowed-out gourd into the cool mountain water. She walked to her father and squatted down so they were eye-level.

"Here, Daddy." She nudged the gourd so that he had to part his hands. "Take this. Drink."

ABOUT THE AUTHOR

Named one of "today's strongest emerging talents in literary fiction and poetry" by the *Huffington Post*, Sybil Baker is the author of two books of fiction, *The Life Plan*, a comic novel, and a linked short story collection, *Talismans*. Her MFA is from the Vermont College of Fine Arts. She spent twelve years teaching in South Korea before returning to the States in 2007. She is an Assistant Professor of English (Creative Writing) at the University of Tennessee at Chattanooga where she is the Assistant Director of the Meacham Writers' Workshop. She is currently on faculty of the first international MFA Program at City University of Hong Kong and is Fiction Editor at *Drunken Boat*.

Photo by George Conley

CPSIA information can be obtained at www.ICGtesting.com
.Printed in the USA
LVOW041637290912

300863LV00001B/2/P